By AUGUSTA LI

NOVELS

On Tinsel Wings

BLESSED EPOCH
Ash and Echoes
Ice and Embers

With EON DE BEAUMONT
STEAMCRAFT AND SORCERY
Boots for the Gentleman
A Grimoire for the Baron

NOVELLAS

Coal to Diamonds
Neskaya

STEAMCRAFT AND SORCERY
Snowdrop

Published by DREAMSPINNER PRESS
http://www.dreamspinnerpress.com

ON TINSEL *Wings*

AUGUSTA LI

Dreamspinner Press

Published by
Dreamspinner Press
5032 Capital Circle SW
Ste 2, PMB# 279
Tallahassee, FL 32305-7886
USA
http://www.dreamspinnerpress.com/

On Tinsel Wings

Cover Art by Paul Richmond
http://www.paulrichmondstudio.com

Cover content is being used for illustrative purposes only
and any person depicted on the cover is a model.

ISBN: 978-1-62380-782-5
Digital ISBN: 978-1-62380-783-2

Printed in the United States of America
First Edition
July 2013

Chapter 1

WITH his arms overflowing with freshly laundered velvet, satin, linen, and brocade, Patrick Harford pushed the door open with his knee and flipped the light switch with his elbow. The stack of gowns, skirts, pantaloons, and bodices reached past his nose, making it difficult for him to see. From memory, he navigated the women's dressing room and deposited his burden on a long wooden table at the center. Patrick slid a box of wooden hangers from underneath and started to hang the garments. While his job at the Allegheny Mountains Renaissance Faire entailed everything from emptying trash bins, cleaning privies, mucking out the stables, and basically anything else that needed doing, caring for the actresses' costumes had always been his favorite task. He turned on a small radio nestled between pots of powder, canisters of rouge, and tubes of lipstick on one of the makeup tables, then adjusted the dial away from the hip-hop to the local college station that played an eclectic mix of classical opera, German cabaret, jazz, ragtime, and even show tunes.

When he finished arranging the clothes on their hangers, he took them to their assigned racks and hung them up. After working here for the past three summers, he knew which article of clothing belonged to which character: Mistress Hattie, the amorous haberdasher; Folie au Deux, the crazy French jester; Grace O'Malley, the Irish pirate queen, and her companion Mary Killigrew; Sayyida the Moor; Fair Bianca the Minstrel; the naughty Sisters of Merciful Ministrations, and the even naughtier wenches of the Saucy Stew Tavern. Of course, the best costumes belonged to Jennifer, the Faire's resident Queen Elizabeth. She had a different gown for every Faire day from the end of May until the operation closed for the year at Halloween, and they were all exquisite.

Patrick dragged the portable steamer into the adjoining restroom and filled its reservoir from the sink. A fog formed on the many mirrors as he steamed the wrinkles out of the garments that required it. A scratchy version of Patti Page's "You Belong to Me" played as he moved through the mist until he came to the queen's gowns. He ran his fingers along the neckline of the pale pink dress he'd just washed, marveling at the rows of elaborate lace, fine embroidery, and intricate beading. Looking down at his own simple shirt, brown trousers, and worn, green doublet, he wondered how it would feel to wear something so incredible. How beautiful Jennifer must have felt when she'd welcomed her subjects at the Faire's opening ceremony! Patrick had never once felt beautiful; most of the time, at school and even here at work, he just felt invisible and ignored.

He reached down and turned off the steamer, his hands trembling at just the thought of what he wished he could do. And why couldn't he? No one would know. All of the customers had gone home hours ago, and any of the remaining actors or staff would be well on their way to drunkenness up at the Stew. The idea of feeling that sinfully smooth satin against his skin made the risks seem worthwhile. Patrick looked over his shoulder in an irrational assurance that he was still alone, and then he bent and tugged off his dusty, battered leather boots. The rest of his clothes quickly followed, and he left them in a sloppy pile as he slipped the dress from the hanger.

First, he tied what they called a bum roll—a padded crescent of fabric like a knee sock stuffed with cotton—around his slim hips, above his Batman boxer briefs. Then he slid on an undershift made of fine, thin linen, thinking maybe he'd made an error and the bum roll should have gone over top. Still, his silhouette in the full-length mirror on the wall fascinated him. He actually looked like he had hips, and they made his waist appear tiny in contrast. He barely recognized the person looking back at him in the gathered layers of lacy ivory. Patrick put the gown on above it all, then struggled to reach behind himself to zip up the back. Luckily Jennifer was almost as tall as he was, and the costume fit well, if a little short in the arms. This dress was one of the simpler ones; Jennifer needed the assistance of at least two other women to get into the heavy, embellished white ensemble she'd wear at the Faire's closing ceremony, along with Elizabeth's signature white makeup.

Patrick put the matching bodice on above the gown and closed the busk, wishing he had someone to lace him up. He couldn't imagine how tiny his waist would look beneath the steel boning, but who in the world could he ever trust with such a request? He'd probably get his ass kicked, so he satisfied himself with adjusting the puffy sleeves, tying on the beaded bracers, and stringing some rosy pearls around his neck. He turned to look at himself again, and his breath hitched at what he saw.

He looked beautiful. The awkward, scrawny boy had disappeared, and in his place... a queen, holding her head high, her back straight, radiating a confidence Patrick had never dreamed of feeling. Excited, he hurried to augment the effect, choosing one of Jennifer's wigs from the row of Styrofoam heads on a shelf. He raked his shaggy layers of red-gold hair off his forehead and put the wig on. A similar color to his natural locks, it cascaded over his shoulders in masses of loose ringlets, transporting him even further from the plain, forgettable person he'd been a quarter of an hour ago. He placed a pearl tiara above the bright curls and adjusted the combs so it would stay in place. Almost giddy at what he witnessed, he lifted his skirts and crossed the room to one of the makeup tables.

When he'd finished experimenting with the cosmetics, he looked a lot more like one of the tavern wenches than the queen, with bright red lips, hard pink lines across his cheekbones, and heavy black eyeliner and mascara. He should have used the pink lipstick, and maybe a softer brown instead of the harsh black on his eyes, but he still liked seeing himself, as the cosmetics had enhanced his large blue eyes and full lips.

As Patrick stood from the stool at the makeup station, careful not to trip over the layers of his skirts, "I Feel Pretty" from *West Side Story* began to play on the radio. He smiled as he twirled, the gown billowing out around him beautifully. He *did* feel pretty. He felt like a princess, or… a queen.

Facing the mirror on the wall, he looked at himself from various angles, holding the dress out in a curtsey, then turning to the side to glance seductively over his shoulder. He got a little excited with what he saw, and an erection tented the shimmering fabric. It was such a novel thrill to imagine he could be so alluring. Neither men nor women had ever shown any interest in him. They found him neither ugly nor beautiful and just dismissed him. Patrick wondered what they would say if they could see him now. Many of the Faire's female patrons only wished they looked as good.

Patrick fluffed his hair and ran his fingers down the beaded bodice, grazing his cock and shivering at the jolt of sensation. Just then, the slam of a door wilted his excitement. He looked around frantically for a place to hide. He couldn't let anyone see him like this. How would he explain it? Terrified, he backed into the restroom, crouched down in one of the stalls, and closed the wooden door as quietly as he could. Who would be in the women's dressing room at this hour? Patrick's pulse echoed in his head as he just prayed whoever it was would leave. Otherwise, the best he could hope for was losing a job he truly loved, and it would probably be worse. He inched his way into the corner between the toilet and the plywood partition, hoping for a miracle.

Shiny black boots appeared outside the stall, and someone knocked softly. "Is everything okay in there?" asked a voice Patrick recognized. God knew he'd spent enough nights fantasizing about the man who spoke, the hottest man at the Faire: Eric, who portrayed the privateer Sir Francis Drake. He was tall and lanky, with just the perfect amount of bulk on his frame, warm but devious brown eyes, long dark hair, and the ideal sprinkling of stubble across his angular jaw.

Patrick didn't know quite how to respond. "I'm taking a leak in here," he said pitifully.

"Patrick? No problem. I'll wait. I need you to help me look for Tracy's phone. She thinks she might have left it in here."

He had to get Eric to go away. "Actually, I'm not feeling very well."

Patrick realized too late he'd forgotten to latch the stall door, and Eric pushed it open. "Jesus, what's wrong? Are you—Holy shit. Patrick?"

"I'm sorry," Patrick muttered feebly, hiding his painted face in his elbow. "Please… please don't kick my ass. I-I didn't mean any harm. I just wondered how I'd look. I love this place. It's all I have. Please don't tell anyone. It would kill me if I lost my job. I'll never do it again. I'm sorry… I just…."

To Patrick's surprise, Eric extended his hand to help him up, and Patrick grasped it, slipping on the tiles in nothing but his striped knee socks. Eric led him from the restroom to the dressing room, where he held Patrick at arm's length and looked him up and down. "Have you done this before?" Eric demanded.

"No. No, I swear. I just… I don't know why I—"

"You look beautiful," Eric said softly. "Look." He grasped Patrick's waist and spun him toward the mirror. Eric stood behind Patrick with his dark hair pulled back and that devastating line of stubble over his jaw. He looked perfect in his T-shirt with the faded Jolly Roger and tight, dark jeans, but Patrick looked heavenly in the pink dress.

"I love the Faire," he said again. "I belong here. Please, I just don't want to lose my job."

Eric pressed his chest against Patrick's back and bent his neck to whisper in Patrick's ear. "Jesus, you look fierce. I can't believe this is your first time."

"I'm sorry," Patrick whimpered.

"For what, baby?" Eric asked.

"I… I just thought…."

"Christ. Get yourself cleaned up, princess." Eric let go of Patrick's waist and stepped away.

"You won't tell?" Patrick asked desperately. "My job here—"

Eric shook his head and held up a hand. "You've done nothing to offend me, but other people might not agree, so clean up. If you want,

I'd like to take you for a drink tomorrow after the Faire. We can talk then. Patrick, it's okay."

"Is it?"

"You know you look gorgeous," Eric said, crossing his arms over his chest. "Maybe a little bit rough, but wow. Seriously, man. Damn."

"Really?" Patrick asked, clutching at his skirts. "You're not angry?"

"Why the hell would I be angry? Listen to me: it's okay, and I'm not going to say anything. I promise. Clean up, and I'll see you tomorrow when we close." Eric found the iPhone in the pink case he'd been looking for on one of the makeup tables, then turned and pushed the dressing room door open before disappearing.

Patrick stripped the gown off, hung it up carefully, smoothed the wrinkles away, and washed his face. His hands shook as he turned off the lights and locked the dressing room with one of the keys he wore on a ring on his belt. As he walked past the still and silent Tudor-style buildings, all decked out in seasonal flowers, he kept looking over his shoulder, half expecting Eric to appear with a group of men to taunt him and beat him up. He just couldn't believe the man who made all the women at the Faire swoon with a wink had no problem with finding him in a pink dress. More likely, he just waited to surprise Patrick when he could impress a few of his friends in the process.

The huge field serving as the Faire's parking lot stood practically empty. Last year, they'd installed lampposts at regular intervals for the safety of the patrons, and they cast golden pools of light on the trampled grass. Patrick jogged through them until he reached his 1989 Plymouth Horizon and unlocked the door. He took the highway and drove for about forty-five minutes, until he reached the small town between the fairgrounds and the outskirts of Pittsburgh where he lived with his father.

Careful to park beneath a streetlight, because he didn't live in the greatest neighborhood and cars were often broken into, Patrick killed his engine and locked up. He walked up the cracked sidewalk, spattered with clumps of grass breaking through the cement, to the dilapidated blue ranch house with dirty vinyl siding, sagging roof, and lawn in need of mowing. His father hadn't bothered to lock the door, and after he crossed the tiny kitchen with its sink full of dishes, Patrick found him in his recliner in front of the television, drinking a beer.

"How was the nerd circus?" Patrick's father asked without bothering to look away from the baseball game he was watching.

"Okay. We have a lot of new staff this year, and they're still adjusting, but it's going pretty smoothly, and the turnout has been up from last year." Patrick didn't know why he bothered; his father had only asked so he could work in the jab about the nerd circus.

The old man swiveled in his chair and looked at his son with bleary eyes. "What the fuck is all over your face?"

Stunned, Patrick reached up and touched his cheek, terrified he'd missed a trace of rouge somehow. "Nothing! Why?" he managed.

His father laughed. "I thought I saw a streak of horseshit." Then he turned his attention back to the game and chuckled.

Patrick clenched his fists. "It's a good job, Dad." He resisted the urge to add, "At least I have one." Someday he'd work up the stones to shoot back when his dad insulted him for no reason, but not tonight. He hurried down the hall to his bedroom, deposited his clothes in the hamper, and stepped into the shower. Though he hadn't worked with the horses today, he'd worked up a sweat and knew he needed to wash. Afterward, he slipped on a pair of sweats and a worn T-shirt emblazoned with the Triforce. He climbed into bed and turned on his TV and Xbox with the controller, then picked up where he'd left off on Final Fantasy XIII. About ten hours into the game, he'd decided the storyline was unfathomable and the grinding terribly repetitive, but the monotony helped him get to sleep, and tonight, with his nerves still crackling and his mind working at double speed, he needed an escape. Besides, the graphics were beautiful. He'd often wished he had baby-pink hair like Lightning, that he could be as strong as she was. Patrick's game console, car, and everything else he possessed of value had come as a result of his job at the Faire. He hoped Eric was sincere in his promise not to tell anyone about what he'd seen. Thinking about it made Patrick remember how he'd felt in that beautiful gown, how he'd felt when he looked at himself in the mirror. For the first time in his life, he'd felt like maybe there was something special about him, and then Eric had called him beautiful….

Patrick paused his game on the inventory screen. He set the controller aside and ran his hand down his chest, recalling the sensation of that decadent satin beneath his fingers. As he imagined Eric's face, he let his fingers wander to the growing bulge in his sweats, and then beneath the waistband. He began to move his hand, picturing both himself in the dress and makeup and the way Eric had looked at him. There'd been something behind his dark gaze that Patrick had always hoped to see from a man looking at him, and just the memory of it drove him crazy.

Chapter 2

WHEN he parked his car outside the Faire the next morning, Patrick was almost afraid to get out. He gripped the steering wheel and took a few deep breaths, sure the other employees and actors waited to gather around him and hurl insults as soon as he appeared. Eric would have spread the word by now. The Faire was the first place where Patrick had ever felt he belonged, and the thought of being driven from it sickened him, though he felt sure it was inevitable. The wet grass darkened the leather of his boots as he trudged toward the gate, ready to just get it over with.

It all seemed surreal as Madge, the Faire's resident herbalist and purveyor of tonics, wearing her usual tatty garments and black hood over her silver hair, waved him through. None of the other employees paid him any mind as they worked to open shutters, erect signs, and put goods on display for the coming day. Hattie waved to him from the stand selling everything from demure bonnets to outlandish pirate hats, and Patrick returned her greeting. The most novice employees filled their baskets with flowers of every color to sell to patrons. At fifteen, Patrick had started as a "rose boy," selling overpriced blossoms and directing guests to various shows and attractions. He'd been just as nervous as this year's young recruits looked, but not half as nervous as he felt today, as he made his way toward the small office building just in front of the actors' dressing rooms.

Inside, the Faire's general manager, Tom, lectured one of the newer employees on her attire. "I agree there's a fantasy element to it all, lass," the older man said in perfect character. "The blue hair I don't mind. But you cannae wear metallic silver boots!" Tom straightened his kilt and lifted his chin as the young woman nodded.

To Patrick's horror, Eric stood sipping a cup of coffee next to Jennifer, both of them already in costume. Jennifer wore the same gown he'd tried on the night before, and Eric looked amazing in snug charcoal leggings that left nothing to the imagination, a billowy shirt, and a black leather vest and bracers. Flushing, Patrick avoided making eye contact, his attention on his feet as he approached Tom.

"Good den, laddie," Tom said, clasping Patrick's hand. Then he dropped his accent and grew serious. "Tim called in sick today. I need you to handle props at the main stage."

"Not a problem, sir," Patrick said. Three shows were performed each day on the main stage: the opening welcome, the human chess match, and the musical finale. It would keep Patrick behind the scenes, fetching swords and lances and helping with wardrobe, which he desperately desired today.

"Good lad. And if you can swing by the Rose Stage in between, just to see if Marianne needs anything, I'd appreciate it." On the Rose Stage, actors played out fairy tales and performed puppet shows for the Faire's youngest patrons. It also offered a sort of babysitting service, entertaining the children with games and crafts so their parents could sneak away to attend some of the Faire's more suggestive performances. Patrick didn't mind the assignment; he'd always been good with young children and actually enjoyed entertaining them.

"Absolutely, Tom," he said, "and… and I just want to say I'm happy to be back at the Faire. Feels like home."

"Aye, son, aye. For all of us." Tom hurried away to speak with the young men who'd be singing in the Gregorian choir, leaving Patrick face-to-face with Jennifer and Eric.

He bowed to the queen. "God save you, Your Majesty."

"God save you, Patrick," Jennifer said with a smile. "Will we see you tonight at the Stew?"

Patrick looked at Eric. Had they actually made plans for the evening? Maybe it had all been a dream. He knew he was expected to say something. "I—"

"Actually, Patrick and I are planning to have a drink," Eric said. "We'll probably meet up with Roger for coffee."

Jennifer reached up and stroked Eric's cheek. "As you will, then, my most beloved privateer."

Eric kissed the back of her hand and fondled her fingers, never breaking eye contact. "I live only to serve, my queen."

Jennifer rolled her eyes as she pushed the office door open and stepped out into the soft late-May light. "If only, pirate."

"Privateer!" Eric protested with a grin. Then he draped his arm over Patrick's shoulder and whispered in his ear. "You're lucky she didn't see you in that gown last night, princess. She might have dropped dead from envy." Eric patted Patrick's shoulder and winked as he left the office, and Patrick hurried off toward the main stage with his cheeks and ears on fire, feeling like he wandered through a bizarre dream. He felt like he still wore the dress and lipstick for all the others to see.

The day went routinely, and after the lengthy musical finale, Patrick found a push broom and began sweeping the stage as the actors left to change. He'd already switched his Faire garb for a comfortable pair of worn jeans, a mint-green polo shirt, and his blue Chuck Taylors. Many of the patrons threw dollar chrysanthemums at the performers, a few threw roses, and now and then they tossed peanut shells, popcorn, or even money. Patrick tucked the bills into his trouser pocket and pushed the rest into a bin. He sang:

"Oh the summer time is comin'
And the trees are sweetly bloomin'
And the wild mountain thyme
Grows around the bloomin' heather
Will ye go, lassie, go?
And we'll all go together
To pull wild mountain thyme

All around the bloomin' heather
Will ye go, lassie, go?
I will build my love a bower
By yon clear crystal fountain
And on it I will pile
All the flowers of the mountain
Will ye go, lassie, go?"

"You have a beautiful voice," Eric said, stepping onto the empty stage. "How come you don't perform here with the rest of us?"

Patrick held the handle of the broom in front of his chest. "I'm not an actor. Just an employee."

"You should audition. At least for the chorus."

"I don't know…."

"And how was your day?" Eric asked.

"Fine. I spent most of it at the Rose Stage, helping abandoned children glue sparkles to cardboard crowns."

"Is it such a bad thing for those children's parents to want a half an hour to themselves?"

"Would it be so much to ask for them to think of their kids and not just themselves?" Patrick retaliated.

"But those kids had a good time with you, right?" Eric asked, canting his head.

"I suppose. I mean, I did my best to show them a good time, but I'm sure they know their parents wanted to escape them. They dump them at the Rose Stage so they can attend the wench shows or go to the Stew."

"Patrick, they leave them in your capable hands," Eric said. "Parenting is hard work, and once in a while even the best parents need to be grown-ups for an afternoon."

Patrick shook his head as he pushed the remainder of the refuse into the dustpan. "However they want to justify it, I guess. I have to finish up here. Did you need something?"

"I thought we'd made arrangements," Eric said, crossing his arms over his chest. "For a drink. Are you backing out?"

"No."

"Then let's go." The broomstick clattered against the wooden stage as Eric clasped Patrick's hand and pulled him away. He didn't let go as he led Patrick across the parking lawn to his black pickup truck. They both climbed in, and when Eric turned the key in the ignition, someone speaking a foreign tongue in a flat monotone played from an iPod plugged into the radio. Eric turned the knob and killed the volume.

Patrick tilted his head as Eric drove slowly across the bumpy field, waving to people loading props and costumes into vans and trailers.

"What are you listening to?" Patrick asked. "Sounded like Italian."

Eric laughed as he pulled onto the dirt road that would take them to the highway. "Very good. I'm trying to learn the basics of the language."

"For the Faire?"

"No," Eric answered. "Roger has always wanted to go to the Mediterranean. I'm taking him on a cruise this winter, and I want to be able to at least get by in Italian and Greek."

"Wait, who is this Roger?" Patrick asked, looking out the window at the lush Pennsylvania farmland whizzing by in shades of crimson and orange as the sun set.

"He's my partner," Eric said. "Five years this Christmas. Hence the cruise."

"I—Oh."

"Oh, shit. I think I see what happened here. Look, you're a cool kid, Patrick, and I like you, just not like that. You're a little too young for me, honey. Besides, I'm spoken for."

"I can't believe you're—"

"Gay. I'm gay, Patrick. It's not a bad word."

"But… you? How do you keep it secret?"

Eric laughed. "I don't. I don't advertise it during the Faire; the attention of the women is good for business. They like to pretend I'm interested, but it's all an act, a fantasy, just like the rest of the Faire. But all my close friends know about Roger. I'm proud of who I am, Patrick, and you should be too."

"Do you think I'm gay?" Patrick asked.

"I really don't care if you are or not," Eric said. "If you are, and you want to talk, I'm here. If you aren't and you want to be friends, great. Tonight I just want you to meet Roger and have a good time. I want you to see you're not alone."

"Okay," Patrick said, apprehensive as they drove into the outskirts of Pittsburgh, heading toward Shadyside.

About an hour after leaving the Faire, Eric parked his truck and they walked to a door in a block of brick buildings. A painted red rose served as the business's only signage. It was a warm night and lots of people filled the streets, lined up in front of clubs or sitting outside at cafes. When Patrick and Eric reached their destination, a big man in a snug black T-shirt held out his hand. "Jesus, Eric. Does this kid have ID?" he asked.

"Easy, Duane," Eric said, taking out some money to pay the cover charge. "I'm not planning to let him drink. He needs to see the show, meet Rog. I'll take responsibility for him, okay? Cut me a break."

"All right, man," Duane said, holding the metal door open for them. "Keep him out of trouble."

"Will do." Eric took Patrick's hand and led him into the bar.

Inside, Patrick couldn't believe what he saw. Shirtless men gyrated beneath lights strobing in every color. It made his head hurt, made him unsure of the solidity of the tiled floor he walked across. Completely disoriented, he followed Eric to a padded booth near a stage with an almost phallic, jutting runway. Before long, a lithe, effeminate young man in revealing black boxer briefs and a bowtie sidled up next to them.

"I'll have a Dewar's," Eric said to the waiter. "A Coke for my friend."

The pretty young man nodded before weaving his way back through the throng of grinding bodies. The bass pounded in Patrick's skull, and the smell of stale cigarette smoke almost gagged him. Eric draped his arm across the back of the booth and surveyed the scene. The waiter returned with their drinks, and Patrick downed half of his, the fizz burning his nostrils. He sputtered, and Eric laughed.

"Relax," Eric called over the music. "The show's about to start." He indicated the runway with the hand holding his drink.

A very large woman in a hot pink taffeta gown and matching beehive complete with birds and butterflies took the stage and lifted the mic from its cradle. The background music faded away. "How are we doing tonight?" the masculine voice asked.

Thunderous approval erupted from the men in the booths and on the dance floor.

"All right," said the lady in pink. "We have got one hell of a show for you tonight. First, a perpetual favorite. Give it up for Lady Regina!"

The men hooted, hollered and clapped as a beautiful woman in a tight white dress and a platinum wig flipped up at the bottom sauntered out onto the stage. She took the microphone from its cradle as the music started to play and then lip-synched along with Marilyn Monroe singing "I Wanna Be Loved By You."

Eric grinned, winked, and pursed his lips as the woman in the white dress extended her hand toward him. God, she was a vision: an angel in white with white-blonde hair, blood-red lips and darkly lined, smoky eyes. The way she tilted her hips and bent her waist enthralled Patrick. He wanted to learn to move like that, because her every gesture captured the attention of the men in the bar. Patrick wanted that level of influence. He wanted love like she received. Attention. At the same time, the thought of that kind of scrutiny scared the hell out of him.

Lady Regina leaned down to flirt with the men pressed close to the edge of the stage, touching their cheeks and taking the money they waved at her.

Her song concluded, and she thrust her full hips up and down as she exited the stage, blowing Eric kisses over her shoulder as she sauntered behind the curtain. Next, a queen called Sha-Queera performed to a Nicki Minaj song. Though Patrick didn't care for the music, he admired her dancing skills and long, muscular legs. He couldn't believe the performer's grace in her six-inch stiletto heels. She even managed a walkover, a midair straddle split, and a backflip. After her act, the big woman in pink announced Anita Lei, and Patrick got the joke when the small Polynesian came onstage in a grass skirt and a tiny yellow bikini top. She strummed a ukulele for a few minutes before setting it aside as Gwen Stefani's "The Sweet Escape" began to play. She tore the skirt away and flung it toward the back of the stage, revealing a miniscule string bikini bottom and a pair of high-heeled Roman sandals decorated with flowers.

Patrick gasped, and Eric chuckled into his drink. "She's beautiful," Patrick said, leaning in so Eric could hear him over the music. "But… how? I mean, where is… everything?"

"I'll explain it to you later."

Patrick sat entranced as Anita finished her song, her tiny garments stuffed full of money. A curvaceous performer known simply as Luscious, wearing a sequined lavender gown that reminded Patrick of a prom dress, danced to Fergie's "Big Girls Don't Cry."

As she left the stage, the pink-clad emcee returned. "That's one big girl who definitely leaves the boys smiling. Give it up for Luscious!" After the applause and catcalling faded, she said, "And now, one last time, the beautiful, the incomparable, my baby girl, Lady Regina!"

The crowd went wild as Blondie's "The Tide is High" played and Regina strutted to the center of the stage dressed in black capri pants, a form-fitting striped off-shoulder sweater, chunky red pumps, and a black beret over a straight, waist-length platinum wig. Patrick found it very fashionable and thought she looked amazing as she danced and lip-synced to the catchy old tune. While all the performers had been very good, Lady Regina possessed an amazing presence that kept every eye riveted to her. Patrick knew every man watching her felt the way he did, like she sang for his pleasure alone. At the conclusion, she bowed and blew kisses to everyone to a cacophony of cheers and shouting. Wrinkled bills fell like confetti across the stage.

For the finale, all of the girls returned, each of them in different costumes except for Lady Regina, to perform a choreographed routine to Lady Gaga's "Born This Way," which made Patrick roll his eyes at the cliché. Afterward, they collected their tips and left the stage. Dance music began to play again in the bar as the patrons queued up to refresh their drinks. The practically naked young men hurried around with trays of neon drinks in shot glasses. The colorful concoctions reminded Patrick of something Madge might make in her cauldron to scare the Faire's children. Eric excused himself and returned a few minutes later with another soda for each of them, accompanied by a handsome young man with close-cropped, dirty-blond hair. He was a little shorter and slighter than Eric, and maybe a few years younger. He wore dark trousers and a red button-down shirt that suited his coloring. He extended his hand and Patrick stood to clasp it.

"Patrick, I'd like you to meet Roger, sometimes better known as the fair Lady Regina," Eric said with a wide smile.

Patrick gasped, barely able to process that he looked at the same person he'd seen onstage. It took a few seconds for him to realize he stood staring with his mouth hanging open, and he racked his brain for something to say before Roger decided he was an idiot. "It's nice to meet you. I really enjoyed the show."

"Nice to meet you too," Roger said. "I hear we have some common interests. Let's sit down and have a drink." They left their table by the stage in favor of a quiet, secluded corner on the other side of the room.

Chapter 3

"I'VE heard a lot about you, Patrick," Roger said and then took a sip of chardonnay. "So you like to put on dresses?"

His chest tightening, Patrick looked all around, irrationally afraid someone might have heard. Then his gaze fell on the large queen in the pink gown, and he realized how silly he was being. He couldn't help feeling a little betrayed, though. "What? You said you wouldn't tell anybody!"

Eric laughed warmly and patted Patrick on the shoulder. "I was pretty sure Rog wouldn't be offended, Patrick. That's why I wanted to bring you here to meet him. I just wanted you to see there's nothing wrong with you, and you're not alone."

Roger lifted his glass in salute. "Wish somebody had done it for me at your age."

The queen in pink approached them, knelt down, and kissed Roger on the cheek, leaving behind a smear of magenta lipstick. "Great show again tonight, girlfriend," she said.

Roger kissed her back. "Thank you, Mama," he said, oozing false modesty. "Join us?"

"Oh, not tonight, baby. I have to be at the hospital for my shift by six tomorrow. Who's your new friend?"

"This is Patrick," Roger said. "He works with Eric at the Renaissance Faire. Patrick, this is my drag mama, Miss Merry Rose."

Patrick was about to say "nice to meet you," or some other obligatory, innocuous thing, but he never got the chance.

"Oh my God," Miss Merry said. "Look at those cheekbones. And lips! And his skin is flawless! When do we get to see this little doll onstage? Hey, I know! There's an amateur pageant at Joe's next month for the Pride Party."

"He can sing, too," Eric added.

Head spinning, Patrick held up his hands. "Wait. I didn't even know I was coming here tonight! Eric said we were going for coffee!"

"Just relax, sweetheart," Roger said. "Mama Merry Rose gets a little ahead of herself sometimes."

"He's got such a pretty face," the older queen protested. "And there's a five-hundred-dollar prize—"

"He's here to enjoy himself," Eric said, cutting in and rescuing Patrick. "Nothing else. Leave him alone, you two. I'm sure his head is ready to explode as it is."

Merry Rose held her hands up in surrender, her rows of plastic bracelets rattling. "All right, all right. I have to get the hell out of here anyway." She kissed Roger again. "I'll see you next weekend, girl. Good night, Eric. Patrick, nice to meet you. You come back anytime, all right, baby?"

"Um, thank you," Patrick managed.

After she'd left, Roger leaned toward Patrick and winked. "So, you wanna meet the girls?"

It occurred to Patrick that maybe he should be nervous, uncomfortable, or confused, but he wasn't. So far, everyone had been nothing but nice, and they'd given him more attention and praise than he'd probably received in the rest of his life put together. "Okay," he said, genuinely excited. "Why not?"

"Come on," Roger said, looking equally eager. "These bitches are going to love you." He stood, and Patrick followed him through a set of double doors marked "Employees Only."

As they walked down the well-lit hall toward a second set of doors, Patrick asked, "How did you and Eric meet?"

"At the Faire," Roger answered. "I went with my sister and her daughters, and I thought Eric was hot, so I went back the following weekend and asked him to have coffee with me."

"Wow," Patrick said, impressed at the courage and self-confidence that must have taken. He wondered if he'd ever work up the balls to do something like that. "But how did you know? I mean how did you know he... that he'd be interested?"

"You're asking how I knew he was gay? You can just tell after a while. I saw it in how he acted with all the women who flirted with him. I mean, he was convincing, but I could see his heart wasn't really in it, not like some of the other guys. Besides, I kept catching him watching me and looking away when I noticed. It was just too adorable. What about you? Do you have a boyfriend?"

Patrick stopped walking and faced Roger. "You think I'm gay?"

"I guess I just assumed. It's not unheard of for a straight boy to do drag, but it isn't the norm."

"I don't really do drag," Patrick explained, wondering what Eric had said to Roger. "It was just the once. I was just curious, and I've always loved the costumes the women wear at the Faire. They're just so beautiful and elaborate. But it's not like I want to be a girl or anything."

"None of us want to *be* girls," Roger said. "So, have a girlfriend, then?"

Patrick shook his head. "I'm not sure I'm straight, either. I like girls' clothes and their hair, and I think it would be fun to play around with makeup, but I'm not sure about the rest of it."

Roger nodded and rested a hand on Patrick's shoulder. "Don't worry, hon. You'll figure it out. Just know that whatever you decide, it's okay. Whoever you end up being is the person you're meant to be. Now, are you ready to meet the girls?"

Patrick nodded enthusiastically, because their conversation had meandered into uncomfortable territory he usually quarantined to the back of his mind and buried beneath as many distractions as he could dig up. A major diversion presented itself as Roger swung the door open and led Patrick into a large, bright room not unlike the dressing rooms at the Faire. Patrick looked around in awe at yards of feather boas in every imaginable color, a veritable rainbow of wigs atop Styrofoam heads covering a long shelf, racks full of costume jewelry in every style, and hangers bending under the weight of sequined garments that sparkled in the light. Some props, like fake flowers, parasols, and plastic candy canes, leaned against the walls. A sewing machine sat on a table in the corner, surrounded by spools of colored thread and scraps of lace. Patrick was so fascinated by all of it he almost forgot about the people in the room.

A portly, balding man in baggy jeans and a Pittsburgh Steelers sweatshirt folded Roger into a hug. It took Patrick a moment to realize he was Luscious, because out of his wig and gown, he seemed so ordinary, one of any hundred men one might pass without a second look at the supermarket or on the street. God, Patrick thought, out of drag, Luscious could have passed for a more wholesome version of one of his dad's friends.

Roger introduced them. "Patrick, this is Larry. Larry, Patrick."

They shook hands, and then Larry explained, "Look, I can't stick around tonight. Me and Bill are still in the middle of remodeling that bathroom, and I've got a hell of a mess at home. I at least want to get the crapper hooked up tonight."

"No problem, hon," Roger said. "I'll talk to you soon." As the other man left, Roger turned to those remaining in the room. "Hey, girls. I have somebody I'd like you to meet. This is Patrick. He's a friend of Eric's from the Renaissance Faire. Patrick, these are my sisters. Sha-Queera, also known as Shawn, and this bitch is Miss Anita Lei, or Aouli."

"Hi, Patrick," Aouli said, turning away from his makeup mirror to wave. He looked magical with his slim, male chest exposed, spiky black hair messy and damp, but a gorgeous face sparkling with impeccable cosmetics. Even beneath it all, Patrick could tell he had handsome, if delicate, features.

Shawn, who wore a tank top and a pair of shorts, was tall, with lean, defined muscles. He wore his hair in a series of tight cornrows and made a very attractive man out of drag. "How are you doing, Patrick?" he asked, extending his hand.

"Nice to meet you," Patrick said, his cheeks heating as he appreciated the curve of Shawn's full lips.

"He's *cute*, Rog," Shawn said. "What are you thinking for him? Innocent and coy? Little Japanese schoolgirl kinda thing?"

"Hey," Aouli said, looking lopsided with one fake eyelash still in place and the other pinched between his fingers. "If anybody's going to be the Japanese schoolgirl, it should be me!"

"Bitch, you're Hawaiian," Shawn teased, and all of them laughed.

Finally Roger caught his breath. "Patrick isn't sure about performing, but he really likes clothes and makeup. Ain't nothin' wrong with that, right, girls?"

"Amen, sister," Shawn said.

"Oh, I have something you just have to try on," Aouli said, discarding the premoistened cloth he'd just used to wipe his face. He went to a rack and selected a spaghetti-strap gown in so pale a pink it was almost white. He held it up to Patrick and said, "I think we're about the same size," and then he pushed the dress into Patrick's hands.

The satin felt as light and soft as a whisper against Patrick's palms. Tiny glass beads sparkled on the straps and accentuated the extremely low neckline. The back plunged even lower, and another set of beaded straps crossed over it. Patrick couldn't help the stir of excitement that moved down his spine at the thought of that fabric against his skin and the way he might look. He cast around the room for a place to change but didn't find one. "I don't know about this."

"Don't be shy," Aouli urged. "We're all family here."

Everyone always assumed Patrick was shy because he'd kept to himself during high school and quietly went about his work at the Faire without clawing for every shred of attention like some of the others. In truth, he rarely felt uncomfortable meeting new people or speaking with customers. He'd just become accustomed to being ignored, existing behind the scenes instead of in the spotlight, and he'd accepted it because it let him avoid inspection. Tonight, he'd been called cute and complimented more than he'd ever expected. These three men wouldn't judge him. Here, he was safe to experiment a little without the fear of someone barging through the door to kick his ass. Feeling a little rebellious, he draped the gorgeous dress over the back of a chair and slipped his polo shirt over his head.

The gown felt like a second skin, and Patrick's nipples hardened as the cool, silky cloth grazed them. Aouli tugged at the waistline and adjusted the straps. Fabric pooled around Patrick's feet, and he reached beneath to unbutton his jeans and let them fall down his legs until he could step out of them.

Shawn pinched Patrick's chin with his thumb and finger. "Girl's got no ass."

"I think it works in a Gwyneth Paltrow kind of way," Roger said. "She just needs the right shoes." He selected a pair of champagne-colored pumps and handed them to Patrick, who toed off his worn Chuck Taylors and stepped into them, his balance immediately threatened as he teetered in the high heels.

"Let's serve Gwyneth all the way," Aouli said, handing Patrick a long dirty-blonde wig with subtle highlights and heavy, blunt-cut bangs.

Patrick put it on and turned toward the mirror where Aouli had been removing his makeup, careful not to tread on the hem of the dress or trip in the shoes. The other three men clapped as Patrick gasped and raised a hand to his mouth. He just couldn't reconcile the invisible boy no one ever noticed with the lovely creature staring back at him from the mirror.

"Girl, you are ready for the Oscars," Shawn said.

Aouli fussed with Patrick's hair. "You look so elegant, Patrick. That whole jailbait thing is totally gone. You look like a *lady*. You would clean up in tips out there."

"Here," Roger said, "give me your hand."

Patrick did, and Roger helped to steady him as he guided Patrick around in a circle. "Now look over your shoulder," Roger said.

Hair like spun gold cascaded over Patrick's slim, bare shoulder but didn't conceal the lean lines of his back. The gown dipped almost to his crack, only the waistband of his boxers ruining the effect.

"Push your chest out a little bit, girl," Shawn suggested.

"And arch your back," Roger added.

"Oh, damn," Aouli said. "You look sickening! Girl, you're a natural. Ooh, can I do your makeup?"

Feeling a weird sense of unreality but basking in all the unfamiliar praise, Patrick smiled wide and nodded. He thought he'd float away, and little electrical tingles danced across his skin. Never in his wildest dreams had he imagined finding not only acceptance, but people who actually encouraged him to do this.

Someone knocked softly at the door, and Patrick instinctively flinched before he remembered no one in this club would have a problem with him or what he currently wore.

"Yes?" Roger called out.

The door opened, and Eric entered the dressing room.

"Hi, Eric," Shawn and Aouli said in singsongy unison.

"Hey, ladies," Eric responded. "Jesus, is that our little Patrick?"

Roger draped an arm over Patrick's shoulder. "Isn't she a doll?"

Eric shook his head. "Yeah. Yeah, she's a beauty, but I should get her home. We have to drive all the way back to the Faire to pick up her car."

"All right, hon." Roger kissed Eric softly on the mouth and stroked his cheek. "Guess I'll see you back at the house. Love you."

"Love you, Rog. Patrick, we should probably head out."

Patrick hurried to change and handed the dress and wig back to Aouli. Then he hugged the cute Hawaiian man, and Aouli kissed him on the cheek. "Thanks for everything. This has been a lot of fun. I'm really glad I got the chance to meet you."

The other two men embraced Patrick and kissed his cheeks. Then Patrick followed Eric out of the club and onto the quiet street, where they walked to the truck.

"You've been smiling since we left," Eric said as he started the engine. "Can I take that as forgiveness for telling you we were going for coffee and talking to Rog about what I saw?"

"Yeah, I guess," Patrick conceded. "I had a really good time."

"Good. I just wanted you to see that there are all kinds of people in the world, and maybe you're not so different. I want you to know there's nothing wrong with you. I know how it feels to think you're alone."

"You? Everybody loves you, Eric."

"They love a character I play. Only a small and special group of people get to love the real me. Quality over quantity, though."

"But how would it be any different if I decided to dress up and perform?" Patrick asked. "It wouldn't be like anybody liking me for me. They'd like the boy in the dress. I'd just be a fantasy."

Eric laughed a little bitterly. "You're too wise for your age, princess."

"You know, if anybody else called me that, it might piss me off."

"I don't mean any offense," Eric said.

"I know. That's why I don't mind. What I don't understand is why you've taken this sudden interest in me. I mean, we've worked together for three years. Why now? You saw me in a dress, so suddenly I'm worthy of your time?"

Eric shook his head as the white lines of the highway whizzed by them. "No, it isn't that. Well, maybe it is, a little. I just know what I went through, what my poor Rog went through, and I don't want you to have to go through it alone. I want to be your friend, Patrick, and I swear that's all. I don't have any ulterior motives. I'm more than happy with Roger. I'd love to see you find a boy your own age and fall in love. Patrick, you'll never be in love again in your life like you will be now, at this age. Christ, I sound like my father. But it's still true. Don't let this time pass you by."

"Find a boy and fall in love," Patrick repeated numbly. "I guess everybody but me has decided I'm gay."

"Have you ever had an interest in girls?" Eric asked, donning his English accent. "Has any one of our voluptuous lasses spilling out of her corset at the Faire made your loins tingle? Have you imagined your face buried in her luscious breasts?"

Patrick shuddered at the thought of all that extraneous flesh. He wouldn't know what to do with it. "No, not really."

"You're what—nineteen?" Eric asked. "You must entertain fantasies about someone."

"Characters from games and movies, mostly," Patrick said, surprised at what he admitted.

Instead of taunting him as Patrick expected, Eric asked "Which ones?"

"Loki from *The Avengers*," Patrick said softly, not ashamed but not proud to broadcast his feelings. "The Tenth Doctor, David Tennant. Zevran from the *Dragon Age* game. I loved him. Did you play it?"

"I did," Eric said, "and that elven assassin was so hot. I like them slutty and not ashamed of it."

"I—yeah, I guess," Patrick said. He remembered watching the sex scene in the game—the scene with Zevran and the male warrior Patrick played—and how he'd gone back to a previous save so he could watch it again. The third time the cinematic had played, he'd masturbated, feeling like a loser more because he'd become aroused by a character in a video game than because the character was male.

"Fantasy men are safe," Eric said. "They can't reject you, but they also can't love you back. You have to take a risk on a real man, Patrick. He might break your heart, but it's better than jerking off to a paused screen on your Xbox, right?"

"I haven't met anyone worth risking it," Patrick admitted as Eric pulled onto the abandoned swath of grass outside the Faire. He fished his keys from his pants pocket and opened the truck door.

"You will," Eric said with a confident smile.

"If you say so."

"I do," Eric replied. "Some man is going to be lucky to have you, princess. So you choose carefully, okay?"

"Okay."

After he parked his truck in the grass, Eric leaned over to kiss Patrick on the cheek. "You've got me, baby, you know that? And Rog. We're here if you need us." He took his phone from the truck's center console and handed it to Patrick. "Let's exchange numbers. You can call me if you want to talk."

They exchanged numbers and, gripped by true gratitude and an irrational impulse, Patrick reached across the seat to hug Eric. His heart dropped when Eric didn't hug him back for a few seconds, and he wished he could take it back, but then Eric wrapped his arms around Patrick's shoulders and patted his back.

"Thank you," Patrick breathed into Eric's sweet, dark curls. "You'll never know—This has meant a lot to me. God, Eric, if it wasn't for Roger…." Eric's skin and hair smelled so good. Patrick pressed his lips to the apple of Eric's cheek and tasted the tang of perspiration when he pulled away and licked them.

Eric kissed him back, just a few inches from his mouth. "I'm here if you want me. Oh Jesus, Patrick, I'm a married man! Don't look at me like that. But come find me if you want to talk. Or call. Anytime. Go home, sweetheart, and I'll see you in the morning."

"Okay," Patrick said as he walked toward his car. Eric waited until he got inside, then started the engine before pulling away. As Patrick drove home, tired but still excited, he had the surreal feeling that something significant had just changed in his life. His next thought was how silly it seemed to think a night in a bar could change a life, but for the first time, he knew how it felt to receive attention, to be told he was worthwhile, to not be ignored. As for the rest of the questions the evening had dredged up… well, he'd consider them later, when he wasn't quite so tired. For tonight, Patrick decided to let himself enjoy the memory of people telling him he was okay just as he was, that he was cute, and that he had a good singing voice.

Patrick put his iPod on random and turned up the volume as Apoptygma Berzerk's "In This Together" played. Patrick sang along, envisioning himself onstage, performing to the music. He'd wear black vinyl in a nod to the Norwegian synthpop band's aesthetic. Or maybe not. A scanty Elizabethan ensemble, with a corset, bustle, and bloomers, topped off with an elaborate lace ruff, could work just as well. Yeah, he liked picturing himself in that, and it would certainly set him apart from the other performers. God, was he really considering this? His father would kill him if he found out. He'd be so ashamed.

Aside from Eric, what would the other Faire employees think? Would they see he wasn't hurting anyone, or would they just see a pervert? Should he care? Patrick didn't know, but as he drove, the details of his costume crystallized in his imagination. There seemed to be an art to drag, in everything from the concept to the execution, and he liked a creative problem to solve. Further, he knew artisans at the Faire who could sell or lend him everything he'd need, if they weren't disgusted by his request. He could think of a few who might not judge....

By the time he got home, Patrick was too exhausted to think anymore. He stumbled through the kitchen and living room, around his father, who'd passed out in the recliner with a dozen discarded cans on the floor around him. Patrick stripped off his clothes and fell into bed. He worried his overstimulated mind wouldn't shut down and allow him to sleep, but seconds after his head hit the pillow, he dropped into deep slumber.

Chapter 4

THOUGH he performed the same tasks around the Faire as he had for three years, everything felt different to Patrick. Sir Francis Drake was now his friend, and that alone elevated his status somewhat. The other actors and employees seemed to take more note of him as he went about his work, smiling and waving when they noticed him. Patrick wondered if they'd always appreciated him and it had just escaped his attention. It was a beautiful late-May day, with a blue sky overhead, a light breeze scattering flower petals and discarded pamphlets across his path, and the ribbons and banners adorning the shops fluttering softly. Tom hadn't given him any specific tasks that morning, so Patrick wandered almost idly, talking to the vendors and seeing if they needed him to fetch change for their tills or watch their booths while they took breaks.

After he'd emptied the trash bins around the food stalls and delivered a case of toilet paper to the privies nearby, Patrick wandered up the hill to the area where the clothing merchants clustered. Tents, stands, and well-established shops sold everything from costume-quality knockoffs to movie-worthy ensembles costing thousands of dollars. Patrick made his way to a pink building with ivory and gold trim called "Madame's Unmentionables." Champagne-colored roses in gilded urns stood beneath the windows, and all three sets of French doors stood open. Banners with silk-screened female silhouettes snapped in the wind. The inside of the store smelled of lavender incense. Neat rows of mostly white, frilly underthings lined the walls, while various colors of hose sat on tables between them. Mannequins displayed full sets of archaic lingerie, complete with bodices, crinolines, pantalets, and bloomers. Several dress forms stood behind the counter, along with bolts of cloth.

Alone in the shop at the moment, Patrick lifted the delicate silver bell and jingled it. Both of the sisters who owned the shop and made the garments emerged from their workroom in the back. The petite young women wore identical pink-and-gold brocade corsets, pink bloomers, white hose, and little, gold, kitten-heeled shoes. Their elaborate powdered wigs, decorated with rows of faux pearls and flowers, and their snow-white makeup and ruby lips stepped a bit beyond the Renaissance look, but the Faire represented a fantasy for its patrons, not a history lesson. Besides, Fifi and Fleur looked as flawless as porcelain dolls. The women who patronized their store wanted to appear as perfect, and so did Patrick.

"*Bonjour, monsieur*," Fifi said, curtseying to Patrick. "How can we help you?"

"This is a bit of an awkward request," Patrick said, wiping his sweaty palms on the sides of his trousers. "I… I'm looking for…. Would you consider making these things for a man?"

"We've done it before. What things are you looking for?" Fleur asked in her overdone French accent.

"Corset, bloomers, and bustle," Patrick said. "Maybe a ruff."

"For you?" Fifi asked. "Why?"

"Just a costume," Patrick hurried to say. "For a show."

Fifi laughed and came around the counter to clutch Patrick's elbow. "*Oui, oui.* Whatever you need, Patrick. Bloomers in a small size should work for you. They are only fifteen dollars. A fully boned bustle will cost around fifty dollars, but the corset will have to be made to your measurements. That will be expensive."

"I don't have a lot to spend," Patrick said. "Could I maybe borrow the bustle? I'll be sure to pass out your business cards, and I'll only be wearing it for one song."

"Just what kind of show is this, *mon ami?*" Fleur asked as she pulled a tape from her belt to measure Patrick's waist.

"A drag show," Patrick said, his cheeks heating. "I'll be dressed as a woman. It's to raise money for gay pride."

The sisters looked at each other, and Patrick held his breath as he waited to see if they'd ask him to leave. Instead, Fifi said, "In that case, maybe we can arrange for a discount on the corset. Come in the back and we can take your measurements."

Patrick followed them beyond some brocade cloth screens into a cluttered workroom with a set of sewing machines, more bolts of cloth, a table strewn with laces and braided cords, and some garments in various states of completion hanging on a rack. Fifi found a notepad and pen as Patrick removed his doublet and the billowy shirt underneath. Gooseflesh covered his skin as she measured his waist, chest, and the length from his sternum almost to his crotch. The bell rang, and Fleur left them to attend to another customer.

"You're so tiny," Fifi said as she draped her tape measure around her neck. "I bet you'll be able to lace your waist down to twenty-four inches after time. You'll need someone to help you get into the corset, though."

"I know," Patrick said. He'd actually helped lace up many of the women at the Faire over the years. "Listen, I'd appreciate it if you didn't tell anyone about this."

"You have nothing to be ashamed of," she said as she tore a sheet of paper from her pad and tacked it to a corkboard.

"I know, I just don't know how people will react. I don't want anyone to feel awkward around me."

"Everybody loves you here," she said.

"And you don't think that might change?"

Fifi put her hands on her tiny waist, almost encircling it, and dropped her accent. "It'll only change if they're assholes, Patrick. And that says something about them, not you. So, when will you need this?"

"By the end of June," he said as he got dressed.

"And what were you thinking for color?"

"I want everything to be black," he said.

"Ooh, how very Goth." She knelt down and sorted through some fabric folded neatly on a shelf until she found the one she wanted and handed it to Patrick.

He ran his hand over the cloth. It was black, but with a subtle iridescence that shimmered violet and turquoise when he shifted it. A delicate, swirling pattern in flat velvety black meandered over top. "This is beautiful. But will it be sturdy enough to lace tight?"

"This is just the icing on the cake," Fifi said. "The actual corset will be constructed from heavy canvas and steel boning. Don't worry; we know what we're doing."

"About the price—"

"How about two hundred for the corset, twenty-five for a black lace neck ruff, and I'll throw in the bloomers if you'll take some pictures for our website?"

"That's really generous," Patrick said, slightly ashamed to accept. A corset like this usually sold for at least four hundred dollars, and the ruffs for fifty or more. He had some idea of the time they took to construct. Many of the Faire patrons wore them season after season and they still looked like new. As well-made, durable, and beautiful as they were, the garments were worth every penny Fifi and Fleur charged. On the other hand, it was still a lot more than he could afford.

"You can make payments," Fifi suggested. "Just put down what you can afford every week. Even if it takes a little longer than June."

"Are you sure?"

She smiled. "Hey, I know where you work. Besides, I think you're going to look so gorgeous me and Fleur will have orders pouring in from everyone who sees you. Just make sure the other drag queens know where to go for all their intimate apparel needs, and don't forget you promised me pictures. This could be a whole new source of clientele for us, and that could really help us in the off-season."

"Anytime," Patrick said and kissed the hand she offered. Her skin smelled of roses and talc.

"I have a friend who's a photographer," Fifi said. "Would you be opposed to posing with me and Tracy—er, Fleur?"

"No, that sounds like a lot of fun. Where do you get your wigs?"

"From a site called Cosplay Kingdom. They're actually cheaper and better quality than most wigs, but they're custom-made and have to come from China, so you'd better order it pretty soon."

Patrick groaned. "I'm afraid to even ask—"

"The one I'm wearing was one fifty," she said. "Me and Tracy do the jewelry and flowers ourselves. I can help you, if you want."

"Thanks for everything," Patrick said.

"Hey, I love this stuff," she answered. "It'll be fun to try something a little more daring. Looking forward to it."

Together, they went back to the counter, and Fifi drafted an invoice. Patrick reached into a leather pouch he wore around his hips and handed Fleur his debit card to offer them at least a small down payment. He thanked them again and left the shop with the intention of finding Tom and asking for more hours.

Outside, someone called, "Hey Patrick! Shopping for a new pair of lacy knickers?"

He turned to see a group of knights waving to him from across the street. For a second, he was terrified Sirs Henry, Ian, and Carlton had somehow overheard, or worse yet, seen what he'd been doing in Madame's. He tried to reassure himself it was impossible; the other young men hadn't been around when he'd gone in, and Fifi and Fleur's workroom had no windows. Patrick took a breath to banish the mini heart attack and walked across the cobbled lane to join the knights.

"I was just talking to Fifi and Fleur," he said, trying to sound casual and not like he needed to defend himself. "Seeing if they needed anything."

"I wish what they needed was a comely, blond knight willing to satisfy their every desire," Henry said, swooning theatrically. "One who would deftly wield his sword on any quest they might choose him to fulfill."

"Aye," Carlton said. "I'd like to be the meat in that French sandwich."

All of them laughed, and Patrick joined in, even though he really wanted to ask the knights to stop talking about the sisters like that. They'd been so kind to Patrick, and what the knights said felt sleazy. Still, over the years, he'd grown accustomed to the current of mild sexual innuendo running beneath the wholesome surface of the Faire. The young men didn't mean any genuine disrespect, and if they'd made the same jokes to Fifi and Fleur's faces, the sisters would have likely bantered right back.

"What are you good knights about this fine day?" Patrick asked.

"We've come in the hopes of enticing some of these goodly people to show their support for Her Majesty and the tourney," Carlton said. He turned to a group of young women wearing floral circlets with their blue jeans and T-shirts. "What say you, lusty wenches? Care to witness our expertise with pole and pike?"

The girls tittered, and some of them covered their mouths. "Um, where is it?" a cute brunette asked, her cheeks red and eyes sparkling as she stepped closer to Carlton.

Carlton scooped up her hand, bowed theatrically, and kissed the back. "If it would please thee, it would be my great honor to escort you ladies to the arena."

"Okay," the brunette said, and her friends nodded enthusiastically, all of them giggling and sharing meaningful glances.

"Right this way," Carlton said, hooking his elbow with the girl's, to her apparent delight.

"I suppose we too must do our part," Henry said, turning to an older couple and bowing. "Good den, my lord. My lady. It doth please me to request you attend the joust in Her Majesty's honor. It will commence upon the hour, just down this hill and upon the field beyond."

Patrick watched as Henry moved up and down the street, trying to encourage people to attend the joust. Patrick found Henry the nicest-looking of the three, though all of the young knights were very attractive. Even more than his bright blue eyes and angular face, Patrick liked the way Henry always seemed to have fun with whatever he did. He always smiled easily and honestly, and his approach soon had a large group of patrons ready to follow him to the arena.

"Will Tom be at the joust?" Patrick asked Ian, who he knew preferred actual combat to interacting with his audience.

"He usually is. Why?"

"Just hoping to talk to him about more work," Patrick said. "Need the money."

"You should ask about joining the cast," Ian suggested. "It pays better than the staff positions. You have any experience performing?"

"Not really," Patrick said.

"You should still ask him," Ian said, brushing his dark hair out of his eyes. "You'd have to give up that shy, quiet thing you have, though. It's cute, but you have to be more of a showman."

"Cute?" Patrick asked.

Ian shrugged. "Plenty of the girls say so."

"They do?"

"Yeah, they like that innocent quality. And nobody knows much about you, so it makes them wonder. Plus, you're, like, the only guy here who isn't always trying to hook up, so they see you as a challenge. Why is that, anyway? You have a girlfriend?"

Patrick froze as Ian crossed his arms over his chest and leaned a shoulder against the wooden lintel of a shop. The way Ian's brown eyes bored into him made him feel like Ian knew, like he could see every buried secret. Shifting uncomfortably, he answered, "No, I just respect women. I don't see them that way."

Ian laughed. "They want you to see them that way, idiot. We might be pretending we're in the Dark Ages here, bro, but we're not. They want it just as bad as you do, and a lot of these girls aren't looking for marriage, if you know what I mean. For some of them, all you have to do is buy a flower, and for some of them, not even that. What makes you think women don't enjoy getting laid as much as men? Trust me. You can probably take your pick at the joust today. Just buy her a rose and ask her to meet up at the Stew. The rest will take care of itself, believe me. Anyway, I have to get going. I'm fighting in the second match. I'll see you there, and hopefully I'll see you tonight at the pub. And not alone."

Great, Patrick thought. Now he had to find a way to wriggle out of asking a girl to the Stew. He wished he could just tell Ian he didn't want to without the suspicion he knew that would raise. He didn't want to lose the few friends he had. Maybe he could just avoid the joust and claim he'd found some work he needed to do. But he really wanted to talk to Tom, and he couldn't lie about who he was forever, could he?

He couldn't help wondering why they all cared so much how he spent his spare time as he wandered down the lane toward the arena. He'd just decided to simply tell Ian he felt like going home, that he didn't owe anyone an explanation, when he saw Jennifer sitting alone on a bench between two buildings. As Queen Elizabeth, she never traveled without her retinue, or at least her ladies-in-waiting. Besides, she should already be seated in her royal box at the joust in her honor. She had to give a speech and choose her champion before the tournament could commence.

Patrick shouldered his way through the throng and dipped into the narrow alley. "Jen? Is everything okay?"

She sniffled, wiped her nose on the back of her hand, and looked up at him with damp, smudged eyes. Then, as people always seemed to do when they were upset and somebody asked about it, she forced a little smile. Patrick sat down next to her and took her hand. He reached into his pouch to offer her a tissue. "Anything I can do?"

She shook her head, making her rich red ringlets bounce around her shoulders and rustle the high, stiff lace collar of her brilliant blue gown. "It's stupid."

"What is?"

"God, I'm embarrassed to even tell you. It's… it's fucking Taylor."

"The Duke of Anjou?" Patrick asked, just to be sure, since a new actor had assumed that role this year.

With a sneer, Jen nodded. "That son of a bitch has been hitting on me since he started, and I kept turning him down. He's sleazy; it's not that 'want to polish my sword, Your Majesty?' joking around we all do with each other. I was almost ready to say something to Tom, because it was getting really uncomfortable when we had to perform together, and then I ended up getting way too drunk at the Stew. Fucking stupid. Anyway, some stuff happened...."

"Did he force you?" Patrick asked in a horrified whisper, an unexpected surge of anger flowing through his limbs and turning his hands into fists without his conscious intent.

"Nothing like that. We just made out in a booth in the back for a while. I was sober enough to put a stop to anything else he tried, thank God. But this morning when I checked my Facebook page in the dressing room, I saw that he posted, saying some really nasty things. People I don't even know are calling me a slut. The worst part is everybody believes him over me. People I've worked with for years are taking his side. Everyone thinks I'd really do something like that, even though I never have before. They've been whispering and staring all day. I feel like I'm back in fucking high school." She balled her fist and pressed it to her lips. "I've been avoiding Taylor all day. I don't think I can face him at the joust."

Patrick stood and offered her his elbow. "Everyone will be disappointed if the queen isn't there. Come on; don't give him the satisfaction of keeping you away. I'll come with you, if you want. And for the record, *I'm* on your side, for what it's worth."

She stood and kissed him on the cheek. "You're so sweet, Patrick. How is it some girl hasn't snatched you up yet?"

As they walked arm in arm, Patrick actually considered telling her the truth. He thought about how much easier it would be if everyone just knew. Right now, Jen needed his support, though, not to have his problems competing with her own. They made their way to the wooden stairs leading to the queen's box. People filled the bleachers beyond the wooden fence, and the smell of horses was strong. Young men and women sold flowers and tiny banners, just triangles of felt attached to wooden sticks, some printed with the Tudor rose for Elizabeth and others with the fleur-de-lis for Anjou. At the foot of the steps, Patrick prepared to take his leave, but Jen clutched his arm and whispered, "Would you mind staying and sitting with me?"

"But—only your courtiers are supposed to sit with you."

Rolling her eyes, she said, "Come on. It's not like I'm a real queen. What are they going to do, execute us? Please, Patrick? I could really use a friend right now."

"Okay," he said. "Of course." The people lining the bleachers cheered when Jennifer waved at them, and the other actors, those portraying the French aristocrats on the opposite side of the field included, stood and bowed.

Jim, who played Sir Walter Raleigh, announced, "Her Majesty Elizabeth, by the grace of God, queen of England and Ireland. God save the queen!"

"God save the queen!" the audience responded.

"Thank you all for joining us on this lovely afternoon," she said. "Please enjoy the tournament." Though she usually offered a lengthier speech and a few mild jokes, Jen just chose Henry as her champion, tied a ribbon from her dress to the end of his lance, and sat down on her padded bench beneath the awning.

From his seat a few feet away, Eric shot Patrick a quizzical look, and Patrick just shrugged. He had no intention of telling anyone what Jen had shared. It was nobody's business but her own, and she could tell Eric if she chose to. Across from them, Taylor indicated Jen with a jut of his chin before whispering something to the woman next to him, who laughed and covered her mouth with a fan. Jen's jaw twitched and her cheeks reddened.

"Just ignore him," Patrick whispered. "He's not worth it."

Though Jen nodded, she looked like she wanted to be sick.

Unlike other Faires, theirs offered a genuine joust; nothing was choreographed, so the knights actually fought and no one knew beforehand who would be victorious. Today, all of the fighters went out of their way to put on an exceptional show, and all of the matches were very close. Henry even suffered a bloody nose, but he bested the French knight chosen by Taylor's companion, to the crowd's great delight. Patrick had never taken the time to sit through an entire tournament, and he enjoyed it, finding himself very caught up in supporting his friends. The fighting even seemed to distract Jen from her worries, and she smiled and cheered for her champion. At the end, she presented Henry with a red rose, and he tossed it into the audience.

The queen stood to more cheers. After a few minutes, she lifted her hand and spoke. Patrick wondered if the audience noticed the cruel curve of her painted lips or the sharp, dangerous glint in her blue eyes. "Kind lords, ladies, lads and lasses, our most sincere thanks. It would seem that, despite the boasting of the Duke of Anjou, his prowess doth not back it up. While any man can bluster, or even utter falsehoods, a true man proves his worth by how he hoists his lance, and, once again, my English knights have demonstrated mastery of their weapons. Perhaps the French skills with spear and javelin have been exaggerated? Perhaps French steel does not remain as straight and rigid as the weapons wielded by our fine, British lads. I will have to remember that."

"The man who needs to brag about the size and strength of his lance is often the least adept at hoisting it," Henry yelled from below. "Remember that, Queen Bess!"

The patrons supporting England cheered, while those on the French side booed. Jen waited for them to calm down before saying, "In parting, we wish to thank our true and loyal friends and subjects. You know who you are, and you have our eternal gratitude. Now, do remember to attend our musical finale at the conclusion of today's festivities, and God save you all."

Eric stood and clapped his black-gloved hands. "God save you, Your Majesty!"

"Thank you, Sir Francis," Jen said, "for all your good service."

As people left the bleachers, a crowd of merchants met them to hand out pamphlets, business cards, and coupons. Carts selling food and drinks offered refreshment, and musicians and acrobats performed for tips. Boys hurried to have their pictures taken with the knights and pet the horses, and Patrick knew the young girls would want to meet the queen. Despite her subtle vengeance after the tournament, Jen seemed reluctant to leave the royal box, even though the wide eyes of her admirers gazed up at her expectantly.

"There are going to be a lot of disappointed little girls if you don't go down there," Patrick said.

"Taylor's down there." She canted her head toward the handsome dark-haired duke surrounded by smiling women.

"Yeah, and who's more important? Those kids who look up to you or that dickhead?"

Jen smiled, shook her head, and brushed Patrick's face with her gloved fingers as she kissed his opposite cheek. "I should have named you my champion. Will you come with me? God, you must think I'm so pathetic."

"It's not pathetic to need a friend once in a while."

"Thanks, Patrick. Come on. Take my arm and let's do it right."

"Yes, Your Majesty," he said with a smile. They descended the stairs and walked around to stand in front of the royal box. Little girls lifted the hems of their Disney-pink polyester gowns to run toward the queen. As Jen knelt down to speak with them and have her picture taken, Patrick's gaze wandered across the field to the knights.

Henry looked particularly valiant with his wheat-blond hair fluttering in the breeze and a line of dried blood flaking beneath his nose. As usual, he offered a sincere smile to everyone who queued up to shake his hand or request a photograph, showing no impatience as kids tugged at his tabard and shouted questions. Carlton stood at the epicenter of a ring of young women, while Ian had retreated to the back of the crowd, near the weapon rack. Ian looked down at his sword, which had been damaged during the tournament, and soon another young man crossed the lawn with long, sure strides. Patrick didn't recognize the slender man in tight gray leggings, simple black boots, a dirty white shirt, and a blue bandana covering his long black hair, but he couldn't take his eyes off him as he took Ian's sword and examined the hilt. Something about the way he moved held Patrick captivated.

Patrick nudged Jen's shoulder as soon as he could capture her attention without interrupting her. "Hey. Who's that?"

She stood and shielded her eyes against the late-afternoon sun. "I think he's Wade the blacksmith's new apprentice. Why?"

"Just wondered," Patrick mumbled, squinting to watch the young man scowl at Ian's weapon before carrying it away in a great hurry. Patrick's unexpected disappointment followed the stranger until he disappeared into the small city of faux Tudor buildings beyond the field. Then he remembered Jen standing beside him and felt guilty for ignoring her, especially the way she felt today. Most of her ardent fans had dispersed in favor of the caramel corn vendor. Patrick knew Jen needed his attention far more than some strange man's ass, no matter how enticing it looked in his skintight leggings. "What do you want to do now?"

"Actually, I'm starving," she said. "All this bullshit had me too sick to my stomach to have any breakfast, and I'm regretting it now."

"Okay. Me too. Where do you want to go?"

"Feel like a turkey leg?" she asked.

"Ugh. Not really. Can you get away for a McDonald's run?"

"Yeah, fuck it," Jen said. "As long as I'm back in time for finale. Damn, Patrick. You can intuit my desire for cow and greasy fries. And a sundae! You're like the sister I always wanted. Oh, I didn't mean that as an insult or anything."

"I'm not insulted," Patrick told her. "Actually... this will surprise you, but I—"

"Moved on already, I see." It was Taylor. "I'm not surprised, but I'm a little offended that *this* is the best you could do to replace me."

"Patrick is more of a man than you'll ever be, you sick son of a bitch," Jen said. "Just leave us alone."

Taylor crossed his arms over his chest and lifted his chin smugly. "This little boy? I guess you'll spread your legs for anybody."

"Anybody but you," Jen said, her voice strong even though her hands trembled.

"That's not how I remember it," he said with a sneer. "And now everybody else knows what their queen really is."

"Oh, and what's that?" Jen asked.

"A slut who puts out after one lousy drink."

"You're a liar, Taylor!"

"You're a whore, Jen."

"Enough." Patrick stepped in front of Jen, extending his arm as if he could shield her from the hurt and humiliation. "Just fuck off, Taylor."

"Or what, bitch?"

Without thinking, Patrick drew back and punched Taylor in the shoulder. He hit harder than he'd intended, and Taylor landed on his ass in the gravel, a cloud of dust rising around him. "Just fuck off and leave us alone, Taylor! You're such a pitiful little child, acting like you're in high school! Who the hell do you think you're impressing with this bullshit? If you had anything going on, you wouldn't have to make up lies."

Taylor scrabbled to his feet and dusted off his velvet breeches. "You're fucking dead, you little bastard!"

Though he'd never been in a fight, Patrick's anger at Taylor's treatment of his friend trumped any anxiety, and he gritted his teeth, ready to throttle the other man. God knew Taylor deserved it, and Patrick raised his fists as they squared off.

Before either of them landed a blow, Tom appeared from behind one of the striped canvas tents. "Is there a problem?"

They looked at each other and frowned, just like two kids on the playground who hated each other but still didn't want to tattle. A bizarre solidarity formed between them.

"No, it's fine," Patrick mumbled. Jen's pleading expression told him she didn't want Tom to know what had happened, what she'd let happen, and Patrick wouldn't embarrass her.

"I just need to change for the finale," Taylor said before slinking away. Before he left the arena gate, he looked at Patrick over his shoulder. "I'll see *you* later. Count on it."

Patrick resisted a strong urge to flip Taylor the bird and turned to Tom instead. "I wanted to talk to you."

"Go on, lad."

"I, um, I've been with the Faire for a while now, and I was kind of hoping to move up a little. Maybe join the cast. I… I could still keep up with my other duties, of course. The truth is, I need the work. So, yeah. If there are any openings in the cast, I hope you'll consider me." Patrick was glad of Jen's supportive presence, her hand on his shoulder as he voiced his request.

Tom smoothed down his wiry gray beard. "The only thing I have right now is an opening for a minstrel."

"What about Bianca?" Patrick asked.

"She's fantastic," Tom said. "But I could use a male minstrel. You understand; for the ladies. Can you play an instrument?"

"I played the cello in elementary school," Patrick said. "But it's been a long time."

"All right, son," Tom said, dropping his accent, which meant he was serious. "Bianca can show you enough about the lute to get you by. You should pick it up pretty quickly if you've played a stringed instrument before. Come up with a character by next weekend, and as long as it's viable, I'll put you on the cast."

Patrick grabbed the older man's hand and shook it ferociously. "This means more than I can tell you, Tom. And I still want to help out on staff."

"You're a good boy, Patrick, but you need to break out of your shell if you're going to perform. Can you do that?"

"Yes, sir. I think I can. Thanks for giving me a chance."

"Yes, well, don't let me down," Tom said as he turned to leave.

"No, sir."

Jen clasped Patrick's hand. "This is awesome! We'll be on the cast together."

Taylor glared at them as they walked by the blacksmith's shop, and Patrick searched the area for the beautiful young man he'd seen before. Who was he, and why did knowing matter so much?

"McDonald's?" Jen asked.

"Do they have champagne?" Patrick asked.

"Huh?"

"Shit, Jen. I'm on the cast!"

"Oh. Oh! Patrick, I'll get you some bubbly, babe. You were totally gonna kick Taylor's ass for me, weren't you?"

"He's a fucking jerk-off."

"Patrick, do you *like* me?"

"Yeah. I love you. I think you're gorgeous, Jen. I just don't want to have sex with you. You're my friend. I—I'm—"

"What?" she asked.

"I'm just your friend," he said.

Jen lifted her hand and Patrick slapped it. "I'm glad," she said.

"Me too." They hooked their elbows together and made their way through the idyllic village toward the gates and the parking area beyond.

"Patrick, I'll find out about the boy at the blacksmith's shop for you."

"I—What?"

Jen shook her head. "I'll find out for you, because I love you and I know you'd like that. This is the first time you ever, um, *wanted to know about* anyone from the Faire. You don't have to say anything. It's cool."

"Is it?" Patrick's hand shook as he opened the car door for Jen.

"Dude. You're gay. So what?"

"I haven't decided if I'm gay," Patrick said as he slouched in the driver's seat.

"I always thought it wasn't a decision," Jen said.

"I—I'm not ready to say one way or the other."

"Okay," she said. "Makes no difference to me, anyway. Jesus, give me a little more credit than that, okay? Let's go get a Happy Meal. God, I'm starved!"

"Yes, Your Majesty." He pulled out of the grassy parking area and onto the road toward greasy fast-food goodness. Even in the most awkward situations, people needed to eat, and he planned to order at least three cheeseburgers. After that, well, he would just have to see what happened. His life had been full of surprises lately.

Chapter 5

THOUGH Patrick spent the rest of the day performing the same duties he always had, a fresh current of energy seemed to run through the Faire, making him as excited, nervous, and happy as he'd been on his first day three years earlier. A crackle of electricity moved through the cobbled lanes below his feet, through the lush leaves of the old oak trees lining them, and through the red and white rosebuds stretching toward the warm early-summer sun. His fantasy-inclined imagination perceived it as enchantment. The colors seemed more vibrant, and the music, which he'd always loved, sounded even sweeter. He was a member of the cast now, a real part of the Faire, and it felt even better than he'd always imagined to finally be fully included. In anything. As Patrick emptied bins and swept sidewalks, almost everyone who passed stopped to clap him on the shoulder and offer congratulations. It felt like he'd materialized after spending his previous lifetime invisible, and everyone took notice. While he enjoyed the accolades, the idea of living up to everyone's expectations frightened him a little bit. No one had ever expected anything from him before, and he swore to himself he wouldn't let them down.

Word had also spread of Patrick's confrontation with Taylor, and he sensed a new respect, especially from the other men.

"Nice going," Henry said under his breath, brushing Patrick's shoulder as he walked by. "Taylor's a douche. I wish I could have been the one to toss him on his ass, but I'm just glad somebody did it."

Ian and Carlton, as well as a group of the French knights, nodded when they saw him, and Eric gave him an enthusiastic thumbs-up. Even Tom shook his head with mock disapproval when he saw Patrick again, but he smiled proudly. For the first time, Patrick noticed the Faire's female employees and patrons watching him, blushing and whispering to each other, looking away when he tried to meet their gazes.

Patrick considered going to the Stew when the workday ended. He wasn't ready for this magical day to be over just yet. At last, his life was falling into place, and he felt he'd finally found the path he wanted to follow amidst all the tangled bracken that had obscured his way until now. He couldn't believe how easily those briars had been cut away. But at the tavern's entrance, Taylor and a group of his fawning friends gathered, smoking cigarettes and looking already drunk as they shouted at the girls sitting at the outdoor tables beneath the grapevine-covered trellis. Since Patrick didn't see anyone else he knew, and knowing he didn't possess the legendary bravery everyone now gossiped about, he decided to visit wardrobe, as Tom had suggested, and then go home to get to work on his character. He didn't want to blow this wonderful opportunity.

Using one of the many keys on the ring at his hip, Patrick unlocked a small shed between the men's and women's dressing rooms. It held all the costumes and props the actors weren't currently using, and it smelled of must and neglect, like a forgotten attic. Patrick flipped the light switch and almost despaired at the rows and heaps of garments. How would he ever find anything salvageable in this chaotic forest of fabric? Sighing with resignation, he went to the nearest rack and started sifting through the old linen and velour. Soon, he realized the shed contained some really wonderful pieces, and all they needed was some care and a bit of creativity to shine again. He felt like he'd unearthed a chest of pirate treasure.

Two hours or so later, Patrick teetered beneath a mound of cloth, leather, and costume jewelry, barely able to free a hand to lock the door. He felt even more elated than he had before as he envisioned altering the garments he'd collected and his character started to solidify in his mind. Though he could barely see over the pile of fabric in his arms, he made his way to his car, opened the back door, and dumped his burden on the empty seat.

As he drove home, Patrick's costume took shape in his imagination. He couldn't wait to start sewing and embellishing. Rolling down all the Horizon's windows, he inhaled as the verdant night air flooded the little car's interior. It smelled new and hopeful, if hope could have a fragrance. No matter what happened, Patrick felt sure he'd always remember exactly how this late-May evening smelled: fresh-cut grass, warm asphalt, cow dung, and stale old velvets. The fragrance of hope was the smell of things just starting out, things with time to grow and see what they'd eventually become. The soundtrack to *The Rocky Horror Picture Show* came on Patrick's iPod, and he turned it up and sang at the top of his lungs:

"Don't dream it, be it...."

When he parked in front of the house he shared with his father, Patrick's happiness started to fizzle away, more like a slowly leaking tire than a burst balloon. The lawn needed to be cut and the walkway weeded; if he let it go too much longer, the town would issue a warning, then a fine. Patrick despised the embarrassing notices tacked to the door, stating that the water or gas would be shut off, or that the home was an eyesore and needed attending. The leaflets were always neon green or orange, just to make sure no one missed them. Patrick saw them as his personal scarlet letters.

Patrick struggled to turn the old brass knob with his arms full of clothes, and then he shouldered it open. Inside, it smelled of stale beer, old socks, and old men who saw no need to wash regularly since they didn't have jobs to go to. The kitchen sink overflowed with dishes caked in drying food, and the garbage bin brimmed over, spewing cans and foil wrappers across the scuffed, linoleum floor. Patrick would have to bag it up, and soon, or he'd miss the truck and it would sit stinking for another week.

In the living room, Patrick's father sat on the sagging sofa with Al and Bernie, two other unemployed drunks. After all these years, Patrick harbored no illusions about his father. Once, as a child, he'd thought his life normal, though he'd slowly noticed his father didn't make it to parent-teacher conferences or the school play like the other dads. He also waited for a disability check to arrive in the mail instead of kissing his family good-bye each morning and going off to work. Patrick had noticed his clothing was shabby and too small compared to what the other kids wore. He had soon found he had to rely on himself to make dinner, even if it consisted of questionable bologna, day-old bread, and mustard. Or hotdogs. Always hotdogs. Patrick couldn't even look at them anymore. He'd spent the last five years of his academic career filling out the free lunch forms himself, just so he could eat something besides hotdogs and greasy bologna. He especially detested the round, marbled, red-and-white conglomerate little known outside Pennsylvania: Lebanon bologna.

To Patrick's horror, the three men sat watching a porno movie. Unmistakable moans and grunts echoed from the speakers, and mounds of flesh jiggled on the screen of the old TV. Patrick Senior and his companions grunted their approval as they slurped their Old Milwaukees. An entire city of empty cans stood on the old coffee table, with wads of foil from Danny's Dawg House and Six-Pack Store forming a topographic moat. Patrick buried his face in the garments he held and prayed he'd make it to his room without notice.

No such luck. "Boy, get tha' six-pack outta the fridge," his father bellowed.

"In a minute," Patrick mumbled. "My hands are full."

"Full o' what?" Al asked, punctuated by a multisyllabic belch.

"Work," Patrick snapped.

"Bunch a fucking dresses," his father said. "Jesus. Get us a beer! Men drink beer, they don't carry around a heap of fucking dresses." The images on the TV screen almost made Patrick retch. He headed down the hall to deposit the clothes onto his bed.

Though he knew he should have just closed the door and stayed in the space he had claimed as his own, Patrick returned to the flashing blue lights of the untidy living room. "I got a promotion," he announced, not sure what reaction he expected or why he even bothered. "I'm on the cast at the Faire now, and my salary's almost doubled."

"Get us a beer," Bernie said in a gassy slur. When Patrick hesitated, he chucked a crumpled can at his head, to the great amusement of Al and Patrick Senior.

Patrick dodged, and the rumpled column of aluminum ricocheted off the battered cabinet doors.

"What the fuck?" Patrick snapped, the delicate matchstick bridge he'd built between himself and his father shattering. "Get your own beers, you fat, lazy old bastards. I've been working for the last ten hours."

"Aw, poor baby," Bernie said.

"Get us a beer, you little faggot," Al demanded.

"Get your own, you prick!" Patrick swatted away the beer can Al hurled. "And don't call me a faggot."

"Yeah, go suck another cock at the fairy ball, you little queer. At least you ain't my son. You even look like a fucking girl. *Faggot.*"

"Fuck you," Patrick snarled, flinging the refrigerator door open. Hotdogs and bologna. Plenty of ketchup and mustard, but nothing to put it on besides pinkish-gray processed meat. Or that hideous loaf of artificial red with flecks of white fat. Looking at it made him feel sick.

"Your boy's a sausage goblin, Patty," Al said, and all of them laughed. "Wearin' fucking panty hose and dancin' around with flowers in his hair."

"Fuck you," Patrick repeated, too angry and disgusted to formulate a wittier reply. "You guys are pathetic—three grown men picking on a nineteen-year-old."

Patrick's father hoisted his bulk off the couch. "Hey! You disrespectin' my friends now, boy?"

"Leave me alone."

"Apologize to Al and Bernie, Patty. They're"—he belched loudly—"your fucking elders. Apologize."

"For what?" Patrick snarled.

"Jus' say you're sorry, boy."

"No."

His father backhanded him, and Patrick pressed his chin against his collarbone as blood filled the hollow between his teeth and lower lip. He spit a red gob on the hideous rust-brown carpet. It was so fouled with refuse a little more wouldn't matter. The threads were already stiff with spills that should have been cleaned up long ago, and it smelled terrible.

Al and Bernie laughed.

"Tell 'em you're sorry, boy," his father repeated.

"I'm not sorry. Get your hands off me, you *sorry* old drunk!" Patrick shouted, shoving his father in the shoulder like he'd shoved Taylor and sending the old man stumbling backward. He didn't know where he'd found this sudden source of strength and courage; maybe it had to do with accepting himself and having at least a few people at his back. "Just stay the fuck away from me!"

"Bitch-boy's got an attitude," Bernie mumbled.

"You want to say something, old man?" Patrick shot back. "Why don't you get your fat ass off that couch?"

"Fuck you, you little cocksucker," Bernie muttered in reply.

"Get up," Patrick said again. "All of you. I'm so fucking sick of living like this!" He kicked one of the rickety chairs away from the table and it shattered against the wall, limbs flying everywhere.

"Ain't no anchor tied to your ass, boy," Patrick's father said. "There's the door."

Patrick rubbed his palms from his chin to his forehead and back in manic swipes, as if he wanted to wipe something away but couldn't scrub himself clean of it. He wanted, *needed*, to get out of here. For now, he retreated to his room, shut and locked the door, and turned on a TV his father only dreamed of owning. He used his Xbox controller to start some old *Doctor Who* DVDs he'd found in the bargain bin at Target and turned it up to drown out the sounds beyond his room. Gingerly he touched his swollen lip and winced. It hurt, but not as much as his father's refusal to stand up for him. Patrick didn't know why it hurt—he couldn't remember the old man ever defending him—but it still felt like he'd swallowed something hot and acidic that now bubbled up into his throat and chest. As much as he wanted to expel it, he knew it would just refill, so he choked it down as he always had.

Patrick stretched out on his twin bed beside the bundle of clothes from the Faire, fished his phone out of his jeans pocket, and scrolled down through the contacts. He didn't want to be in this house tonight; he needed to be anywhere but here until Al and Bernie stumbled up the street to their houses and his father passed out on the recliner in a mushroom cloud of his own gas. He wanted to be with somebody, somebody who might congratulate him on his promotion, who'd be sincerely happy for him, or at least polite enough to fake it. As he looked at the names whizzing by on his screen, Patrick realized he didn't really have any friends. He'd had a few in school, acquaintances he sat with at lunch, but he'd always been too embarrassed to invite them here and they'd lost touch after graduation. More than that, Patrick realized he'd never reached out to people on more than a superficial level, never formed any deeper ties. He's always assumed others wouldn't understand or accept him, and he'd never given them the chance to prove him wrong. Even his budding friendship with Eric had been accidental rather than anything Patrick had instigated. Jen had been right; he'd never given anyone the benefit of the doubt. Looking at her name and number, Patrick considered calling her, but he dismissed the idea when he remembered her recent drama.

He wished Dylan could be here with him, could stand beside him against their father. But then, did he really want Dylan subjected to this? Was it only selfishness that made him wish he had an obligatory ally?

However it had started, his friendship with Eric was better than nothing. Patrick touched Eric's name and pressed the phone to his ear. Eric picked up on the third ring, and Patrick nervously said his name.

"Patrick?" Eric responded. "Is everything okay?"

"Yeah," Patrick said, trying to keep the trembling out of his voice. "I… uh, I was just wondering if maybe you and Roger wanted to do something. Go get something to eat."

"Honey, are you sure you're all right?" Eric asked. "You sound like you've been crying."

"No, nothing like that. I just... I just got a promotion today at work, and I kinda wanted to celebrate with somebody." Patrick hated how needy he sounded. "I just thought maybe we could go for a pizza or something."

"Oh, we'd love to, but we're babysitting Rog's nieces tonight, and we just managed to get them to sleep. Those two girls can be hellions when they're hopped up on soda and cupcakes."

"I understand," Patrick said.

"Listen, we're thinking of having a cookout on Wednesday, so why don't you come by then?"

"Okay," Patrick said.

"Great! Lots of people from the Faire will be there, so just come by around four. I'll text you the address."

"Okay," Patrick repeated. "Um, should I bring anything?"

"You can if you want, but you don't have to," Eric said.

"I'll think of something," Patrick said.

"Patrick, are you sure you're okay? You're not in trouble, are you?"

"No, I promise. Listen, Eric, I don't want to keep you. I'll see you on Wednesday."

"Congratulations on joining the cast," Eric said. "Good night."

"'Night," Patrick said softly before disconnecting the call. His stomach rumbled, reminding him he hadn't eaten since lunch. Going out for something meant getting past his father and his friends again, and if he ordered delivery, those three drunks would snatch it up before he ever made it to the door. Instead, he turned his attention to the heap of garments, hoping to distract himself from his hunger. Some ideas about his costume already floated around his head, and they began to solidify as he sorted through the fabric. He found two pairs of velour leggings, one green and one rust-red. He took a small pair of scissors from the drawer of his night table and began to pick apart the inseam threads of the emerald pair. By the time Patrick's eyes started to lose focus from exhaustion, he'd hand-sewn the separated pieces together so he had a pair of trousers with one reddish-brown leg and one green. He held them up, pleased with his work. He'd save the discarded bits of velour to add detail to the ensemble later in the week. Yawning, Patrick stood, stretched, and shifted the pile of clothing to the floor. He put his scissors and sewing kit back in the drawer and stripped down to his boxer shorts before crawling into bed and turning his TV off with the controller. Thankfully, only quiet came from the living room. Patrick set his alarm so he could wake up and do his laundry before his father rose, hungover and grouchy. Then he'd get some breakfast and mow the lawn. The garbage, he thought with grim resignation, would have to wait till the following Sunday.

He looked at Dylan's picture on his night table and blew it a kiss before turning out the light.

BY WEDNESDAY, Patrick had completed his costume: the dual-colored leggings, a floppy, muffin-style hat made from triangles of leftover velour, and a simple beige linen doublet he'd enhanced with some gold cord. It would do until he could make or afford something a little more impressive. Having it finished meant he could spend the day thinking about the cookout at Eric and Roger's house, which he looked forward to attending.

As usual, he got up earlier than strictly necessary so he could shower and leave the house before his father woke up. The place smelled in the early summer heat, and Patrick looked guiltily at the dishes in the sink and the fruit flies circling the bin. He knew he should at least stay long enough to tidy up, but he was sick of being the only responsible one, of basically being the parent since he'd been nine or ten. He tried to convince himself he deserved to be a teenaged boy for a day and go to a picnic, to enjoy what everyone always told him would be the best years of his life before they passed him by. Why should he feel ashamed? Still, he did, but he slammed the door decisively anyway.

The day outside could have been painted by a happy child, with its bright blue sky, puffy white clouds, and flowers of every color just beginning to bloom. A tender breeze ruffled the dark-red hair that now reached past Patrick's collarbones. The farther he got from the house, the further away his worries felt, as if he'd left them locked in that dark and fetid place. He got into his car, tossed his backpack on the passenger seat, rolled the windows down, and turned on the radio.

Before leaving his dilapidated little neighborhood, he stopped at a deli called Tony's a few blocks away. Like most of the buildings in the vicinity, it had a shabby exterior marred with black streaks left by the exhaust of passing vehicles and a sagging roof, but the food it served rivaled the fancy cafes in the city and then some, and everything inside was sparkling clean. Patrick bought a container of fruit salad and one of the deli's famous (at least locally) red potato salad. Then he programmed Eric and Roger's address into his phone's GPS and followed its directions to their home in Pittsburgh's Mount Lebanon suburb. Just as he pulled into the driveway, he got a text message from Jen:

R U @ Eric's?

Just got here. Why?

Have a surprise 4 U! Be there soon!

Patrick shrugged and stuffed the phone in his pocket before collecting the food and heading toward the brick Craftsman-style house with tan and hunter-green trim. A plump oak cast refreshing shade on the front lawn, and ferns lined the walkway. Fifi and Fleur, or Tish and Tracy, as they were known outside the Faire, parked their silver Volkswagen Beetle on the street just as he reached the bottom step. Without their elaborate wigs, both had messy pixie haircuts, Tish's platinum blonde and Tracy's an almost neon hot pink.

"Hi, Patrick," Tracy yelled, waving, as Tish got out of the car, carefully balancing a three-layer cake with white-gold icing and pink roses. It reminded Patrick of the lingerie in their shop, somehow. Everything about it was frilly, feminine, and meticulously perfect. "Come on. Everybody's probably out back."

He followed them around the side of the house to a large yard obscured from the neighbors by a tall hedge. Some picnic tables had been set up, and all kinds of food covered their surfaces. As Patrick and Tish added their offerings, she whispered, "Those things you wanted should be done by the weekend."

"That was fast!" Patrick's pulse sped up at the thoughts of owning those beautiful garments, of wearing them, of seeing how they'd look on him, and of others seeing him in them.

"It was a fun project," Tish said, "and I can't wait to see—"

His expression must have been sufficiently horrified, because she stopped talking and rolled her eyes. "Anyway, come by Friday or Saturday."

"Okay," he whispered, like he'd agreed to take part in some conspiracy, and feeling a similar illicit thrill.

The back door opened, and Roger emerged carrying a large platter of beef patties and hotdogs. He stretched his neck to kiss Eric as he set them down on a stand next to the grill. Eric sipped from a bottle of India Pale Ale as he cooked. Soon the smell of charcoal smoke and savory food filled the yard, and more guests arrived: Tom and his wife Susan, followed by Henry, Ian, and Carlton, and then Shawn and Aouli soon after. Everyone settled onto the benches and padded lounge chairs. Patrick sat down next to Tish and Tracy, absently crunching barbeque chips as he watched for Jen and her mysterious surprise.

"Hey, Patrick," Eric called from within his curtain of smoke. "Hotdog or hamburger?"

"Hamburger," Patrick said quickly.

"Bacon and cheese?" Eric asked.

"Yeah, definitely!"

"Well, come and get it," Eric said, motioning Patrick over with a wave of his spatula.

Patrick grabbed a paper plate and a roll and hurried to receive his feast. Just as Eric placed the fat, juicy burger on the bun, Jen came around the side of the house with a catlike grin. She wasn't alone: two of the actresses who portrayed her ladies-in-waiting were with her…

and so was the boy from the blacksmith's shop. Patrick almost dropped his food as he watched the other young man stride with unassuming confidence into the yard. He wore fitted, dark jeans and a tan T-shirt with a distressed floral pattern that hugged his slim but muscular chest and showed off arms sculpted by hours a day at the forge. Jen tipped her head in Patrick's direction and winked, and he just wanted to find a place to hide. He wasn't even sure if he was interested in the blacksmith's apprentice or if he'd just mentioned him to gauge Jen's reaction. Sure, he was nice-looking…. Actually, he was *really* nice-looking, so much so Patrick seemed unable to tear his gaze away. His heart flopped around in his chest like a fish out of water, and his fingertips tingled as he clutched the edges of his plate in both hands. He even felt a little dizzy.

"So, this is Eric and Roger," Jen said to the attractive stranger. "This is their house. And these are their friends Aouli and Shawn. I think you've made weapons for everybody else here."

"Not for me," Tracy said, sauntering over with a glass of bubbly pink wine in her hand. "Although maybe that needs to change. I'm Tracy, known as Fleur at the Faire."

The young man grasped the hand she extended, while Jen glared at them both. "What would you like?" he asked.

"To know your name," Tracy said.

"It's Yu. Yu Elion."

"Well, then, Yu, how about something I can hide in my corset?" She took a step closer to him without releasing his hand.

Yu, looking impassive, neither impressed nor annoyed, said, "We actually make a line of those. The handle curls over the edge of the bodice so it just looks like jewelry, or a decoration."

"Let's not talk about work," Jen said. "Yu, come meet everyone else. This is my friend Patrick. He just joined the cast."

For what seemed like hours, Patrick just stared at the hand Yu offered him. Then, feeling like an idiot, he set his plate down to shake it. Yu's grip was firm but not overpowering, and his palm was warm and covered in rough callouses. His full, deep-rose lips curled in a small smile. Patrick just stared. When he'd seen Yu from a distance, he'd thought his hair was black, but it was actually a rich, deep brown streaked with bronze and copper. His eyes were almost a caramel color, and he smelled good, like soap and fresh laundry.

"Uh, nice to meet you," Patrick said.

"Likewise," Yu said, letting go of Patrick's hand.

"Would you like something to drink?" Roger asked. "We have wine, beer, soda, and iced tea."

"Iced tea will be fine, and thank you very much." Yu turned away to follow Roger, and Patrick was forgotten.

Patrick was used to being forgotten, though. He sighed and retrieved his plate, then went to find a seat on a bench. At first he thought he'd lost his appetite, at least until he tasted the burger. He finished it quickly and took a second one, along with a large helping of potato salad, some of Jen's homemade mac and cheese, baked beans, and deviled eggs.

"You're going to ruin your girlish figure," Aouli warned.

"Leave the boy alone," Shawn said. "He's still growing."

"Ugh, I miss the days when I could eat like that," Aouli said, sipping chardonnay and nibbling on a slice of melon.

"Bitch, you're twenty-four," Shawn teased.

"I think you look great," Patrick said.

"Aw, thank you, sweetheart," Aouli said, feigning surprise and batting his lashes.

Across the lawn, Yu sat with Ian, Henry and Carlton, picking at his food and engaging in polite conversation. From what Patrick heard, they spoke mostly about weapons and armor for the joust. From his posture, Yu didn't seem quite relaxed or comfortable; he sat stiffly while the others reclined on lawn chairs. He didn't smile nearly as often as the three knights. Patrick softened a little toward the other man. He had no right to be angry with Yu. Likely Jen had just invited him under the pretense of friendship, to get to know some of the people at the Faire, and that was what Yu was doing. What had Patrick expected, that

Yu would propose to him or something? Yu obviously had no inkling of Jen's intentions, so how could Patrick be bitter toward him for not playing along?

He watched Yu a little longer as Aouli and Shawn teased each other at the edge of his vision. Yu moved with an easy, understated elegance, and his hair looked both soft and shiny in the afternoon sun. He'd come here to make friends, and while Patrick might have entertained some silly fantasy about more, he could also use friends.

"Excuse me," he said to Aouli and Shawn before he stood to dispose of his plate and join Yu and the knights.

"Well, if it isn't our resident ass-kicker," Ian said, raising his beer bottle.

Heat spread across Patrick's cheeks as he perched on the edge of a wooden chair.

"I wish I could have been there to see it," Ian continued. "What did Taylor do, anyway?"

"He was just being a dick to Jen," Patrick said, burrowing his toes into the grass. "And all I really did was push him. I don't think we should bring it up, though. It might upset her."

Yu narrowed his eyes and regarded Patrick, as if he'd decided Patrick was one thing and now wondered if he might be something else. Or maybe Patrick read too much into it, and Yu just squinted against the sun.

"Well, I'm sure he deserved it," Henry said with a tone of finality. "He acts like he's better than the rest of us because he went to acting school or some shit."

"Let's just forget about him," Patrick repeated. The conversation lulled after that, and Patrick cast around for a topic to break the awkward silence, but nothing came to his mind but lame statements about the food or how nice the weather was. Though he knew he might embarrass himself, he took the risk and asked, "So, Yu, where did you learn to be a blacksmith?"

Yu perked up a little, though he kept any excitement he might have felt tethered tightly to him. "I learned basic forging techniques at a folk school in North Carolina. It gave me a good foundation, and it was a unique experience, but it focused more on functional items, and I've always wanted to make weapons. That… wasn't so well received on what was essentially a hippie commune. Don't get me wrong; I'm grateful for the knowledge, and I got a solid foundation there, but I felt it was time to move on."

"Is that where you're from?" Patrick asked, finding the conversation came easily when he had no motive other than genuine curiosity.

"No, I grew up outside DC," Yu said, a little frown pulling at the corners of his lips as he stared into his tea and churned the ice cubes around. Patrick had enough bittersweet memories of his own to recognize them swirling behind another's eyes. He didn't pursue the topic.

Carlton spoke. "So, are you…?"

"What?" Yu asked.

"Like… Chinese, or what?"

Patrick rolled his eyes, but if Yu took offense, he didn't show it. "My mother's family is Japanese-American, and my father is of German and English descent," he explained in a flat, formal way. Patrick could tell he didn't like talking about his past and his family, and he wondered why even as he understood completely.

"Are you in school now?" he asked, hoping to change the subject.

Again, Yu brightened, and Patrick felt like the sun broke through the clouds and shone down on him. "I'm hoping to start again in the fall, at Pitt, majoring in Studio Art with a minor in Medieval and Renaissance Studies."

"Cool," Patrick said, genuinely impressed. "I never thought about making a career out of Renaissance Studies. I've always felt a connection with that period, and I think we can learn a lot from it."

"I wish my parents agreed with you," Yu said. "They think I'm being foolish, and they're not willing to pay for it. They say I'll never find a job, but I'm trying to get into the work-study program and make up the rest with loans. I'm fascinated with traditional methods of forging and with the history of arms and armor. I can't imagine being happy doing anything else. What about you? What are you studying?"

"I... haven't decided what I want to do yet," Patrick said. He'd done quite well in high school and knew he'd be accepted into a good college if he applied, but he had no way to pay for it. "Right now I'm just working at the Faire in the summer and at a gas station during the off-season, trying to save some money."

"What do you love?" Yu asked, his bluntness catching Patrick off guard. "What's your passion?"

"I guess I haven't found it yet," Patrick said softly and not entirely honestly. Working on his minstrel costume had stirred something buried within him, and so had designing and commissioning the ensemble he hoped to wear at the drag pageant. So had putting on Jen's pink dress, watching himself transform, but he didn't want Yu turning away from him in disgust or dismissing him as a freak. "I'd just stay at the Faire forever if I could."

"That sounds like love," Yu said.

Patrick looked up, right into unblinking eyes edged in thick, dark lashes, eyes like afternoon light shining through amber, eyes that, for once, seemed to look at him and into him instead of past him or through him as everyone else seemed to do. Patrick smiled in gratitude, but then he quavered and blushed. Why on earth would a talented, dedicated young man like Yu take an interest in the aspirations of the kid who emptied the bins? It was all wishful thinking.

The soft tap of a fork against glass drew everyone's attention, and they turned toward Eric, who stood next to the grill with his beer raised. "Glad you could all make it," he said in his commanding, Francis Drake voice but without the accent. "I'd like to propose a toast to one of our dear friends and most loyal supporters, a young man who has worked hard for years behind the scenes and is now about to take his rightful place in the spotlight. To Patrick! Congratulations on joining the cast! We're very fortunate to have you."

"To Patrick," everyone said, raising their drinks. Many people clapped, and Tish cheered out loud, hooting as she punched the air.

Patrick's face and ears burned to rival the coals in the grill as everyone smiled at him and called his name, but it was a pleasant heat, like the sun beaming down, and not the hurting fire of mockery or humiliation. He looked at the happy faces of the people around him— his friends—and smiled in return.

Yu reached out and touched Patrick's shoulder, making Patrick flinch. "Congratulations," he said, his eyes crinkling to crescents as he offered Patrick one of his sparing smiles. "Maybe you'll find your passion after all."

"Thank you," was all Patrick could manage.

"Will you be needing a sword?"

For once, Patrick actually wished for the cheesy double entendre everyone at the Faire used when discussing anything longer than it was wide, but he knew Yu didn't mean it that way. Somehow he knew Yu wasn't the type to make sleazy jokes. "I'm afraid I don't know how to use one," he said, the split meaning still appropriate.

"Well, we can fix that!" Henry said brightly. "You should come by the stables for a lesson."

Patrick dragged his mind out of the gutter with some effort, banishing the images of the three young knights teaching him how to handle his sword before his body betrayed him.

"Totally," Ian said. "You should be able to handle a weapon. It'll give a whole other dimension to your character: the cute little minstrel boy who can kick your ass!"

"Defender of the kingdom's fair damsels!" Carlton agreed.

"Yes, our secret champion in motley clothes," Jen said, as she came up behind Patrick and leaned down to kiss his cheek. "Congratulations, Patrick. I want to get together and work out a few skits with you." She ruffled his hair and returned to her friends on the other side of the yard.

"Holy shit!" Carlton whispered. "Dude, are you hitting that?"

"That? Jen is a person, not a thing," Patrick said. "And no. She's my friend, and I don't like anyone talking about her that way."

Carlton held his hands up in surrender. "Chill, man. It's just an expression. But just to be clear—you're not with Jen? Not trying to be? 'Cause if you're going for her, I'll stand down. But if not—"

"I'm not going for her," Patrick said. "We're just friends. But I will take offense to anyone who doesn't treat her with the respect she deserves."

For some reason, that made Yu smile, or else Patrick imagined it again.

Chapter 6

THROUGHOUT the day, a dozen people from the Faire stopped by the cookout and stayed for an hour or so. Patrick got to meet Rog's sister Kate, her husband, and her two little girls, Naomi and Melissa. By the time the sun set and the suburban sky deepened to rich cobalt washed over in streetlight orange, only Eric, Rog, Aouli, Shawn, and Patrick remained in the yard. They'd pulled their chairs around a chiminea and sat within the bubble of light it provided. Fragrant twigs popped and hissed within, and music played softly on the radio.

"Glad you could come," Eric said to Patrick. "Did you have a good time?"

"I really did," Patrick said. "Thank you so much for inviting me."

"You're welcome here anytime, darling," Rog said, sprawled out next to Eric on a chaise lounge and running the pad of his thumb along the stubble of Eric's jaw. "Maybe next time we all get together, it'll be for your coming-out party."

Eric swatted Rog playfully on the shoulder. "Don't pressure him. He'll come out when, and if, he's ready."

"He'll be happier when he's honest with himself and proud of who he is," Rog argued, braiding his fingers with Eric's.

"I'm worried about how everyone at the Faire will react," Patrick said. It felt good to give voice to the concerns he'd felt for so long.

"I'm so comfortable there, and everyone's comfortable with me. I can't stand the idea of them seeing me differently or not wanting to be around me. It's kind of been my home, the place I felt safe and accepted over the years."

Eric sputtered out a laugh. "You're worried about the people at the *Faire*? Jesus, princess, the Faire is already a collection of outcasts. It's a place where nerds and freaks feel accepted. The whole idea of the Faire is that people can come and be themselves without fear of judgment. Nobody is going to care that you're gay."

"I'm not…. I don't know if I…."

Rog sat up and rested his elbows on his knees. He looked Patrick right in the eye. "You do know, honey. What are you afraid of? Look around. Nobody here is going to be offended. Even if you're not ready to say it to anybody else, say it to us. Say it to yourself."

"I… I guess I do like… maybe…."

"Be proud, honey," Shawn said. "You got *nothing* to be ashamed of."

"I am," Patrick said softly. He'd known it for a long time. "I'm gay."

Aouli got to his feet and jumped up and down, clapping. "This calls for some champagne! No more holding out on the good stuff, you stingy bitches!" He went to the cooler, dug through the ice, located the bottle he wanted, and popped the cork. Foam shot out and crawled down the curve of the green glass. Aouli poured the golden liquid into his glass, then Shawn's, and then Roger's.

"Wait," Eric said. "How old are you, princess?"

"Nineteen," Patrick said. "Almost twenty. I… I guess I shouldn't."

"Oh, Eric!" Aouli said with a theatrical pout.

Eric rolled his eyes. "I only wanted to say, if you're drinking, even one, then you're staying here tonight. Okay? Your parents won't mind?"

"My dad will never even notice I'm gone," Patrick said with a prickle of guilt. Who would wash the dishes? Would his father bother to eat? Would he eat something bad and get sick, or leave the stove on and start a fire—?

"Well, then, it's a party," Aouli said, filling a glass and then handing it to Patrick. "Let's drink to our baby sister!"

"To Patrick," Eric said, raising his disposable plastic flute.

"I don't know about all this," Shawn said. "Skinny bitch is gonna make me look bad."

"Does this mean you want to perform?" Rog asked, excitement wafting off him like the heat from the chiminea.

It all felt surreal, like a beautiful dream, and Patrick banished his doubts and just went with it, let it carry him along like a rose petal on a gentle breeze. "I do. I talked to Tish and Tracy about a corset and bloomers, and I've ordered a wig. I think I want to give the amateur pageant a try. I mean, I'm sure I won't win—"

"The hell you won't," Shawn said, standing. "You never get on stage with that attitude. You get up there thinking, *knowing*, you're the fiercest bitch in the house. You got it?"

Patrick nodded and downed the rest of his champagne, a little intimidated by the almost angry passion of Shawn's declaration.

"Well, let's see it," Shawn said, hands on hips. "I wanna see you be fierce. Go on, get up."

"I don't know—"

"Honey, if you can't strut your stuff in front of us, how the hell you gonna get up on stage in front of a hundred people?" Shawn persisted.

Aouli poured Patrick another glass of champagne and then went to the stereo. He fiddled with the controls until a catchy beat thumped out of the speakers. Then he knelt down in front of Patrick and rolled Patrick's jeans up to his knees. Taking the bottom of Patrick's shirt and looping it through the collar, he fashioned a sort of halter top that exposed Patrick's entire midsection. Then he turned the music up. RuPaul's "Supermodel" captured Patrick's pulse, and he sauntered around the ring of chairs.

"No," Roger said, coming up beside Patrick. "No, honey. You're too stiff. Use your hips. Watch. Thrust your hip, take a step, hip, step. See? You've got to work it. Twist at the waist. Know you're sexy. Tease. Use your whole body."

Watching Roger, Patrick tried again, his body feeling looser, more fluid. He let his pelvis sway and his waist bend as he walked to the back porch steps, turned, and strutted back to the fire. His stomach muscles stretched and contracted, and he twisted his body and tossed his hair.

"That's hot," Shawn said. "Exaggerate it. You got to be better than real. Shake that booty, hon!"

Patrick let his ass swing from side to side as sweat broke from his pores. He'd never been the object of everyone's attention like this, and of course he enjoyed it. The small amount of alcohol helped him relax, and he ran his palms down the taut muscles of his belly as he moved to the music. God help him, he was getting a little turned on. What would Yu think if he saw Patrick now? Would he find it a travesty, or would he like the way Patrick's damp skin caught the firelight as he shimmied and twined?

"Here. I'm going to teach you how to walk, sister," Aouli said, coming to stand beside Patrick. Side by side, they put their hands on their hips. "Now, you're used to walking like a man. You've got to walk in a straight line, one foot in front of the other. Heel to toe. Big, bouncy steps."

Aouli demonstrated, Patrick copied, and Shawn, Rog, and Eric clapped.

"Not bad, princess," Eric said.

"Again," Aouli said, pirouetting back toward the porch. Patrick mimicked the gesture and lifted his feet in tandem with the other man. Together, they strutted to the back steps, spun, and walked back to the chiminea. "Lift your feet, Patrick. Make every movement count!"

After two more rounds, Patrick was sweaty and his muscles twitched with tension, but he felt amazing, sexual and enticing. He felt like he could demand attention instead of hoping for a cast-off scrap of it. For the first time, he felt worthy of adoration, and he couldn't wait to show this newfound side of himself to the world. Maybe to Yu Elion.

Eric handed him another glass of wine, white zinfandel this time, and Rog asked, "Want to try it in heels?"

"Okay," Patrick said, his confidence soaring, eager to continue showing off and earning praise.

Rog went into the house and returned with a clunky-looking pair of white pumps that reminded Patrick of something a grandmother might wear to church. Still, he unlaced and pulled off his canvas sneakers and slid them on. When he stood and tried to walk, he stumbled, his center of gravity thrown off.

"Put your weight on the ball of your foot," Rog coached. "It'll make you stick your ass out, but that's the point."

"Your calves look amazing," Eric said from his seat by the fire.

"Bend at the waist," Shawn said. "Put your chest out."

"Nice," Aouli said as Patrick took their advice. "You were born for heels, honey. Your legs are to die for."

After half an hour's practice, Patrick could walk in the shoes without staggering. Aouli replayed the RuPaul song, and the three of them practiced walking back and forth while Rog and Eric offered tips and encouragement. When the song ended, Patrick collapsed on the edge of the chaise, body strained and tired, but feeling beautiful, feeling right. Aouli poured him more white zinfandel.

"So what are you thinking for the pageant?" Aouli asked, stirring the coals in the chiminea with a stick.

"I know just what song I want to use," Patrick said. "'In This Together', by Apop."

When the other four men looked at each other, clearly not familiar with the song, Patrick fished his iPod out of his pocket and went to the stereo. "I really connect with it," he said as the music played.

"It's a really nice song, Patrick," Rog said.

"But?" Patrick asked.

"It's an unusual choice. Most people won't recognize it, and it's a man singing. That's a risky choice for a queen, especially an amateur."

"I really want to perform to this song," Patrick said. "I can—I can make it work. I know I can."

"It's got a good beat," Shawn offered. "But Rog is right. Audiences usually respond better to songs they recognize."

"It has to be this one," Patrick said. "I can't explain. I just feel like it has to."

"Okay," Rog said. "And what do you have in mind for a costume?"

Patrick described the beautiful garments he'd commissioned from Tish and Tracy, as well as the wig he'd ordered and the makeup he planned to wear. Only silence awaited him at the end of his account. "What? What's wrong?"

"It just might be a little over most guys' heads," Rog offered gently.

"A little too artsy," Aouli agreed.

"But it will be different," Eric said. "He'll stand out."

"Yeah," Shawn said. "I just don't know if everybody will get what he's trying to do. Most dudes go to a drag show to see a hot queen and maybe have a laugh. I'm not sure they want something they have to think about this much. It could work against him."

"So he should dumb it down?" Eric argued. "I don't agree with that at all. Let him go out there in the things he loves, to a song he loves, and if people don't get it, that's their problem."

"But he's trying for some prize money, babe," Rog said. "This might just be too weird for him to win."

"Then let him pick," Eric said. "Do you want to go safe and mainstream, do what people will expect, or do you want this to be art, Patrick?"

"Art," Patrick said without a second's hesitation. "The money would be nice, but I don't care if I don't win. I'd rather leave people with something to think about, something they'll remember after the show. I want a reaction, whether it's love or hate."

"Oh shit," Shawn said. "We have created a monster."

"No," Patrick said. "The feminine arts, at least in the Renaissance, were all about understatement and mystery. Poets talked about women like these unfathomable goddesses, like they were something more than human and completely enigmatic. They wrote verses about them because they couldn't comprehend them. Things people can't fully understand will intrigue them, make them question what they find beautiful. That's what we do, right? Make people redefine their ideas of beauty?"

"You're too damn smart for your own good, princess," Eric said, though he looked both pleased and proud as he smiled at Patrick over the rim of his wine glass.

"I think I found my passion," Patrick said as he sipped his wine. The other men sat down around him, relaxing and looking up at the stars shining dimly against the glow of the nearby city. "What do you guys think of Yu?"

"The cute Asian boy?" Aouli asked. "I'd say he's a tough one to call."

"How do you mean?"

"I mean, my gaydar's usually, like, 99 percent," Aouli said. "But I got nothing from him. Either way."

"Some high walls up around that one," Shawn agreed. "Very guarded. That usually means trouble."

"I like him," Patrick said in a frail whisper.

"I can see why," Rog said, clasping Patrick's hand. "He's a hottie. But, hon, I just don't think he's interested, so don't waste your time."

"So anybody who doesn't want me for… like that… is a waste of my time?"

"No," Rog said. "Of course not. Go ahead and be his friend. He seems like he could use one. Just don't fool yourself or waste your energy where it isn't welcome. Believe me, it just leads to heartache."

"I know," Patrick said. All through high school, he'd fantasized about boys who would never give him the time of day. To protect his fragile psyche and its delusions, he'd told himself he wanted to be like those boys, not that he wanted them. He'd transferred his admiration of them from physical longing to envy, and it hadn't been much of a stretch. Everyone loved them, those boys he'd pined for while walking the corridors of his school like a ghost. Of course he'd wanted to be the one everyone adored, but he'd also wanted to be with those gorgeous young men, confident in the prime of their lives, and he was only just beginning to realize it. He also realized no amount of longing would sway a person's desires. If Yu wasn't interested in him like that, so what? It was no fault of Yu's. Patrick found Yu interesting, and he would be his friend. Yu certainly didn't owe Patrick any devotion, especially a fondness that might not be in his nature to feel.

"There'll be others," Aouli said. "Wait until guys see you in a pair of lacy panties."

"You'll have to be very careful," Eric said in a more serious tone. "You'll get a lot of attention, and guys might want to take advantage of you. Some of them can be very convincing."

Patrick nodded, though he still pictured the lace panties. "Um, that reminds me. How exactly do you guys…. I mean… what do you do with… everything? Aouli, you were wearing a swimsuit. Where does it all go?"

The other four men laughed. When Rog finally caught his breath, he came and sat down next to Patrick. "Honey, we're not laughing at you. It's just that we can relate to the curiosity."

"I know," Patrick said.

"Anyway, think about what happens to your body when you get really cold," Rog explained.

"Everything shrinks up," Patrick said, hoping Rog wasn't going to tell him he had to put ice down there.

"It does more than shrink up sometimes," Rog continued. "Have you ever been so cold it felt like your nuts were crawling back up inside your body?"

"I guess so." He'd felt that way a few times, working at the gas station in the winter.

"Well, before you grew up, when you were still just a young boy, they were up there, inside your body. For some guys, they go back in when it's cold enough. What I'm saying is there's a place where they can go. You can pop them back up in with a little practice. And once they're out of the way, you just tuck your penis between your legs."

"No," Patrick gasped, shocked at what he heard, sure Rog was teasing him, trying to get him to believe something ridiculous.

"It really doesn't even hurt as long as you don't try to force them," Shawn said. "And if I can keep *my* shit out of sight, you shouldn't have any trouble."

"Oh, puh-lease," Aouli said. "Patrick, just give it a try some time when you're relaxed. Lie down on your back and just... see what you can do. You'll want to shave everything first, and it's a lot easier if you don't get aroused, so you might want to take care of that before you try."

Patrick nodded, surprised the others spoke so frankly of such intimate matters, and even more surprised the conversation didn't embarrass him. These men just wanted to help him, and they felt no shame in talking about his body or their own, and their ease put Patrick at ease. He poured himself another glass of wine, kicked the granny pumps off, and wriggled his toes into the dew-damp grass. He leaned back in the chair and looked up at the sky, feeling completely content and delighted to finally be a part of something. Two things, really; he was now a full cast member at the Faire as well as an initiate into the clandestine society of these beautiful creatures. They'd shared their secrets with him and called him their sister. Patrick tried, but he couldn't imagine how the others could benefit from helping him. Maybe they truly just liked him and wanted to see him succeed....

Hope, like a little moth with translucent wings, circled his head as if drawn to the warm light he felt inside. Though frail, it drew closer, and Patrick thought if he stayed still enough it might even land on his shoulder....

The next thing he knew, Patrick was bolting up as Eric gently removed the empty glass from his hands. "Time for bed, princess. Come on. I'll show you to the spare room."

It took a moment for Patrick to remember his surroundings. When he looked around the lawn, he noticed Aouli and Shawn had left. Roger collected paper plates and wadded-up napkins and put them in a black plastic bag. The embers in the chiminea had all but gone out, leaving the small yard dark and much chillier than it had been before Patrick had fallen asleep. The stars shone brightly, as if to compete with the distant glow of the city, and the moon had fallen below the horizon. Shivering, Patrick yawned and stretched his arms over his head before standing up to follow Eric into the darkened house and up the stairs to the second floor.

"You'll have to forgive the décor," Eric said as he flipped the light switch. "Rog keeps this room for his nieces. He just adores those little girls."

The room had a lovely bay window with a padded bench in front of it overlooking the backyard. Ivory and pink striped wallpaper covered the top half of the large space, and distressed, whitewashed paneling skirted the bottom. Crown molding with a similar finish accented the juncture between wall and ceiling. Two beds with lacy white canopies and rose-printed quilts sat on either side of the room, each with a night table and lamp nearby. A long, rectangular white rug covered the hardwood floor between them. A small crystal chandelier sent prisms to dance along the shelves of books and toys, mostly things from the Faire like hand-carved wooden soldiers, sculpted cloth fairy dolls, clay dragons, and ceramic unicorns. A Tudor-style dollhouse sat on a stand with a pair of upholstered stools in front of it.

"This is so beautiful," Patrick said, trying to imagine growing up in a household where someone valued him enough to go to so much trouble. "It's right out of a fairy tale. Naomi and Melissa must love coming here."

Eric chuckled, crossing his arms as he leaned against the doorframe. "They love it because Rog spoils them rotten. He'll have to get a handle on that if we're ever going to raise kids of our own, or they'll turn out to be monsters. Anyway, the bathroom is just through there, if you want to wash up or anything. I'll let you get some sleep and see you in the morning."

"Eric, thank you. This... this has been one of the best times I've ever had. I... just wanted to thank you for inviting me."

"You are very welcome. Good night, Patrick." Eric softly latched the door.

Patrick stripped to his boxer shorts and crawled between the pink satin sheets, just glad he'd managed to stop himself before he'd asked Eric to take him in, be his father, and let him stay in this wonderful place.

Chapter 7

PATRICK spent the next day with Eric and Roger. They had brunch at a charming little French bistro and bakery, and then spent the rest of the day scouring thrift shops and vintage clothing stores for items both Rog and Patrick could use in their acts. At first Patrick had wanted to buy everything he saw, but he'd reminded himself how badly he wanted to move out of his father's house and restricted his spending to a few items he simply couldn't pass up: a pale green skirt made of layers of tulle and chiffon; a necklace with three strings of faux pearls and a big cameo in the center, plastic but still with an antique feel; and a snug tank top with a Union Jack made of rows of sequins. It reminded him of the one Rose Tyler had worn in an episode of *Doctor Who*—the first episode to feature the drop-dead gorgeous Captain Jack Harkness—so he couldn't pass it up. At a consignment shop, he found a short black vinyl skirt for only two dollars. Roger also took him to a shoe store specializing in larger sizes, and he bought a pair of black satin kitten-heeled pumps to wear at the pageant. He planned to glue some white velvet roses to the toes and maybe add a row of beads. After hours of shopping, they ate dinner at a Korean barbeque before returning to the house in Mount Lebanon so Patrick could retrieve his car.

When Patrick got home, he left his treasures hidden in the trunk of his car, planning to sneak them inside while his father was out or asleep. The fluctuating blue light behind the stained curtains told him he wouldn't get the opportunity tonight. He stood on the stoop, his hand on the greasy brass knob, wishing he didn't have to go inside. But he needed to put a few finishing touches on his minstrel costume and practice the few tunes he'd managed to pick up on the recorder. Then he needed to work on mastering that damn lute. Steeling himself and planning to rush straight to his room and lock the door, he went inside.

A familiar stench hit Patrick like a brick wall: body odor, musty clothing, and cheap alcohol. His father intercepted him in the kitchen and blocked his way. Al sat at the table next to an empty plastic bottle that had probably been filled with vodka. Patrick Senior swayed and grasped the edge of the counter to steady himself. Apparently they'd started early. What else would they do on a Thursday afternoon?

"I been thinking," Patrick's father slurred out, his curdled breath almost making Patrick gag. "I ain't getting no more child support from your bitch mother, and you're a grown man now, Patty. So I been thinking, if you wanna keep staying here, maybe it's time you started paying your own way. You're too old for me to keep letting you sponge off me. Give me fifty bucks."

"So, you're out of drinking money?" Patrick asked.

His father grabbed him by the collar and shoved him. Patrick's back hit the corner of the old refrigerator before he landed on his ass. Al laughed as Patrick's father stood over him with his fists balled.

"You can give me the money or you can get the hell out of here tonight."

"I don't have that much, Dad," Patrick said as he scrambled to his feet. "I have to pay my car insurance, and I paid the water bill last month so they wouldn't shut it off."

"Waa-fucking-waa," his father said, pretending to wipe his sagging eye with his fat fingers. "You give me something, or you get out."

"And go where?" Patrick struggled not to cry, not to give the old prick that satisfaction.

"What do I care? I'd be happy to get you off my ass. Give me twenty dollars, or pack your shit and go."

"You'd really do that?" Patrick asked. "Kick me out with nowhere to go? You really don't give a shit what happens to me?"

"I never wanted kids," his father said. "I told that bitch to get an abortion. Maybe if you'd been in that car—"

Patrick reached into his pocket and threw a wad of crumpled bills, a twenty and a few ones, on the table. It was all he had left in cash; the rest was safe in an account at the credit union Faire employees could join. His weakness disgusted him, and as much as he wanted to leave, he had nowhere to go at the moment. The words his father had finally spoken aloud had shredded him up inside, and he felt no more worthwhile than the hotdog wrappers lying on the floor by the bin. Damn it, he'd always tried to believe somewhere, deep down, his father loved him, even if alcoholism and despair prevented him demonstrating it. The proof that he'd been deluding himself was both devastating and liberating. Patrick felt like he could finally leave without the burden of guilt. He could leave and not feel like he'd abandoned his father to wallow in his own filth and drink himself to death.

Couldn't he?

God help him, he wanted to be with Dylan, in the soft, perfect, golden realm he imagined Dylan inhabited, drifting along on the downy wings Patrick's imagination provided. He wanted to be there with Dylan, transcending all this bullshit. Free. Safe. Finally cherished.

Patrick Senior picked up the money, waved it in the air, and hooted in triumph. "Let's go get some more of this Nikolai shit. Al, can you drive?"

"Oh yeah," Al said. "Hey, I got an idea first. Let's get pretty Patty here to suck our dicks. Just looking at the top of his head, we can pretend he's a chick, and a blow job is a blow job, right? He looks like he's got the lips for it. Just like a bitch."

Patrick held his breath and waited for his father to explode, to finally grab the other drunk and say, "That's my son, damn you. This time you've gone too far."

Instead, the old man shrugged and muttered, "Whatever. The liquor store closes at nine, though."

Patrick couldn't quite bite back the sob that tore from his throat. He rammed his father with his shoulder as he ran past, and he yanked the money from the old man's hand on his way to the door. Tears blurred his vision by the time he got outside, and he turned his face toward the twilight sky and screamed. He kicked the rotted old post, and the roof above him shuddered, threatening to fall down on his head. He hurried to get into his car and away from the house before the two old men could pursue him.

As he pulled onto the highway, driving too fast and letting the night air smack his cheeks and twist his hair around his face, Patrick cried out loud, sputtering and choking as snot ran from his nose and over his lips. He pressed down on the gas pedal, his Horizon's engine revving. He just wanted to reach the one place he'd always felt at home, accepted and valued, the place he knew would never just dismiss him and tell him to leave, that he wasn't worth anything.

The Faire parking area was empty when Patrick slammed his brakes, tearing up grass and damp soil. The amber lights gilded the wet grass and the wildflowers as they stood still against the clear cobalt sky. Patrick unlocked the gate with the key on his ring and wandered slowly up the lanes, past the pseudo daub and wattle buildings with their colorful banners, curving balconies, well-tended flower gardens, and winding cobblestone paths. The Faire felt different at night: quiet, empty, all his. At night, Patrick could roam the lanes between the storybook buildings as a prince. He didn't have to share his kingdom with anyone else. He found it easy to pretend the rest of the world and all its ugliness didn't exist beyond the Faire's wooden fences and the old trees marking its boundaries.

He pulled the recorder from his pocket and played a slow, atonal tune as he walked in the direction of the food court. The turkey leg stand, the pie shop, the bakery, and the sandwich stall stood boarded up, so Patrick sat on a bench near the central fountain. The tinkling of the water kept the rhythm as he played another tune. Though he knew it was a silly fantasy, a childish dream, he wished he could live here, in a Wedgewood-blue house with white lintels and pansies spilling from the window boxes. If only the fantasy society they'd created here could actually exist, and Patrick could buy his bread at the bakery, his wine at the Stew, his clothing at Madame's, and… and something from Yu.

Thinking of Yu, he wandered in the direction of the tournament field and past the striped tents where the knights rested and changed, toward the blacksmith's shop.

The horses nickered softly from the paddock as Patrick passed the stables. He found the smell of hay and manure familiar and comforting, so different from the insidious odors of rotting garbage and stale booze back at his father's house. Would his life have been better if he'd been born five hundred years ago? Unfortunately, Patrick knew enough of history to realize it wouldn't have. He'd still be a nobody struggling to eke out a living in an indifferent world. The Faire provided a rose-tinted view of medieval life, he knew, but sometimes indulging in imagination soothed his soul, so he let himself step beyond the reality of his existence as he wove between the octagonal canvas structures.

It surprised Patrick to see light coming from the blacksmith's shop. Reddish-orange illumination surrounded the open structure, broken only by black strips where the rough-hewn columns supported the wood-shingled roof. Patrick crept closer and closer, until he stood concealed by one of those former railroad ties, his breath catching at what he saw inside the low, stone wall.

Yu worked at the forge with his shirt off and a leather apron draped over the front of his battered jeans. The glowing coals accentuated his musculature as he alternated between pumping the bellows and hammering the piece of metal on his anvil. Patrick watched his sinew move beneath his flawless golden skin as he worked. Sweat coated Yu's willowy limbs and ran between the ledges of his chest and belly muscles, disappearing beneath the waistband of his worn denim. A navy bandana held his shiny dark hair back, and the glow of the embers lit the planes of his perfect face. Yu lifted the sword he'd been working on and plunged it into a pail of water. With a hiss, steam rose to surround him like a halo, the vapor making his bared body gleam. The white cloud hovered just below the shop's ceiling, torpid tendrils curling out and along the roof before twisting slowly into the sky.

With his hands protected by heavy leather gloves, Yu lifted the newborn blade out of the water and took it to a grindstone. He positioned it, but stopped suddenly. "Is someone there?"

Patrick stepped out from behind the column. "It's just me. I didn't mean to startle you."

"Patrick. What are you doing here?" Yu looked annoyed at being interrupted.

"Nothing. Just checking up on things. I have a key."

"So do I," Yu said, and the two of them stood looking at each other.

"I didn't mean to disturb your work."

"It's all right," Yu said, setting down the fledging sword and slipping off his gloves. "I need a break anyway. Hey, are you all right?"

"Fine. Why?"

"Because you don't look fine," Yu said. "Are you upset about something?"

"Just stupid family stuff," Patrick said.

"I know how that can be," Yu said.

"Yeah."

Yu took two bottles of water from a cooler and handed one to Patrick. Patrick opened it and drank, thirstier than he'd realized. Yu rested his hips against a wooden sawhorse and poured some of his water over his face. Patrick watched as the liquid traced the contours of his taut body, highlighting every bump and dip of muscle. Yu had such a long, graceful neck. God, Patrick wanted to get down on his knees and lick the droplets from the gully between Yu's stomach muscles. Instead, Patrick crossed his legs to conceal his body's reaction to what he saw.

"Are you sure you're okay?" Yu asked again.

"Yeah."

"So what are you doing wandering around here so late?" Yu asked.

"I just like it here," Patrick said.

"So do I. And I think you're a good person."

"You do?" Patrick asked, a little stunned. Yu's declaration came out of nowhere.

Yu nodded. "You could have bragged about pushing Taylor, but you put Jen's feelings before your own. I respect that. I also like the way you stood up for her to Carlton. Are you sure she isn't your girlfriend?"

"No, just a friend," Patrick said.

"Just a friend," Yu repeated. "She's lucky to have you to defend her, to have your loyalty. Most men would have boasted about making a fool of Taylor, or used it as a way to win affection from her, but you didn't. Why is that?"

"Because it was stupid," Patrick said. "And he was being an ass. If we leave it alone, the drama will just blow over. We're all here to do a job, and crap like that doesn't make it any easier."

"Agreed."

"I hated high school," Patrick admitted. "All that useless conflict."

"So did I."

"We're adults now, and we should act like it."

"You'd think so," Yu said, pushing the bandana off his hair and using it to mop his sweaty face. "You behaved admirably, at least."

"Thanks, I guess."

"I don't expect gratitude," Yu said. "I'm just happy to know someone I can trust to be honest. If you wouldn't mind, will you tell me what you think of this sword?"

Patrick looked at the blade resting on the anvil. "I'm no expert, Yu."

"Honest, at least. You admit when you don't know something instead of pretending you do. Just give me your opinion of it, if you don't mind."

"I don't even know what to look for. I guess there are no ripples along the blade's edges. I understand that's good. The hilt is very pretty."

"I'm glad you think so. Will I be making something for you in the near future?"

"I don't know," Patrick said. "I don't really have the money. I'm trying to save up for an apartment. I've got to get away from my father."

"Why?"

"He's a drunk," Patrick said. "A raging alcoholic. It's no good living there."

"I see."

"Do you?"

"Yes, to an extent," Yu said. "I'm not close with my family, either. Well, I should probably get back to work."

"Would you mind if I sat here with you for a while?" Patrick asked.

"Why? Why do you want to watch me?" Yu asked.

"I just don't want to be alone," Patrick answered.

"All right, then." Yu slipped his gloves back on and replaced his bandana while Patrick took a seat on a wooden crate in the corner. Yu spent the next hour or so forging hooks for coats and curved garden stakes for hanging baskets. Patrick found the rhythmic ping of his hammer against the hot steel soothing in its regularity, and he couldn't deny he liked watching Yu's bare torso in the low light of the shop. Slender and defined, his body looked like carved and polished wood as it reflected the red glow of the coals. He moved gracefully and efficiently, not expending any unnecessary energy as he went about his work. Smithing was still strenuous, though, and by the time Yu slid his gloves off and wiped his palms on his apron, a patina of sweat covered his skin. God, he was beautiful, and as much as Patrick tried to ignore his desire to touch the other young man, he couldn't quite eliminate it. He just hoped his feelings wouldn't be obvious enough to make Yu uncomfortable around him.

Yu wiped his face on a pale gray T-shirt before shaking the wrinkles out and slipping it on. Then he poured a bucket of water into the forge, extinguishing the embers with a spectacular geyser of steam that left his hair and eyelashes sparkling.

"I hate the repetition of making a dozen of the same stake," Yu said as he meticulously organized the shop, put all the tools away, and placed his new creations on shelves to be sold. "Too bad we sell twenty of them for every original commission we get. I suppose I shouldn't complain. They're good practice for me as a novice."

"I know exactly what you mean," Patrick said. "Most people don't appreciate an artistic risk. They prefer safe things they can understand over things that make them think or wonder. I think that's kind of a shame. Personally, I like pieces like this"—Patrick picked up a heavy candle holder covered in the dents of the smith's hammer—"where you can see the evidence of the human hand that made it. I don't like things that are too refined, you know? There's a different kind of beauty to this. I don't want to live in a world where people have to conform to survive. Where everything has to be completely regular and identical to everything else. It's one of the things I hate about our modern society."

Once again, Yu gave Patrick a quizzical look, like he'd completely misunderstood Patrick and was pleasantly surprised to be wrong. "I wish more people felt that way. I usually only hear an opinion like that from another artist. But you're a performer, so I guess you can understand."

"I haven't really performed yet," Patrick admitted. "But when I do, I hope it will be memorable and give people something to think about."

"I'm sure you will," Yu said.

"Would you…. Are you hungry?" Patrick asked, grinding his toe into the gravel on the floor of the shop. "Do you want to go get something to eat?"

"I don't think so," Yu said. "I'm filthy."

"I don't mind," Patrick said, a little too quickly.

Yu narrowed his eyes and tilted his head. "You just say whatever's on your mind, don't you? You're strange. I can't quite figure you out."

"What do you want to know about me?" Patrick asked.

The other young man shook his head and smiled. The rarity of Yu's smiles made them even more precious, like hidden diamonds scattered on the ground. "Patrick, I don't even know what to ask."

"I'm starving," Patrick said. "We can go to a drive-through or something. I mean, unless you don't want to."

"I do," Yu said, folding his leather apron neatly and then setting it on a shelf.

Patrick fished his car keys from his pocket, and the two of them crossed the glistening field together. After he wiped the fog from the windshield with his arm and unlocked the doors, Patrick got behind the wheel and started his car. Yu sat next to him, and Patrick could smell his damp skin combined with the scents of charcoal and heated metal, along with a faint hint of leather. The intoxicating aroma almost made it hard for Patrick to drive. He couldn't believe Yu was here with him, in his car, and he didn't want to waste the opportunity, even if they were only ever destined to be friends.

Instead of a drive-through, Patrick stopped at a locally owned all-night market and bought some fried chicken, potatoes, coleslaw, and iced tea, because he remembered Yu requesting it at Eric and Rog's cookout. When he got back in the car, he handed the white plastic bag to Yu. "I hope you don't mind a little bit of a picnic," Patrick said.

"Where are we going?" Yu asked.

"Just a place I like," Patrick answered. "As long as you don't mind."

"If I minded, I'd let you know," Yu said in his painfully honest way.

Patrick liked it, liked knowing exactly where he stood without having to interpret subtle signs. He drove to a roadside rest area overlooking the city, parked, and took their dinner from Yu's lap. He carried the bags and plastic bottles to a picnic table with a view of the sprawling, sparkling lights of Pittsburgh miles beneath them. Yu sat down across from him, and Patrick opened the Styrofoam containers and shrink-wrapped plastic silverware. He handed Yu a fork and slid a bottle of tea in front of him.

"This is so lovely and romantic, I have to wonder if you planned it all along," Yu said.

"I didn't!" Patrick said. "I didn't even know you'd be at the Faire. I went there to be alone."

"I know," Yu said. "You seem to have quite a flair for dating, in that case."

"Dating?" Patrick asked. "I've never been on a date in my life, and I didn't mean it that way."

Yu looked disappointed. "I just wanted you to know this is all very nice."

Patrick sensed he'd screwed something up, and he had no clue how to fix it. "You thought I wanted to take you on a date?" Damn it, that sounded accusatory, like Yu had been the one to read too much into the simple meal. "I—I never meant to presume."

"I wouldn't mind if you presumed," Yu said, looking up from his chicken and right into Patrick's eyes. "I presumed."

"You did?"

"I hoped," Yu said.

"Really?"

"Really. If I saw something that isn't there, I apologize."

"Don't apologize," Patrick said, his appetite gone despite the enticing aroma of the chicken. He considered, and then, deciding he couldn't screw the night up any worse, said, "I think you're really cute."

"I think you're cute too, Patrick. I like you, and I want to know more about you."

"Like what?"

"Have you ever dated a guy?" Yu asked.

"No. I never dated anybody. I really didn't plan this. I just thought we could hang out, and I like it here. I think I might like you. As a friend, at least."

"Don't be so defensive," Yu said. "I like it here too. I'm just surprised you've never had a boyfriend. You're really cute. Ha. I guess I already said that, though. I can't be the first one to notice."

"Nobody seemed to think so when I was in school," Patrick said. "Besides, I only really decided I was gay a week ago."

"Wait," Yu said. "You decided?"

"Admitted, I guess," Patrick answered.

"Did you come out to your family?" Yu asked.

"No. Not yet. I'm not looking forward to it."

"Yeah, I know," Yu said, brushing his fingertips over the back of Patrick's hand. "So I guess I can safely assume you're single?"

"Yeah."

"Good news," Yu said, lifting his bottle of tea in a toast.

Patrick tapped the rim of his bottle against Yu's. "Is it?"

"It might be. I'd like to see you again, and the next time I'll buy dinner. How does Sunday after the Faire sound?"

"Really?" Patrick couldn't believe Yu Elion wanted to take him out.

"That innocent, insecure thing you do only goes so far," Yu said. "Yes, really. Patrick, I'm asking you out to dinner. Out on a date. Do you want to go or not?"

"I really, really want to go," Patrick said softly, his skin tingling, still feeling like he'd wake up from this beautiful dream at any moment.

"I'm glad," Yu said, tucking into his meal. "I'm really glad I met you."

"Uh, thanks. Me too. That I met you, I mean."

"I wish you wouldn't be so nervous," Yu said. "If anybody's going to say something wrong, it'll probably be me. I never really mastered the arts of flattery or flirting. I've been told by many people that I can be too direct, that I don't know when to keep my opinions to myself."

"I prefer it that way," Patrick said. "I'm no good at deciphering signals. So, your family knows about you? What was it like?"

"It was no fun. My mom cried because she thought she'd never have grandchildren. For the longest time, my dad thought I was just going through a phase, rebelling or something. He didn't think I could possibly like guys since I wasn't effeminate. He thought since I played sports and liked working with metal I had to be straight. He accepted it in time, though. Not like when I switched my major from engineering to art. That was the last straw. I haven't spoken to my parents since then. They think I'm throwing my life away."

"I'm sorry," Patrick said, amazed at how little it took for people to cast others away, to decide they weren't worthy of love or devotion. He reached across the table and squeezed Yu's hand, earning a surprised smile from the other man.

"Do you think your parents are going to react badly?"

Patrick shrugged. "My dad is just looking for a reason to kick me out, I think. He was pretty young when my mom got pregnant, and I don't think he ever wanted a wife or kids. He saw us as something that stole his freedom. My mom… I don't know. She has a new family now, and when I used to go to their house to spend the summers, I always felt like her botched first attempt, you know? Like a leftover from her messed-up former life before she tried again and got it right. She'll probably see it as just something else wrong with me, another defect. And I know I remind her of Dylan."

"Who's Dylan?"

"He was my little brother," Patrick said. "He died when I was three."

"How?"

"Car accident. Both of my parents drank quite a bit back then, and they didn't have Dylan strapped in properly. I used to wonder how things might have been if it hadn't happened. If my parents would have stayed together. I really missed my brother growing up, even though he was still a baby when he died. I was really lonely, and I would have liked a friend. But then, sometimes I think he got lucky. I know that sounds horrible, but I can't stand to imagine him growing up in that filthy house with my father. Geez. I'm sorry. I didn't mean to dump all that on you."

Yu turned his hand over beneath Patrick's so their palms pressed together, and then they interlaced their fingers and just sat listening to the sounds of insects and the light breeze in the trees. The silence settled between them, not in the awkward way of people who had nothing to say to each other, but in the comfortable way of people content to just sit together without the need to fill every second with meaningless words. After a few minutes, they smiled at each other in a nonverbal agreement to finish their now cold food. After they did, Patrick gathered up the bags and wrappers and took them to the can.

"It's getting late," Patrick said. "Do you want me to take you back to the Faire?"

"I wouldn't mind sitting here a little longer," Yu said.

"Okay." Patrick moved to sit back down across from him.

"You can sit beside me."

"Okay." He sat down on the bench, his knee pressed lightly against Yu's. Yu took his hand again and lightly traced his thumb along the back. Below them, the city glimmered like a pool of fairy dust settled between the darkened hills. Patrick was afraid to say anything, almost afraid to move or breathe, as if the slightest motion would pop the iridescent soap bubble he currently inhabited, and it would all disappear. Perfect moments like this came to others, not to him, and he worried somehow the universe would realize it had mistakenly put him in someone else's place.

"When I first got my car and learned to drive, sometimes I just drove around when I had to get out of the house," Patrick said. "I like coming here, looking down at the city, and thinking about the thousands of people living there. When I think about the lives some of them lead, my problems seem a lot smaller in comparison."

"That's a beautiful idea," Yu said.

"Thanks."

"We should probably get back," Yu finally said. "We have to work tomorrow, after all."

"Yeah," Patrick said, standing and taking his keys from his pocket. "Thanks for listening to my drama."

"Thanks for bringing me to your special spot," Yu said, brushing a strand of hair out of Patrick's eye and tucking it behind Patrick's ear. "I bet you don't share this with everybody."

"No. You're the first."

"I'm honored. I hope I can return the favor someday."

Chapter 8

WHEN he arrived at the Faire the following morning, Patrick felt sure everything that had happened that week had been a dream. His life just couldn't be going this well, with a promotion at the Faire, people who wanted to care for and support him, who accepted him and encouraged him while asking nothing in return, and a date with the most attractive young man he'd ever met to look forward to. As he entered the gate, he waited for someone or something to pull the rug out from under him. God, maybe he had a brain tumor or something and he really had imagined it all.

Jen, in a brilliant yellow gown embroidered with flowers and accented with lace ruffs at the neck and wrists, waved Patrick over. A young woman with a basket of roses—pink, white, and red—stopped Patrick before he reached Jen and handed him a dewy scarlet blossom.

"This is from the young man at the blacksmith's shop."

Jen's eyes went wide, and she lifted her skirts to hurry over. "Patrick. It looks like you have a secret admirer."

"It's not really a secret," he said, grasping her elbow and guiding her behind a copse of hemlock trees. "It's from Yu. We ate together last night, and he asked me to dinner on Sunday."

"That's awesome," she said, squeezing his shoulder. "I have to say, I didn't think he was really into you."

"He's just, I don't know, kind of quiet and reserved. He said I was cute."

"I'm so happy for you," she said.

"I'm happy too. I keep feeling like I'm going to wake up and realize it was all a dream."

"Why?"

"Things like this just don't happen to me."

"Well, it looks like they do now," Jen said. "Come on. We should get to the main stage for the opening welcome."

"What, me too?" Patrick asked.

"Well, yeah. You are in the cast now. You're not nervous, are you? After all these years you must know the songs in your sleep. Just stay with me. I really do like the idea of making your character into my secret bodyguard and spy. And you can say things that would be improper for the queen to mention. That'll be fun."

"I can sing, too. And play a few chords on the lute," Patrick said, pinning his flower to his hat. "I've been practicing."

"What do you want to sing? Nothing too bawdy, I hope. Tom likes to keep the more risqué numbers for the finale."

"No," Patrick said. "I thought I'd sing 'The Minstrel Boy' by Thomas Moore."

"But that song is so sad," Jen said. "Doesn't the minstrel boy die?"

"Yeah," Patrick said. "I guess maybe it isn't a good idea."

"No, it'll be fine if you want to sing it. I'll announce you right after we sing 'The Star of the County Down'. Tom will be delighted. He loves it when we dip into the source material."

They'd reached the stage, and people filled the benches in front of it, some in costume but most in T-shirts and shorts. Patrick and Jen hurried up the steps to join the rest of the cast backstage. Eric waved at them in greeting, and Taylor crossed his arms and scowled. Tom was onstage addressing the crowd, and at the end of his speech, they all queued up to join him, the English from the right and the French from the left. They sang "Johnny Jump Up" and "Wild Mountain Thyme" before Jen moved to the front of the group.

"We are most pleased to have all of you as guests in the kingdom on this fine day," she said. "And it is a fortuitous day indeed, for we also have as our guests the distinguished Duke of Anjou and his retinue from France."

"I thought I smelled stinky cheese," Patrick called out, earning a laugh from the audience and a nasty scowl from Taylor.

"In honor of the Duke," Jen continued, "we have planned many amusements, including a human chess match on this very stage and a tournament and joust between our knights and the chevaliers from France. We hope you'll all be able to grace us with your presence. And for those of you attending today's festivities with young lads and lasses, you will note that those shows in your program marked with a red kiss may be a bit too bawdy for the little angels. However, our Rose Stage offers stories and crafts for their entertainment, should you wish to attend. And now for a special treat, we are pleased to introduce our new minstrel, performing here for the first time."

Patrick's pulse sped up as he stepped to the center of the stage and strummed his lute. He worried his voice would crack from nerves, but he thought about Jen, Eric, Tom, and all the rest of the people standing behind him and silently offering support. All those people believed in him, and he didn't want to let them down. He took a deep breath and sang in a strong, clear voice:

"The minstrel boy to the war is gone,

In the ranks of death you will find him;

His father's sword he hath girded on,

And his wild harp slung behind him…."

The audience applauded when his song reached its conclusion, stunning him a little bit. For a few moments, he'd forgotten all about the people on the bleachers as he'd concentrated on the lyrics and keeping his singing and playing together. He held his instrument out to the side and bowed with a flourish before returning to the chorus.

"Good job, lad," Tom whispered, patting him on the shoulder.

Jen introduced Eric as Sir Francis Drake, and some of the women in the crowd catcalled at him as he sauntered to the edge of the stage. He made a few off-color jokes and talked about some of the other attractions, then they all sang a sea chanty called "All For Me Grog." By the time he'd finished, the flower vendors had started moving through the crowd to hawk their wares, and people rose from the benches to wander in the direction of the food stalls. Some of the patrons approached with cameras to take pictures with members of the cast, Jen and Eric being the most popular.

Tom came up to Patrick. "I need you to be at the Rose Stage between three and six, and then back here for the finale at seven."

"I'll miss the joust," Patrick said. He'd been hoping to catch a glimpse of Yu, and he'd hoped to make a little time for his lesson with the knights so he'd have more in common with his new friend. But this was his job, not a place to watch shows and envision new ways to impress the boy he liked. "I mean, no problem."

"Good lad. That'll pretty much be your schedule from here on out: opening welcome, the Rose Stage in the afternoon, and finale. In between, walk around with Jen and interact with the customers. They'll appreciate a personal serenade now and then, particularly the girls. Oh, and would you be interested in doing some maintenance around the grounds during the week? Trimming up the roses and whatnot?"

"Absolutely," Patrick said. "That would be great. Thanks, Tom."

"You're a good boy. Make sure you take a lunch break. Drink plenty of water. It's getting hot."

"I will. Thanks again."

Tom nodded once and went to speak with some of the other employees. Fifi appeared at the bottom of the stage carrying a large black box tied up with pink ribbons. It matched the black corset, crinoline, and cage bustle she wore, as well as her elaborate pale pink wig with ringlet curls and a pair of shimmery, fake doves perched among its tiers. Patrick hurried down the steps to meet her.

"It's ready," she said.

"I hope I'll look half as good as you," Patrick said, taking the box. "I'll pay on it as soon as I cash my check."

"No worries," she said. "Listen, I can't stick around. The shop's already busy." She kissed him on the cheek, curtseyed, and hurried away.

"Wow, is that another gift?" Jen said under her breath as she passed Patrick. "Maybe I should have gone after him."

Soon after, Eric pushed his way out from the center of a group of women, Faire regulars who referred to themselves as the Wench's Guild. One of them smacked his ass as he stumbled away, pulling a lacy white napkin from his pocket to wipe away the many red smears their lipstick had left on his face. He grinned and rolled his eyes when he saw Patrick watching him.

"Don't look so smug, my young friend," he said as the two of them fell into step together. "Your time is coming. Plenty of those lusty wenches had their eyes on you while you sang."

"They did?"

"Oh, aye," Eric answered. "Watch out for them. They'll eat a tender young lad like you alive."

They both laughed. "Eric, is Roger performing tonight?"

"Every Friday and Saturday. Want to come to the club?"

"I'd like that," Patrick said. "I got my corset and things from Tish and Tracy, and I want to see what everyone thinks of it. Actually, the truth is I'm dying to try it on, and I can't get into it and lace it up without help. Do you think they'd mind?"

"I think they'll be delighted," Eric said. "They love you already. Jen tells me you have some other good news?"

Patrick nodded, and his jaw almost hurt from smiling. "I have a date."

"So I heard."

"I'm really nervous about it," Patrick admitted. "I've never been on one. And… and he's so hot. I can't believe he's interested in me."

"You need to stop beating yourself up," Eric said, growing serious as he stopped walking and faced Patrick. "It remains to be seen if *he's* good enough for *you*. Remember that."

"Okay."

"I mean it, Patrick."

"I will, I promise," Patrick said, smiling at Eric and wondering if this was how it felt to have a real family.

THUNDERSTORMS, spurts of drizzle, and high winds kept Faire attendance to a minimum on Sunday. Most of the actors huddled on the covered stages, in the pavilions, or just gave up and went to spend the day in the tavern. Though Tom officially cancelled the joust, the knights decided to fight anyway. Since they didn't want to risk their horses slipping in the mud, they opted for a hand-to-hand match. Patrick didn't have any children to entertain at the Rose Stage, so he sat in the royal box with Jen and watched Henry, Ian, and Carlton enjoying themselves as they wrestled and slid around in the mire.

"So where's he taking you?" Jen asked Patrick.

"I have no idea," Patrick said as he took his phone from his pocket and pulled up the cryptic text Yu had sent him a few hours ago. Tom would go ballistic if he saw any of the cast on their phones—the actors weren't even allowed to use plastic silverware where the patrons could see—but at the moment no one was around, so Patrick showed Jen the message that simply said:

Wear something nice.

"Ooh, how mysterious," Jen said. "You'll have to let me know how it goes. I think I'll just go to the Stew."

"Won't Taylor be there?"

She shrugged. "Probably, but I'm sick of letting him ruin my life. I like going to the Stew, all my friends are there, and I'm not going to let him keep me from doing something I enjoy. I mean, we were here first, right?"

"Right." Patrick held up his hand, and Jen slapped it.

The rest of the afternoon dragged on, partly due to Patrick's excitement over his date with Yu and partly because the weather prevented him from doing much of anything to pass the time. Finally they performed an abridged version of the finale, since no one had come to watch, and Patrick said good-bye to his friends, most of whom intended to dry off and warm up at the pub.

Since he didn't want his father sinking his buoyant mood, and because he didn't want to answer questions about his attire, Patrick went to his car and fetched his old backpack from the trunk. Then he crossed the campground where some of the vendors, artisans, and employees lived in RVs for the summer, or, in the case of the purists, canvas tents. Beyond them was a stone building where the staff could shower. Patrick went in the men's side and found it empty, thankfully. He took off his Faire garb, readied a towel from his pack, and took his soap, shampoo, and razor into the stall and pulled the vinyl curtain closed.

After he'd washed, Patrick dressed in a pair of khaki pants, a light-green shirt, and a brown argyle sweater vest. He didn't own a pair of dress shoes, so he hoped his old Chuck Taylors would do.

Yu met him at the gate, standing beneath a black umbrella. He looked amazing in a pair of charcoal trousers, a peacock-blue shirt, and black blazer. He wore his straight dark hair loose, and it tumbled over his shoulders. He looked like a *GQ* model—better—and Patrick felt suddenly very shabby. He reached up to smooth down his unruly waves of auburn hair.

"You look nice," Yu said, leaning forward and placing a light kiss on Patrick's cheek, stealing Patrick's breath for a few seconds.

"You look incredible," Patrick said as he followed Yu to his car, a newer black Ford SUV. Patrick wasn't quite sure of the model. "This is a nice car, too."

"I'm surprised my parents let me keep it," Yu said as he opened the passenger door for Patrick. "But let's not talk about unpleasant things this time."

"Good idea," Patrick said as he hooked his safety belt. Though he'd been nervous all day, he felt completely comfortable now that they sat together. With Yu, he knew he didn't even have to struggle to keep the conversation going. Only meaningful statements interested Yu; Patrick had discerned that much. He saw no need to talk unless he had something to say.

They drove into downtown Pittsburgh, and Yu pulled into the parking lot of a small, unassuming bistro. The rain had finally tapered to a fine mist, so they didn't bother with the umbrella. Once again, Yu held the door for Patrick and they went inside. The restaurant, called Avenue B, looked warm and inviting with its brick walls, fuzzy lighting, and simple wooden furnishings. Yu spoke to the maître d', and he showed them to a secluded table in a corner near the window.

"Can you bring us a bottle of Cloudline Pinot Noir?" Yu asked their waitress when she appeared.

"Sure thing."

"Yu," Patrick whispered, "I'm not old enough to drink."

"Oh. Well, it's only wine. Pinot Noir goes with most everything. The cuisine deserves wine. This place has a very creative menu, but the best dishes are the seasonal offerings here on the chalkboard." He pointed. "The chef changes it daily based on the availability of fresh, local ingredients. Let's see. What do you want to start out?"

Patrick looked at the items listed on the board, things like nori scallops, Kobe beef gyoza and coconut bisque. Then he saw the prices and felt his appetite depart. Yu couldn't afford a meal like this working at the Faire and trying to save money for school. "I… I don't know. You didn't have to go to all this trouble. I mean, I bought you fried chicken from a convenience store."

Yu met his gaze. "I didn't bring you here to try to make you look bad, or to outdo you somehow. The last thing I want is for you to feel uncomfortable. You shared a place you love with me. I just want to do the same, so don't worry about it and just enjoy. Please?"

"Okay. I think I'll let you order, though."

Their waitress returned with the wine, and Yu said, "I think we'll have the mussels and the grilled artichoke and prosciutto flatbread."

"Very good," she said, writing the order down. "I'll get those in for you."

"I just realized you're a foodie," Patrick said.

"I suppose I am, a little. It's like anything else. I prefer creative things made with great care. A chef can also be an artist. If I have to pay to eat, I'd rather give my money to someone who deserves it, someone with a passion for his craft."

"That's a good point," Patrick said. "Do you cook too?"

"Not at all," Yu said. "I never learned."

"So how did you get Wade to take you on as an apprentice?" Patrick asked, and then he took a small sip of his wine. "He's got kind of a nasty reputation for wanting to work alone. It's a nightmare when he has to do the demonstrations for the school groups who come to the Faire. To be honest, we all avoid him like the plague."

"He's not a patient man, but he's one of the best blacksmiths in the country, and one who knows the traditional techniques for forging weapons and armor. He's won many awards and is respected as one of the foremost experts on the subject. It's a fair trade."

"But how did you get him to agree?"

"I just didn't take no for an answer," Yu said. "When I came to his shop two summers ago, he told me my work wasn't good enough and to go away. I worked harder, and I went back last year. He told me I still wasn't good enough, so I asked him specifically what I needed to improve. Over the winter, I emailed him pictures of some of my pieces, even though he ignored most of them. This year I came back, and Wade asked if I was ever going to stop pestering him. I told him no, not until he accepted me as a student. He finally gave in."

"Wow," Patrick said, impressed.

"I hate to think of all of these techniques being lost," Yu said. "I really love doing this work. It isn't something most people can understand, the extra time it takes to make things by hand that can be manufactured now. They usually don't see the point. Especially since I'm never going to get rich doing this."

"Money isn't everything," Patrick said. "It's not worth doing something you hate for the rest of your life."

"Or giving up something you love," Yu said, just as the waitress arrived with their appetizers.

Patrick sat practically mesmerized as Yu picked small chunks of meat from the shiny black shells and dipped his bread in the dark-red broth, slurping a little as he savored it. The wine gave a purplish sheen to his full lips. He darted out the tip of his tongue and mopped his top teeth, and a shudder spilled down Patrick's spine. He picked up a piece of the flatbread and nibbled the edge.

"You should try these," Yu said, spearing one of the mussels on his fork and holding it out to Patrick. Slowly, Patrick parted his lips and accepted it, though he barely noticed the flavor because all his attention focused on Yu's smile. "Do you like it?"

"Can I try it again?" Patrick asked.

Yu's smile widened, making his eyes crinkle adorably, as he fed Patrick another bite of the mussels. This time, Patrick tasted wine, garlic, and smoked tomatoes over the briny flavor of the crustacean's tender flesh. When he took a sip of his wine, he found new flavors in it after the food: sweet cherries with a smoky, earthy undertone. It tasted a little like the Faire grounds smelled after a spring rain.

"Are you gentlemen ready to order?" the waitress said.

Patrick looked back at the chalkboard. "Can you order for both of us?" he asked Yu, afraid he'd make a fool of himself. Besides, he trusted Yu, at least when it came to food.

"I can. Do you like meatloaf?"

"Sure," Patrick said.

"A Kobe meatloaf. I'll have the pan-seared walleye and smoked trout."

"This has got to be the best thing I ever tasted," Patrick said after their entrees arrived. "I can't believe this is meatloaf. Thanks for bringing me here."

"I'm glad you're having a good time. What would you like to do next?"

"I know a club we could go to," Patrick said, eager to gauge Yu's reaction to his newfound hobby. Maybe, if Patrick was lucky, Yu would like the way he looked in drag as much as the others had.

"No, I hate bars. They're just meat markets full of people saying things they don't mean and trying to get strangers to sleep with them. Do you spend a lot of time at places like that?"

"Some," Patrick said, finding Yu's normally refreshing honesty a little judgmental in this case. "I go with Roger and Eric, but not for those reasons."

"Why, then?"

"To hang out with my friends," Patrick said. "And I really like watching some of the performers. Some of them are truly artists." Yu should be able to appreciate that.

"No, I don't like those places," Yu said.

"Okay. Maybe we can just rent a movie."

"And watch it at your house?" Yu asked.

"We can't go to my house," Patrick said in a voice soft with shame. "My dad will be there, maybe some of his friends. They'll be drunk, and they won't be all right with us being there together. Sometimes my dad gets violent. I'm sorry. You have a place of your own, right? Could we go there?"

"No," Yu said.

"Oh."

They ate in silence for a few minutes. Of course Patrick wondered why Yu didn't want to take him to his apartment, but he had no right to demand it, either. He wasn't ready for the night to end yet, especially not on the discordant note it had struck. He carved little crisscross patterns in his goat-cheese mashed potatoes with his fork and forced himself to finish his food, though his appetite had gone and it sat cold and heavy in his stomach. Still, he couldn't bring himself to throw away a thirty-dollar meatloaf.

"I didn't mean to upset you," Yu said, dabbing at his shiny, wine-stained lips with his napkin.

"I'm not upset," Patrick said, unable to keep the pout from creeping into his tone. "I guess maybe we should just call it a night." He looked up at Yu, holding on to a scrap of hope Yu might disagree, or suggest something else, but Yu looked closed-off, unreadable.

"All right, then." Yu asked for the bill and slid his credit card into the leather folder. When the waitress brought it back, he signed, stood up, and pushed his chair in.

Patrick had no choice but to follow him across the sparkling asphalt and around pools of water like molten metal beneath the city lights, then sit silently beside him as they rode back to the Faire. They got out of the car and stood a few feet apart, just watching each other, each of them waiting for the other to say or do something.

When Patrick couldn't take it any longer, he said, "I had a nice time. The restaurant was very… nice. Thank you."

"You're welcome. Have a *nice* evening, Patrick. Good night." Yu cupped Patrick's shoulders but didn't squeeze, and Patrick stood stiffly as Yu leaned in to kiss his cheek, just a chill, chaste brush of lips against his jawbone. It made Patrick want to cry, so he hurried to mutter his own good night and retreated to his car.

Patrick sat in the Horizon's dark interior as Yu started his car and pulled away, his headlights cutting sparkly green swaths from the darkened field as he bounced along and then disappeared down the dirt road. For the first time, the grounds looked cold and lonely, blurred and distorted by the sheet of mist rising from the ground. Patrick took his phone from his pocket and touched Jen's name in his contacts.

"Hey Patrick!" she shouted over the sounds of music and other loud voices. "Hang on a sec. I'm going outside."

The background noise faded away, and Jen inhaled sharply, probably lighting a cigarette. "How was your date with Yu?"

"Weird," he said. "Everything was going really well. He took me to a fancy restaurant. He's kind of a foodie. Anyway, we were talking, and it felt like we had a lot in common. Then after dinner, I said we should go to his apartment and watch a movie, and he just kind of shut down. We didn't talk much after that, and he brought me back here and dropped me off. Oh my God! Do you think Yu thought I was trying to…. That, um, my intentions were less than honorable?"

She laughed. "Jesus, Patrick. Less than honorable? You've been at the Faire too long. You can't even bring yourself to say 'trying to get in his pants', so if he thought that, he's an idiot. Yu doesn't strike me as an idiot."

"What then?"

"I don't know," she said. "That is weird. Maybe it's just not meant to be, you know?"

"But it was going so well," Patrick argued, more with his inner voice that agreed Jen might be right than with his friend. "He was telling me all about himself, how he learned to forge, what he liked to eat...."

"First, that's not telling you anything about himself. Those are superficial details. And besides, the good ones don't talk about themselves the whole night. They ask about you."

"It really wasn't like that," Patrick said, even as he realized maybe it had been.

"Where are you?" Jen asked as a few bars of music drowned her voice for a moment. Someone had probably opened the tavern door.

"In the parking lot."

"Here at the Faire?"

"Yeah."

"Well, come up to the Stew," Jen said. "Tom's playing the bagpipes, and Henry and Ian are here. Everybody will be glad to see you."

"Okay. I'll be there in a few minutes." Patrick wasn't in the mood for the chaos of the pub or for watching the actors try to hook up with each other, but he decided he'd rather watch his friends get drunk than his father.

Chapter 9

PATRICK spent the next week landscaping at the Faire during the day and practicing his routine for the pageant with Roger, Shawn, and Aouli every night. His wig arrived on Wednesday, and luckily he managed to find the package before his father. With his whole ensemble ready, he experimented with different makeup techniques with Aouli and learned dance moves from Shawn. In the few moments between, he practiced his lute and tried to memorize a few more songs for his minstrel to sing and play at the Faire.

One traditional tune particularly inspired him. It was called "The Lusty Young Smith," and Patrick had some interesting ideas about how he could change the young damsel in the song to a young minstrel. He could keep the gender of the minstrel ambiguous, just so no one took offense. But with the pageant only a week and a half away, he had to concentrate on his drag performance.

"I think this is the winner," Aouli said, setting his makeup brush down on Eric and Roger's dining room table and handing Patrick a mirror. "See what you think."

Patrick loved what he saw looking back at him from the little oval. He looked like a porcelain doll in white foundation, bold, red blush covering his cheeks, his crimson lips painted in a way that made them look perpetually puckered. Aouli had affixed thick, black faux lashes over the kohl lining Patrick's eyes and painted his lids with scarlet and pink. Patrick had doubted Aouli's suggestion to line his brows in black, but he adored the look of them beneath the ringlet curls of the elaborate ivory wig. Aouli had even painted a black dot resembling a mole at the corner of Patrick's mouth and glued tiny, clear crystals to the inner corners of his eyes. The entire look conveyed just the excess, decadence, and defiance of nature Patrick craved. Madame Pompadour could eat her heart out.

"What do you think?" Aouli asked again.

"It's exactly what I wanted," Patrick said. "Thank you so much."

Aouli squeezed his hand. "What are sisters for?"

"Let's see the whole picture," Shawn said. "Get up, girl. Show us what you got."

Patrick stood, finally getting accustomed to his corset. It made him breathe differently, more shallow, but he'd managed to lace his waist to twenty-three inches. On the advice of the others, he'd augmented his chest only with small, silicone inserts women wore inside their bras, giving him maybe the equivalent of a B-cup. The others assured him that with his slender frame, it was enough.

"The French always say more than a handful's a waste," Eric had told him.

The cage bustle, covered in black netting and edged with rows of lace, made any hip or buttock padding unnecessary. Patrick pranced from the dining room to the adjoining living room in the exquisite garments Tish and Tracy had made, his cosplay wig, kitten heels, and the pearl necklace he'd bought at the secondhand store. As he walked, he thrust his hips up and down as he'd been instructed, twisted his waist, stretched his legs, and took long strides as he rolled his shoulders in opposition to his steps. When he reached the front door, he took a wide stance and looked over his shoulder, winking and pursing his lips. Then he spun on the ball of his foot and walked back into the dining room.

Aouli hopped up and down and clapped his hands. "We've got a runway girl, ladies. My God, will you look at those legs!"

"Girl, you could make a straight boy hard," Shawn said. "You are fierce."

"Something's missing," Rog said. "I'll be right back." He hurried up the steps and returned with a pair of elbow-length, black satin gloves.

Patrick slipped them on, feeling even more beautiful and confident than before. Dressed like this, he felt ready to demand attention. He wouldn't take no for an answer, and he wouldn't be ignored.

"Perfect," Rog said. "I'd like you to keep them."

"Oh, Rog, I couldn't," Patrick said. "You've done enough for me already."

"You hush," Rog said, taking Patrick's satin-encased fingers. "I wore these the first time I performed, and they brought me luck. They'll do the same for you, and I want you to have them. You listen to your mama, now."

"Rog—okay, Mama. Thank you."

"No crying, Patrick," Eric said from the sofa where he sat with a cup of coffee. "You'll ruin Aouli's work. You either, Rog. Let's see her perform instead. Do you have your iPod, Patrick?"

"In my jeans." Patrick pointed his chin toward the faded denim draped over the back of a chair.

Eric chuckled as he stood to fetch it. "I see the queen has spoken. Your servant, m'lady."

He took the iPod from Patrick's pocket and plugged it into the stereo. "In This Together" began to play, and Patrick sauntered to the center of the living room to perform the routine he'd practiced at least a hundred times. Lip-synching came easily as he knew the words by heart, and his body remembered every move that coincided with every beat. He performed for his friends with every ounce of enthusiasm he had, trying to make it all as perfect for them as he would for his audience and judges in a little over a week. By the time the song ended, he fought to catch his breath in the corset as he tingled with adrenaline.

"Um, honey, there's just one little—or, damn, not so little—thing you're gonna have to take care of," Shawn said.

Horrified, Patrick clapped his hands over his half erection. "I'm so sorry," he mumbled, completely humiliated.

"It's perfectly normal," Rog said. "Performing can be a real turn-on. Really, it's like making love to an audience, but you don't want that happening next week."

"You should take care of it beforehand," Shawn said.

"Have you tried tucking?" Aouli asked.

"Not really," Patrick admitted. "I'm afraid it's going to hurt."

"You're going to have to get it figured out before the pageant," Aouli offered gently. "Just get your cute Japanese boyfriend to take care of you, and you shouldn't have any trouble."

"I haven't talked to Yu since last weekend," Patrick said. "Our date was a little awkward."

"So why haven't you talked to him?" Rog asked.

Patrick sat on the sofa next to Eric and slipped off his shoes. They took the most getting used to, and they still made his arches ache. "Jen said I shouldn't call him, that I didn't want to seem desperate. She said making him think I didn't care might pique his interest."

"Oh, that is such bullshit," Aouli said. "You should talk to him, not play stupid games."

"I don't know," Eric said. "Men do tend to want what they aren't sure they can have. They like a challenge. Don't forget, we're hunters by nature, Miss Anita."

"Oh, hell," Aouli said, fanning himself with his hand. "All that testosterone is a turn-on. But, Patrick, Yu is a human being. All human beings want to communicate and be heard and understood. You should talk to him. Be the bigger person."

"But if he still wants to be a dick, you cut him loose," Shawn practically threatened. "You can do better, sister."

"I really like him," Patrick said.

"Then call him," Aouli advised.

Patrick nodded. "I think I will. Now, can somebody unlace me? I need some air." He leaned forward and Rog picked apart the cords and loosened the corset. The fabric and strips of steel released Patrick's body, and his ribs expanded as he finally took a full breath.

"So have you decided what you'll call yourself?" Rog asked.

"What do you mean?"

"Have you picked out your stage name?" Eric clarified.

"Oh," Patrick said. "With everything else going on, I forgot about it. That's pretty important, isn't it?"

Rog nodded. "Especially if you decide to keep performing. You need a name people will remember."

"I think you should call yourself Tinker Bell or something," Aouli said. "You're like a magical creature. A little fairy princess of a pixie. Ethereal."

"There are Peaseblossom, Cobweb, Moth, and Mustardseed," Patrick offered. "Those are the eventide fairies from *A Midsummer Night's Dream*."

"Oh no," Shawn said. "Honey, you can't call yourself Mustardseed or Moth."

"And certainly not Cobweb," Rog agreed.

"I know," Eric said. "You look like royalty, so name yourself after a queen. The fairy queen. Call yourself Titania."

Everyone clapped with approval, and Aouli called for champagne.

"To our fairy queen!"

PATRICK spent the night at Eric and Roger's, then worked power-washing the Faire buildings all the next day. By the time the sun set, he knew he couldn't avoid going home. He'd run out of clean clothes and he needed a shave. Besides, he looked forward to an evening of escaping all his worries in the fantasy world of the Skyrim video game. Killing dragons sounded like a vacation after the week he'd had.

Before he left the Faire, he sent Yu a text: *How have you been?*

Busy, was the response.

Me too. Do you want to get together this weekend?

Lunch on Saturday? Yu sent.

I'd like that, Patrick typed. *Can I bring something to you at the shop?*

Okay.

Cool! See you then.

Patrick used his phone to research some of the area's best restaurants. He wondered if sushi would be too cliché, and then decided the menu at Umi looked enticing, and the reviews were generally very positive. The sixty-five dollar price tag the woman quoted when he called shocked him a little, but he ordered the food anyway. Yu was picky about what he ate, and Patrick wanted to impress him.

He left the Faire just after the welcome to drive to Shadyside and pick up their meal. When he returned, he hurried to the blacksmith's shop carrying two pretty paper bags printed with watercolor cherry blossoms. He arrived just as Yu was washing his hands and arms in a metal basin, scrubbing up with the gritty green soap everyone whose work got them especially dirty seemed to use. He wore his hair in a tight bun at the back of his head, and his loose white shirt hung open, revealing the smooth golden skin of his chest. Smiling, eyes sparkling, he joined Patrick on the gravel lane outside the shop.

Yu's eyes went wide when Patrick lifted the bags. "You got Umi?"

"You don't like it," Patrick assumed, crushed.

"No, I love it. It's just very expensive. I admit I assumed you'd just get something here at the Faire."

Patrick had already decided he wouldn't attempt to play a game to which he didn't understand the rules. "Getting to have lunch with you means a lot to me. I wanted to make sure it was special. All of this is so pretty. I can't wait for you to see."

"I don't know what to say, Patrick."

"Don't say anything," Patrick answered, feeling like little birds twittered inside his ribcage. "I only have an hour break, so let's find a place to eat. I love this warm, golden part of the day. Let's not waste it."

With a wide smile, Yu caught Patrick's hand and wriggled his fingers between Patrick's. As they walked together, Patrick worried someone might see them at first, but then he decided he was too happy to care. They were just two people enjoying lunch on a beautiful day, holding hands and relishing their time together. They weren't hurting anyone, and they had nothing to be ashamed of.

Yu led Patrick past the knights' tents and the tournament field to the edge of the woods surrounding the grounds. They sat together in the warm fragrant grass beneath the dappled shade of an old mossy oak, and Patrick took the small containers from the bag and set them down. Each of them slid their chopsticks from the paper sleeves and broke them apart.

"Are we just sharing everything?" Yu asked.

"Is that okay?"

"Sure. Thank you for this. I haven't had sushi in a while." Yu carefully picked up a slice of yellowfin sashimi and dipped it in the soy sauce.

"Have you ever been to Japan?" Patrick asked, worried as soon as the words left his mouth. Why hadn't he asked Yu if he'd been to England or Germany?

Yu just nodded as he finished chewing and swallowed. "A few times. My fondest dream is to study with a weaponsmith there. A swordsmith."

"That would be really cool," Patrick said. "Why haven't you?"

"There are only maybe half a dozen men left in the world who still know how to make Japanese swords in the traditional way. It's far more involved than medieval western smithing. The steel in a katana is a special kind, *tamahagane*. It has different carbon levels than western swords, and the quenching techniques are completely different as well. The polishing alone can take two to three weeks. Wait. I don't want to talk about swords. I've told you all about myself, and I know next to nothing about you."

"I like hearing about how the swords are made," Patrick said. He especially like the way Yu smiled and became more animated when he described them. "It's probably more interesting than anything I could say about myself."

"You shouldn't be so self-deprecating," Yu said. "Tell me something about you."

"Like what?"

"Well, what do you do when you're not working?"

"I like to play video games," Patrick said. "I like to read, especially history and things from the Renaissance. Especially the poetry. Sometimes I feel like I'm all wrong for the world, for this time in it. Is it weird that I've never felt more at home anywhere than I do here?"

"No," Yu said. "The world can be a difficult place for creative and passionate people, or anyone who doesn't completely conform. Tell me a poem."

"Oh! Okay." Patrick cleared his throat. "I'll tell you one of my favorites." He began to recite Andrew Marvell's "To His Coy Mistress."

"Had we but world enough and time...."

"You chose a love poem," Yu said, his eyes glossy and unfocused as he rested his cheek against his palm, his chopsticks dangling forgotten from his other hand. "It's beautiful. And rather tragic. Who wrote it?"

"Andrew Marvell," Patrick said, staring back at Yu and feeling just as fuzzy and dazed as Yu appeared. "He's one of my favorites. I'm not sure if I like that poem best, or his 'Definition of Love'."

"Tell me that one," Yu said, his voice lower and huskier than it had been, his cheeks flushed and his eyes dilated. "Please."

Patrick recited the poem; he knew it by heart. "I think he's trying to say sometimes you have to defy fate for love, and that hope can be fragile, but also beautiful. I love how he calls it 'tinsel wing'. I've always pictured hope like a little fairy sort of buzzing around me, just out of reach. I'm afraid if I try to grab it, it'll just disintegrate in my hands."

Yu reached up, cupped Patrick's face in his warm, rough hand, and looked into Patrick's eyes. "You're beautiful. My God, how could you ever think for a second that you aren't interesting?"

"Yu—"

"Tell me another."

With a trembling hand, Patrick grazed Yu's knuckles and let his fingers trail down his wrist and over the wiry muscle of his forearm. "I could tell you Robert Herrick's 'Delight in Disorder', but I don't think that one suits you."

"Why?"

"Because your art is all about precision. Perfection," Patrick said, watching a shadow move across Yu's face as a cloud flitted in front of the sun. "You don't seem like you'd appreciate 'a sweet disorder in the dress'."

"I might." Yu traced his fingers down Patrick's neck, making Patrick shudder, before pinching the rumpled collar of Patrick's too-large shirt and pulling it up from where it had drooped past Patrick's collarbone, exposing almost the entire freckled globe of his shoulder. "Now I know you do. You can learn almost everything about a person through what he loves."

Patrick laughed, partly because it was funny and partly because he was just so happy it had to spill out somehow or he'd explode. "We're a couple of nerds, you know that? Me with my cheesy poetry and you obsessed with archaic weapons. We should probably go watch a football game or something."

"No," Yu said, just above a whisper. "I'd rather defy fate." He leaned a little closer to Patrick, and Patrick smelled charcoal and the ferrous fragrance of molten steel. He let his eyes flutter shut as Yu moved his hand around the back of Patrick's neck, beneath his hair.

A trumpet sounded in the distance, and Patrick's eyes sprung open. "Shit! I have to get to the Rose Stage!" For a few minutes, maybe since they'd sat down to lunch, he'd actually forgotten all about the Faire and the hundreds of people expecting him to entertain them or care for their children. He hurried to his feet, shoving the empty take-out containers into the bags as he went. He deposited them into a bin disguised as a wooden barrel, calling to Yu over his shoulder, "Sorry! I really have to go. I'll text you later."

Yu blew Patrick a kiss, and it sailed like an arrow through his heart. Patrick rolled his eyes at his own foolish imagery. Maybe he needed to distance himself from love poems for a while. But Yu made him want to recite sonnets to anyone willing to listen. Hope was indeed a magical, beautiful, shimmering thing fluttering around the edges of his imagination. Patrick only prayed it didn't flap its feeble wings in vain.

Chapter 10

THROUGHOUT the season, the Faire held a variety of themed weekends, and the upcoming Freebooter's Retreat was one of the best attended and most popular. Patrick spent the week hanging Jolly Rogers, draping fishing nets over fences, and hoisting gibbets containing plastic skeletons wearing bandanas and eye patches. Guest vendors selling pirate items set up booths in the square, and musical acts appropriate to the occasion would perform throughout the weekend. In addition, pirate enthusiasts from all over the state and beyond descended on the Faire, pitching their red and black tents alongside the employees and flying their colors proudly.

On Thursday, after he'd finished draping the main stage with skull and crossbones banners, Patrick texted Yu. They'd both been busy and had found little time to spend together aside from a few rushed lunches. Now and then, Patrick had sent Yu little snippets of Renaissance poetry, things like "Shall I compare thee to a summer's day? Thou art more lovely and more temperate," or "O my luve's like a red, red rose, that's newly sprung in June. O my luve's like a melodie, that's sweetly play'd in tune." Once, he even felt bold enough to send a line from "The Lusty Young Smith": "Young smith with your hammer come hither tomorrow. But please could you use it once more 'ere you go!"

Yu had responded: *!!!!*

Now, Patrick wrote: *How R U? Can U hang out?*

No, I'm sorry. Wade insists I make two dozen pairs of manacles before the weekend. Apparently the pirate crowd will buy them all. I'll have to be at the forge morning to night if I have a chance of finishing.

Why's he torturing U?

He's not, Yu responded. *He's testing my dedication. He wants to make sure I won't quit if it becomes too difficult. I still have to prove myself to him.*

Miss U, Patrick typed on his touch screen.

I miss you too, Patrick. Would you like to go to dinner on Saturday night?

Patrick considered how to respond. *I can't. Have to work at my other job.*

You have another job?

Yeah. I perform. Do U want to come C me?

I should work, Yu answered. *Can I see you Sunday after the Faire?*

Yes and I can't wait, Patrick wrote.

You're adorable, Yu said. *I'll talk to you on Sunday, but stop by the shop over the weekend if you can. Seeing you makes me smile.*

Seeing U makes ME smile. Patrick typed a smiley face with a colon, dash, and parentheses. *C U soon.* He wanted to write *I love you*, because he was almost entirely certain it was true, but he knew, without Jen or anyone else telling him, it was too soon, and he didn't want to scare Yu away. He also wanted to say it in person, looking at Yu's face, and not in a text message.

THE evening of the pageant, Patrick arranged to leave a couple of hours early. He drove to Eric and Roger's house, where he met Rog, Aouli, and Shawn. Of course, the pirate community coveted and expected Eric's presence at the Faire, though Eric promised he wouldn't miss the show for love nor money. Jen had also agreed to come, along with Tracy and Tish. Patrick put his costume and props in the back of Eric's truck. He and Rog got into the cab, while Shawn and Aouli prepared to follow them into downtown Pittsburgh.

Joe's Ballroom was a huge club in a turn-of-the-century building. The stage and dance floor lay beyond a large bar and lounge area. The dressing room waited past the long runway, and Rog accompanied Patrick through the single door. Pageant regulations said Patrick had to apply his own makeup, but they permitted Rog to help him lace into his corset. The atmosphere in the room couldn't have been more different from the easy camaraderie Patrick had experienced when he'd gone backstage at Miss Merry Rose's club. Queens shouldered past each other and elbowed their sisters out of the way, fighting for space at the makeup mirrors and hurling snarky accusations at each other. Patrick felt like he'd been dropped into a cage full of angry cats. There was no family love or support beneath the cloud of hairspray in this crowded room.

"You just ignore it, baby girl," Rog said softly next to Patrick's ear. "You're better than this."

"I will, Mama."

"I always wanted somebody to call me that," Rog said. "Now get undressed. You're gonna make me proud, and the rest of these haggard bitches are gonna be crying in their wine coolers. You don't sink to their level, baby girl. You're gonna win by being better, not by being petty. You're too good for that."

"Yes, Mama." Patrick started to tear up and choke, surprised by the onslaught of emotion. God, he'd never had a mother to guide and care for him like this…. It felt nice, like a soft old blanket wrapped tight around his shoulders, and it almost overwhelmed him. "I won't let you down, Mama. I love you."

"I love you too, honey," Rog said. He positioned the corset and pulled the center laces tight. "You are the hottest bitch in this room. Go out there and own it, my fairy queen."

"I… I will."

"Bend," Rog instructed.

Patrick folded at the waist and grabbed his tiny fake tits. Rog pulled the lace until Patrick could hardly draw air. Then he pulled some more, first at the center then up and down from that point.

"*Il faut souffrir pour être belle*. One must suffer to be beautiful," Rog said, giving the lacings a final tug. "You're sickening. Get your face on, honey, and give a mother something to brag about."

Patrick wasn't scheduled to perform until second to last. As he sat in the dressing room waiting, he tried not to listen to the music or imagine the other queens' performances. Some of them looked exquisite in sequined gowns and miles of blonde hair. Seeing them worried Patrick, made him feel invisible in comparison. He decided he wasn't going to be invisible, not ever again. He'd *make* the world see him, pay attention to him. He went over his routine in his mind, feeling confident until he was summoned onto the stage and his song began to play.

The audience members looked dead and skeletal beneath the cold blue lights. Patrick decided he'd bring them to life as the lyrics began and he lip-synched along. The announcer's voice boomed over top of the synthetic beat: "Ladies and gentlemen, give a warm welcome to Titania, the fairy queen!"

The men in the audience clapped as Patrick sauntered to center stage. They didn't start cheering or waving money right away as they did when Regina or Anita appeared; instead they just stared, looking a little confused. Good. They weren't just seeing a pretty drag queen. They didn't know exactly what they were looking at, which meant he had them thinking. Even the judges at the table watched him with canted heads and furrowed brows. Patrick smiled coyly at them and looked each of them in the eyes in turn. He wouldn't give them too much attention, though: just enough that they'd miss it when he snatched it away.

Patrick snapped his shoulders back and pranced to the other side of the stage, flawlessly executing all the moves he'd practiced with Shawn. An appreciative shout rose from the crowd when Patrick turned his back to them, spread his legs with one foot in front of the other, and touched the toe of his satin shoe with both hands. Then he rose slowly, one vertebra at a time, dragging his palms up his calf, his thigh, the front of his bloomers, letting it linger at his flattened groin. He knew the netting of the bustle concealed some, but not everything. The audience would see the shape of his ass through the veil-like material. Just as a synthetic instrumental interlude began, Patrick leaned back, basking in the cold blue light shining down on him. Then, feeling confident, he made a choice and leaned back even farther, bending backward until he arched over and caught himself on his hands. He held the backbend to thunderous applause, then lifted his leg and stretched it out straight.

Shawn had said he wasn't ready to attempt the move, especially in a corset, and Patrick had agreed. He'd been as wobbly as a newborn foal practicing in Eric and Rog's yard. Something about the lights flashing, the song he'd always loved blaring out of the speakers, and the hungry eyes of a hundred men on his body had made him daring enough to try, and his limbs were as sturdy and pliant as steel cords. When he pushed with his hands, got back to his feet, and spun to face his adoring crowd, bills waved from the men's hands like a sea of grass—tens, twenties, even fifties. Patrick twirled around the edge of the stage, letting the lace hem of the bustle billow out around him. Now and then, he bent down to pluck the money from a patron's hand, petting their cheeks as he rose. Others stuffed bills down the front of his bodice or tucked them into his bloomers. As the song reached its conclusion, Patrick made his way back to the center of the stage and positioned himself beneath the shaft of light shining down. The final chorus played, and Patrick sank into a straddle split, adrenaline negating the twinge he usually felt in his inner thighs. Wads of money rained down on him as he lifted himself onto his knees, legs still spread wide. He fell backward, catching himself on his left elbow and draping his right arm over his face. Eric, especially, had approved of Patrick's final pose, calling it a classic archetype: the performer willing to sacrifice everything for the pleasure of his audience. A symbolic death.

When the lights faded to black, Patrick hurried to stand and rushed off the stage. As soon as he reached the hall, Patrick collapsed against the purple-painted plaster and hugged his ribs, gasping for air. He giggled; he'd felt divine out there, the object of everyone's adoration. Looking back, he didn't know how he'd found the courage to go through with it all. It was like he'd been possessed, like the lights of the stage and the music had swept the dust from some long-buried facet of his personality, this goddess he and everyone else had tried to throttle into submission until she hung her head and slinked away in shame. They'd ignored her and told her she wasn't good enough for so long she'd begun to believe it, to cower away from the scrutiny of others. Well, Titania was back, and she was here to kick some ass.

Patrick kept to himself when he returned to the dressing room, sitting on the edge of a folding chair in the corner with his hands folded in his lap. The other queens cast vicious glances in his direction and narrowed their eyes at him as they whispered. Patrick ignored them; Roger had been right and they weren't worth his time. He knew he'd made them angry by being better and that they were jealous. At least he had them thinking, thinking about him.

Surprisingly, one of the queens, a slender, probably Hispanic girl—it was hard to tell for sure beneath the heavy makeup and layers upon layers of caramel-colored curls—came up to Patrick and smiled. "You were really good out there," she said, extending her hand. "You've got some impressive moves, and a really different look. You know how to stand out."

"Thanks a lot," Patrick said. "What's your name?"

"My real name is Chris. This bitch you see before you is Alejandra Fantasia."

"I'm Patrick, or—"

"Titania the fairy queen. Honey, I know. Everyone knows. Just ignore the rest of these bitches. You were sickening out there, and any one of these skanks who says otherwise is just jealous. How long have you been doing drag?"

"Um, about three weeks."

"Jesus," Chris/Alejandra said. "I kind of wish you were dead. Just kidding. Good luck."

"You too," Patrick muttered.

Not long after, one of the brawny stagehands, muscles ready to shred his tight black tank top, came backstage to announce the judging would soon commence. Queens fought for mirror space to powder their noses and adjust their wigs before queuing up to strut back onto the stage in the order they'd performed, which left Patrick near the end of the line. As they stood beneath the harsh white lights, all of them thrusting out their chests and plastering on their best faux smiles, Patrick realized how desperate they all were to be recognized, how hard they fought to be acknowledged, and he felt a camaraderie with the others, even the ones who'd been less than charitable to him.

An older queen in a red cocktail dress went to the microphone at the center of the stage. "Everybody having a good time? Enjoy the show? Ready to see which of these fabulous divas is tonight's winner?"

The audience shouted their assent. Eric, Roger, Aouli, and Shawn stood at the edge of the stage, clapping and yelling wildly.

"Okay," said the queen in red, brushing her long blonde hair off her shoulder. "Before we announce the winner, we want to thank all of you for coming out tonight. Remember, all of our profits will go to charities supporting GLBT youth. If you want to contribute a little bit more, you can buy a purple rose from the stand out in the bar, maybe for one of these special ladies. All proceeds go to the kids, so don't be tightfisted, bitches. I'll turn this over to our one and only beloved daddy. Ladies and gentlemen, Joe!"

The audience cheered as a burly man with a salt-and-pepper beard and tattoos covering his thick arms came to take the mic. He pulled a folded piece of paper from the pocket of his leather pants.

As Joe stood talking about the suicide rate among GLBT kids and how everyone could help, Patrick thought back to his performance. He'd been good, he knew, and that fairylike, gossamer creature called hope flitted around him, drizzling sparkling dust down on his shoulders. Patrick knew if he tried to clutch it, it would disintegrate in his hands, leaving nothing but a sparkling trail on his satin gloves. Hope had to fly free; it couldn't be captured, but the desire to trap and hold onto it grew stronger and stronger as Patrick stood on the stage.

Finally, Joe prepared to announce the winners. "In third place, and receiving a fifty dollar gift certificate to the bar, is Miss Midori!"

A curvy blonde queen in an extravagant gown and feather boa stepped forward to accept her prize. She blew kisses to the crowd as she sauntered off the stage and down the steps toward the dressing room.

"And in second place," Joe said, "the spicy Latin queen, Miss Alejandra Fantasia! She'll receive a one hundred dollar gift certificate to Miss T's Beauty Lounge right here in Pittsburgh, and we're going to donate one hundred dollars to the Trevor Project in her name! Congratulations, sweetheart!"

Patrick winked and gave the other queen a thumbs-up as she went to accept her prize, even though he felt a little disappointed. He'd never expected to win the pageant—he was a rank amateur and his act was weird—but he'd thought he might take second or third. Now, it seemed that wouldn't happen. Patrick tried to console himself by remembering how glorious he'd felt onstage, but it still stung to fail. He looked down the line of contestants and tried to predict which of them reigned supreme. Maybe bitterness compelled him, but they all looked the same in their tacky gowns, overteased hair, caked-on cosmetics, and huge, silicone boobs. Patrick had still made a good amount of money in tips, and he'd known his act was risky, that it probably wouldn't be understood or appreciated, but he'd taken that chance for his art. Unfortunately, it seemed it had been a bad gamble.

"The winner tonight is clear," Joe said. "Both in the judges' scores and audience reaction. I can't say I've ever seen anything like her before. Give it up for the beguiling, magical creature who caught us all in her spell tonight. The winner of Joe's Pride Pageant is the fairy queen, Titania!"

At first Patrick just stood stunned, sure he must be hallucinating. His friends cheered at the edge of the stage, Eric punching the air and Rog scrubbing at his tears. The queen next to him gave Patrick's shoulder a small shove, and he walked in a daze to the microphone. Thank God his legs seemed to move on their own, because he didn't feel like he could will his feet to lift from the stage floor.

"Anything you want to say, baby?" Joe asked, his voice sweet and gentle despite his size and intimidating appearance.

Remembering the award-show speeches he'd seen on TV, Patrick took the mic and said in a scratchy voice, "I have to thank my family. I wouldn't be here without them. God, is this a dream?"

"Go ahead," Joe urged. "You're doing just fine."

"Okay. This, all of this is because of Roger, Eric, Aouli, and Shawn." Tears gathered in Patrick's eyes, but he'd already won—he'd won!—so he didn't have to worry over his eyeliner. "Thank you, Mama. Thanks to my sisters, and Eric, my friend. Oh my God. Thank you all. I am so grateful to have all of you."

He hurried to pass the microphone back to Joe before he broke down sobbing and made an utter fool of himself. As soon as he could, he hurried from the glare of the stage. His friends met him in the hall.

"Eric, did that really happen?" Patrick panted, clutching Eric's T-shirt. "Was that real? They—they really chose *me*?"

"How can you even be surprised?" Rog asked, cupping Patrick's face, his eyes sparkling with happy tears. "You were a vision up there. Just so beautiful. It was like magic."

"You were born for the stage," Aouli said in a voice soft with awe.

"You nailed those moves," Shawn said. "I was afraid you were going to break your back, but you pulled it off. Nicely done, doll."

"Congratulations, Patrick," Eric said. "You went with your gut and it worked out. I'm so proud of you. I knew the only thing you lacked was confidence."

"No," Patrick said. "It wasn't confidence. I needed friends to support me. A family. Thank you all so much." He opened his arms, and all five of them hugged and held onto each other.

"You're welcome," Eric said. "But this was your victory. You should go get changed so you can meet your adoring public."

The dressing room was almost empty by the time Patrick reached it. Roger helped him out of his corset and then went to wait for him at the bar. Patrick pulled out all the bobby pins holding his wig in place and put it carefully into its round cardboard box. After he stripped out of his costume, he placed the exquisite garments carefully back in the package Tish and Tracy had given him, stroking them softly before he closed the lid. He'd have to have them dry-cleaned soon, but they'd be safe in his car until he could drop them off. If he took them in the house, he risked his father finding them....

No. He wouldn't let his mind veer onto that cold and shadowy path tonight. He'd done well tonight, and he had people who valued and supported him. They were waiting. They wanted to be with him, and they wouldn't dismiss him or throw him away. Patrick used half a dozen cosmetic wipes to clean his face. Wadded up in the bin and streaked with pinks and reds, they reminded Patrick of variegated roses, which he supposed was a silly idea. Everything just looked more beautiful beneath the warm lights of love and triumph. He could almost hear the flutter of hope's iridescent wings, as if it sat on his shoulder next to his ear. He still didn't dare to lay a finger on it, though.

Patrick untucked. He never would have dreamed he'd become accustomed to having his testicles jammed up inside his body cavity, but while he'd performed he'd almost forgotten about them. Stretching his skin and clenching his inner muscles, Patrick let them drop back down where they belonged. Then he slipped on his comfortable plaid boxers, loose jeans, T-shirt, and sneakers. In the mirror, he ruffled his hair with his fingers so it wasn't plastered so flat against his head. Before he joined the others, he took out his phone and called Yu. After a few rings, it went to voice mail. Though it was only around ten thirty, Yu wouldn't hear the phone while working, especially if he had his headphones in to listen to music. Patrick sent him a text instead:

Had the best night! Want to share it w/U. Text if U R still up! Then he typed a little heart.

In the lounge area beyond the stage, Patrick sat at a table with his friends. A steady stream of men and even a few women came to congratulate him and offer him one of the purple roses. Before long, their velvety violet petals almost obscured the rippled glass surface of the table.

Several good-looking men asked Patrick to dance, but he politely declined. He tried to be gracious to everyone who complimented him, but working at the Faire all day and then performing had left him exhausted. He just wanted to go back to Eric and Roger's house, curl up on the sofa, maybe watch an episode of *Supernatural* on Netflix, and then go to sleep in the fairy princess room upstairs. Being at their home made him feel safer than he ever had, and he knew he'd sleep better there. Before he suggested they leave, he checked his phone again, but Yu hadn't gotten back to him. He must've already gone to bed.

"Do you guys think we could get going? Me and Eric have to work at the Faire tomorrow morning, and I'm pretty tired."

"That's probably a good idea," Eric agreed. "The Freebooter's Retreat is one of our busiest weekends. Especially for me. I have two extra shows a day, and a gaggle of amorous wenches to outrun."

"Yeah, we can get going, honey," Rog said, squeezing Eric's hand.

"We're gonna stay a little longer," Shawn said. "You guys have a good night. Congratulations again, Patrick."

"Thank you." Patrick reached for the strap of the large duffle bag containing his cosmetics and clothing. Lately, he'd gotten into the habit of keeping a spare set of street clothes and a clean costume for the Faire on hand in case he got the opportunity to stay anywhere but his father's pigsty.

"Leaving so soon?" It was Joe, the club's owner, with another rose for Patrick.

"Work in the morning, I'm afraid," Eric said.

Joe responded with a warm belly laugh and said, "I gotcha, bro. Been there. I just wanted to thank you all for coming, and especially you, Queen Titania. You were absolutely enchanting, darling. It's been a while since I've seen a show like that."

"Thank you, sir," Patrick said.

Joe looked serious for a moment, and then he arched a brow and grinned. "I only like to be called sir under very specific circumstances. Call me Joe. I have a proposition for you. We're having another show next month, and I'd like you to come back and perform. This is a show, not a pageant, so you'd get a guaranteed booking fee plus your tips. Interested?"

"Absolutely!" Patrick said.

"In that case, you'll be performing three numbers."

"That'll be a lot of work, Patrick," Rog said. "You have to realize that's three costume changes, and three songs to memorize and choreograph. Are you sure you want to take this on along with your job at the Faire?"

"I'd really like to do it, Mama. I can use the money, and I felt amazing up there tonight. I like the person I become onstage." Maybe he could make a career out of this. It would certainly be better than going back to the gas station when the Faire closed for the season.

"I'll help you as much as I can," Rog said. Then his inner mother lioness clawed to the surface, and he turned to Joe. "I'll give you a call tomorrow to talk about his booking fee. I know what he's worth. And I expect him to be escorted to his car, or anywhere outside the club."

"Settle down," Joe said. "We provide security to all the girls. Some of my brothers from the motorcycle club volunteer to do it. I can guarantee nobody's gonna fuck with your girl. Call me here tomorrow, though, and we can discuss the details."

"Oh, you can count on it," Rog said, casting a defiant look at the man towering over him. "This is my family now."

Patrick gasped as a strange, warm feeling enfolded him, like sliding into a hot, fragrant bath. All the tension and anxiety drained out of him, and he finally knew how it felt to be defended. It felt wonderful, so wonderful he wanted to cry. "Thank you, Rog. For everything."

"You're welcome, baby." Rog began talking quickly, clearly excited. He pinned one of the roses behind Patrick's ear and they left the rest behind. "Now, if you're serious about going pro, the first thing we should do is get some promotional posters made up for you. I can Photoshop your name onto them, and I know a great site where we can get them printed up for cheap. We can even get you some postcards, though word of mouth is the best way to get more gigs. Do you happen to know a photographer? Maybe somebody at the Faire?"

Outside, the night was warm and clear, the stars shining brightly even through the jaundiced light of downtown. A group of men smoking around the side of the building clapped and hooted when they noticed Patrick, and one of them yelled, "Nice show, beautiful!"

"She'll be here again next month," Rog called. "You won't want to miss it!"

They'd made it almost all the way to Eric's truck on the other side of the parking lot when an older, balding man stopped them. He handed Patrick a bouquet of probably two dozen lilac roses. At ten dollars each, they made an expensive gift, and that made Patrick uneasy. Buying one for a good cause made sense, but this—this was a little creepy. A little too much.

"Excuse me," the man said. He wore a tacky purple shirt and a dark tie. He was a little pudgy and seemed very nervous. Beads of sweat covered the dome of his bald head. "I saw you in the pageant, and I want you to have these."

Eric must have also sensed something amiss, because he came up behind Patrick and stood so close Patrick's back pressed against his chest. Patrick was beyond grateful; Eric could be intimidating, and he made Patrick feel protected as he gingerly accepted the roses.

"Um, I think it's great that you donated so much to charity," Patrick said, the fine hair standing up on the back of his neck.

"I... I have never seen anything like you," the man said. "So sweet and delicate. Strong but vulnerable, just like these flowers. You are like a rose just beginning to bloom." He reached out to touch Patrick's face, and Patrick saw the strip of pale skin where his wedding ring usually rode, and he flinched.

Eric grabbed the man's wrist. "Hands off."

"I would never hurt him," the man protested. "I'm not a bad guy. I would treat him like the treasure he is. I'd never be anything but gentle. I would spoil him."

"I'll ask you one time to be on your way," Eric said. "If I have to ask a second time, it's going to hurt. Do we understand each other?"

The stranger backed away, his hands held up in front of him. "Did I do something wrong? Was it wrong of me to try to talk to a young man? Do you think I don't know what young men like him are looking for when they come to a place like this and prance around in their underwear?"

"That's enough!" This time Roger came forward and shoved the man in the shoulder. "Get the hell out of here!"

"And what are you going to do?" the man asked.

Just as Eric moved in front of Patrick to stand beside his partner, two very large, bearded men in black leather vests came around the corner. Like Joe, ink seemed to cover every inch of their skin. The one with the spiderweb tattoo on the side of his shaved head asked, "Is there a problem?"

"Yeah, there's a problem," Rog said. "This pig is harassing us. We asked him to leave us alone, but he won't take the hint. Look, we just want to go home."

"Take a hike, buddy," said the other biker, a mountain of a man in a black bandana with goggles over top. He slipped his fingers into a pair of brass knuckles. "And don't let us see your face around here again."

The man stuttered, clearly outraged but also ready to piss himself: a coward who only threatened those he perceived as weaker. He turned and ran a few feet, then yelled some nasty slurs back at the five men.

"Yeah, come back here and run your mouth, bitch," the bouncer in the bandana shouted, while his companion only shook his head. "Come on, guys. We'll walk you to your car, just to be on the safe side."

"Thanks," Patrick said. "I… we appreciate it."

The bouncer with the spiderweb tattoo grinned and offered Patrick his elbow. It felt like chivalry and kind of fun, so Patrick took it. "This way, my queen."

They reached the truck and Patrick thanked the bouncers again. The two bikers wished them a good night, and the three of them got into the cab.

The vehicle's interior smelled strongly of roses. Rog sat between Eric and Patrick, fiddling with the knobs on the radio until he found a jazz station.

"Does that happen a lot?" Patrick finally asked.

"I'm afraid it happens more than it should," Rog said. "When you put yourself on display, sometimes you attract the wrong kind of people, and unfortunately, a lot of them think drag queens and dancers are just glorified prostitutes. That guy is probably some closeted asshole who thinks having some money means he can treat people however he wants."

"He is," Patrick said. "I saw the tan lines from his wedding band. And look at this. He left his business card in the flowers. Mr. Mark Emmeck. He works for the state government."

"Figures," Rog said. "He probably feels entitled to act like a dick and treat other people like his underlings. I've seen the type before. You know, if you're going to perform, especially outside the city, you might want to get somebody to go with you."

"Really? Like a bodyguard?" Patrick asked.

Rog nodded. "I bet you could hire one of Joe's friends. They're good people, and nobody's going to give you shit with a seven foot bear of a biker standing behind you."

The stress of the day, good and bad, caught up with Patrick, and he rested his head against the cool glass of the window. "What about a samurai?"

Eric laughed. "Princess, where are you planning to find a samurai? Oh. Oh, I see. I guess he's cold enough to be at least a little scary."

"He's not," Patrick said, starting to doze off with his face drooping into the cool dewy petals, their perfume enveloping him. "He just makes you earn it." He couldn't keep his eyes open, so he let himself sleep the rest of the way home. A long day awaited him tomorrow, and at the end of it he'd finally get to see Yu. That thought made him smile as he surrendered to dreams.

Chapter 11

PATRICK thoroughly enjoyed the final day of the Freebooter's Retreat. He and Jen spent the time between their performances happily wandering the grounds, joining in every errant performance they happened upon. Practice had made Patrick competent enough on the lute to accompany most of the musicians, and Jen's gorgeous singing voice was never unwelcome.

Some remnant of his Titania persona stayed with Patrick, lending him the confidence to banter flirtatiously with women and even willing men. Of course, his allegiance to the queen always gave him a convenient escape if things progressed too far. Their matching red hair led many to ask if the queen's minstrel might be an unacknowledged brother.

"Acknowledged or not, this is our sweet little brother," Jen said before one crowd after a pirate quartet performed. "We cherish him as dearly as the roses do the sun, rain, and soil. We could not do without him, and value him above all others."

"Your Majesty?" Patrick asked, shocked.

"Peace, troubadour," Jen said, squeezing Patrick's arm. "'Tis all true. To the last word." Then she addressed the crowd. "And before tongues begin to wag, we tell you all, on our honor, this is our brother and nothing more."

"Can I have 'im, then, Queen Bess?" shouted a member of the Wench's Guild.

"Nay, my dove," Jen said, "for we cannot do without him."

At the back of the crowd, Taylor stood with his arms crossed, scowling at both of them. When the audience dispersed in search of other amusements, he came up to Patrick and said, "So, you think you're an actor now?"

"I'm in the cast," Patrick answered. "So, yeah."

"Just putting on a costume doesn't make you an actor," Taylor said.

Jen looked around to make sure none of the Faire's visitors heard her. "Fuck you. I never took an acting class either."

"Obviously," Taylor said.

"Just what's your problem?" Patrick asked, stepping in front of his queen. "What did we ever do to you?"

"I saw you having lunch with your little boyfriend," Taylor said. "I saw you two queers holding hands and sniffing each other's hair like a couple of dogs. I almost puked. There are kids at this Faire, for God's sake."

"You're such a douchebag, Taylor," Jen said. "What, are you jealous that Patrick has a boyfriend when no one here will give you the time of day?"

"At least I'm not a faggot."

Jen took a step closer to him, her chin lifted. "No. You're just a loser who thinks you can get ahead by bragging without the talent to back it up. Everyone here thinks you're an asshole. Go ahead and ask them if you don't believe me. Ask anyone."

"You cocktease bitch," Taylor snarled. "One of these days you're going to find out what you passed up, whether you like it or not."

"Over my dead body," Patrick said, getting between them.

"Fine by me."

"Oh yeah?"

"Yeah. What are you going to do about it, you little fag?"

"Try me," Patrick said, his fists balled and adrenaline coursing through his veins. "Go on. Let's see you do something besides run your mouth."

A large group of Faire patrons pointed at the queen and came to stand beside her for pictures. More than a few wanted photographs with Patrick as well, and Taylor, disregarded, soon skulked away.

When the crowd broke up, Patrick turned to face Jen and took her hand. "We have to go to Tom about Taylor."

"Oh, Patrick, I don't think we have to do that."

"Yes we do," he insisted. "He threatened you, threatened both of us. Should we wait around until one of us gets hurt?"

"He wouldn't really—"

"I don't want to take that chance," Patrick told her. "Not of something happening to you. Let's tell Tom what's happened and let him decide what's best for the Faire. Jen, there's no sense in waiting until it's too late. If we don't say anything and he does something—"

"Okay," she whispered, tearing up. "I know you're right. I just don't want to be responsible for him losing his job. I feel like a tattletale."

"Taylor did this to himself," Patrick argued. "It's not like we're making it up."

"I know. It hasn't even felt like Faire because of him this season. I usually love coming back here, but he's made me dread it."

"Tom needs to know that," Patrick said. "We're in this together, working to make the Faire the best it can be, right? It's not a competition."

"You'll come with me?" Jen asked.

Patrick rolled his eyes. "You have to ask? Come on. Tom should be at the joust right about now. We'll have some time to talk to him before you have to appear."

They found their manager outside one of the tents, talking to the French knights. Patrick took Tom aside, and together he and Jen relayed Taylor's infractions, beginning with the Facebook incident.

When they finished, Tom put a hand on Jen's shoulder, a grave look in his pale, blue eyes. "I wish ye'd come t'me sooner, lass. This Faire is a family, at least t'me."

"Tom, enough with the accent," Jen said, wiping her eyes on her sleeve.

"Sorry, Jen. But I meant what I said. You kids are important to me, and I feel like a father to all of you. I'll have a talk with Taylor."

"Thanks, Tom," Jen said, hugging the older man and burying her face against his shoulder. "I just can't stand feeling scared coming to a place I've loved for so many years."

"I can't stand it either," Tom said. "I'm going to put an end to it right now. That arrogant little bastard won't bother you again. I'm sorry I didn't see this sooner. I'm glad I gave you your minstrel."

"So am I," Jen said.

"Good lad, Patrick," Tom said. "Stay with her."

"Yes sir."

Patrick and Jen climbed the steps to the royal box and prepared to watch the joust. Across the field, Tom approached Taylor. Tom spoke, and Taylor stiffened and took a step back. Then the Faire manager reached for Taylor's elbow, attempting to lead him somewhere more private to talk, but Taylor pulled free of Tom's grasp and stuck a finger in Tom's face. Tom held up a hand in a calming gesture, but Taylor's face grew red. The two men obviously argued, and then Taylor threw his fancy, velvet hat adorned with peacock feathers onto the ground and stamped it beneath his boot. He stomped off in the direction of the parking lot, and one of the ladies of his entourage lifted her skirts to run after him.

"Holy shit," Jen whispered. "I think Tom fired him."

"Good," Patrick said. "He had no business here."

"It's my fault," she said.

"No, it's his, for being a dick. Everyone else here gets along and treats each other like family. I'm glad he's gone. Tell me you won't feel better coming here next weekend and knowing you won't have to deal with him. You can finally have a good time."

Jen lifted Patrick's hand and kissed his knuckles. "Bless you, you're right. Do you think—"

"What?"

"Do you think Sir Henry believes all that bullshit Taylor was saying?"

Patrick understood, and it made him smile. His friend had chosen well. "No, Your Majesty. Sir Henry could care less about gossip. He's a very straightforward and honest man. A good man, if I'm any judge. He's a man who will feel honored and humbled by your attention, as any man ought."

Jen kissed his cheek. "We could say the same of you, our dear, dear, friend." She abandoned her accent as she wrapped her arms around Patrick's neck. "God help that boy if he hurts you, Patrick. I'll see he regrets it. Hell hath no fury like a pissed-off big sister."

"Oh, I know that's true," Patrick said. He'd seen it firsthand.

THE cast sang their finale as the vendors leisurely boxed up their goods and secured their shops until the next weekend. Then the kingdom's merchants and laborers gathered around the stage to join the actors in song. Many of the customers, particularly those loyal patrons who came to the Faire in costume, also lingered for what they all referred to as "The Last Huzzah."

The men stood on one side of the stage, the women on the other, with the crowd beneath them similarly divided. Patrick sang along with the lads, though it felt a little strange:

"If all of the girls were bells in a tower, and I was a clapper, I'd bang one each hour!

"Go roll your leg over, roll your leg over. Roll your leg over the man in the moon."

The women responded: "If all the young laddies were big as they say, then nary a lass would be walkin' this day!"

The lads booed and shook their heads before singing: "If all them young ladies was bricks on a pile, then I'd be the mason, and I'd lay them in style."

"Oh, would ye now?" yelled Grace O'Malley, the Pirate Queen. "Ye'd have to learn some style first, as well as how to please a woman, ye knaves!" The audience laughed and applauded. Many of the women left in the crowd knew the lyrics and sang along:

"If all the young laddies were waves in the sea, I'd be the shore and I'd let them lick me!"

"You'll be disappointed, Captain Grace!" someone called out.

"Aye, that's what women are for!" another woman shouted. Grace O'Malley had quite a following among a particular segment of the female Faire-goers.

Eric stepped forward and held his hand over his heart, saying, "You cut me to my core, sweet lass!"

"Put your mouth where your money is, pirate!" another woman yelled.

Eric sang: "I wish all of the lasses were fish in a pool, and I was a whale with a waterproof tool." He grabbed his crotch, much to some of the women's delight.

"I'm watertight, Sir Francis," one of them yelled. "Just like yer ship! I can ride the waves just as hard, lovey!"

It was great fun, and Patrick hated to see it end. He'd have been happy to sing until morning with Yu beside him, but Yu never attended the finale. Maybe Wade just kept his workload too heavy. As Patrick finally wandered down the stage steps, he couldn't help wondering if Yu loved the camaraderie of the Faire or if he simply wanted training. As if summoned by his desires, Yu appeared at the fringe of the audience, apart from everyone else, still in the tight gray leggings and billowy white shirt he wore in the workshop. Patrick didn't mind seeing him in his Faire garb at all, and he loved Yu's smoky scent when he hugged him and buried his face in Yu's hair.

"This show is completely vulgar," Yu said. "You sing beautifully, though."

"You should see me when I'm onstage in drag," Patrick said, watching Yu's face to gauge his reaction.

Yu's reaction was hard to read. "I have a difficult time imagining you looking feminine. I'd like to see you perform, though. It can't possibly be more suggestive than this finale."

"It's fun," Patrick replied. "We could stay and sing. Of course, this will all move to the Stew before long."

"I'm no fan of the Stew," Yu said. "Can we go somewhere else?"

"Where?" Patrick asked, Yu's scent and the sensation of their bodies pressed close making everything else fade into triviality.

"Come with me." Yu took Patrick's hand and led him away from the very vocal crowd. They walked through the dewy grass, past the blacksmith's shop and stables, to a quilt spread on the ground and surrounded by candles in mason jars. "I cooked for you. I hope it will at least be tolerable."

A wicker basket sat beside a bottle of chardonnay in a bucket of ice. Sticks of incense sent curlicues of smoke into the deep blue sky. Patrick and Yu sat down facing each other as Yu removed dishes from the basket. Down the hill, the Faire patrons and cast still indulged in bawdy music. The stage lights formed a dome against the descending night.

"I love fireflies," Patrick said, watching the neon-green flickers and swirls moving across the grass. "They're so magical."

"You find beauty in everything," Yu said. "In the simplest things."

"Or the most complex and inexplicable things," Patrick said, running his fingertip from Yu's temple to his round chin.

"Are you talking about me?" Yu asked, letting his eyelids droop until only a sliver of amber showed beneath his thick dark lashes. "I'm not so complicated, am I?"

"The universe is full of magical things patiently waiting for our wits to grow sharper."

"Andrew Marvell?" Yu asked.

"Eden Phillpotts," Patrick said. "A pastoral playwright."

"And do you refer to me when you quote it?" Yu asked. "Am I a magical thing, or the one whose wits need to grow sharper?"

Unsure exactly how to answer, Patrick asked instead: "What did you make?"

Smiling, Yu opened the basket and took out a few small glass dishes, which he arranged between them. Then he handed Patrick a china plate edged in little pink rosebuds, a white linen napkin, and a fork. One by one, he removed the lids from the containers, releasing a mélange of tempting aromas. "I made a Thai-style mango salad, smoked salmon, Brie, and arugula sandwiches with capers, green beans with almonds, pesto, and truffle oil, and a summer berry terrine for dessert."

"Wow," Patrick said, looking down at the precise little dishes that looked like they'd come from the pages of a magazine. As he'd predicted, the people remaining at the Faire paraded up the hill, still singing boisterously, toward the tavern. Soon only the sounds of crickets and banners snapping in the breeze broke the silence. "How did you find the time to do all of this?"

Yu shrugged and poured Patrick wine. "It wasn't so hard after I found the instructions on my phone. Most of this is pretty fresh, so it involved very little actual cooking."

"Did you finish those manacles for Wade?"

"I did, and an extra eight pairs as well," Yu said.

"Wade must have been happy," Patrick said, carefully picking up one of the work-of-art little sandwiches.

"I think I actually disappointed him by removing anything he could criticize," Yu said, shaking his head. "Not being able to yell at me ruined his entire weekend."

"He must be hard to work with," Patrick said.

"At first. He's hardly an affectionate man, but his praise means so much more because it's so rare. A single kind word from him is the highest compliment."

"I feel that way about you when you smile," Patrick said. "Some people walk around with phony grins plastered on their faces all day. But you don't. You save it for when you're really happy, so I know you mean it when you smile."

"I'm happy now," Yu said, smiling wide.

"So am I." They touched the rims of their flutes together and sipped their wine as they sampled the delicious food Yu had made. It was as good as or better than anything from an expensive eatery, particularly the berry terrine. Patrick told Yu how wonderful it all looked and tasted.

"I made one more thing," Yu said. He reached into the basket, then handed Patrick a little cotton drawstring pouch.

Patrick opened it and took out a small, metal sculpture: an androgynous human form with its arms spread and spine arched backward, as if in flight. The upturned face conveyed joy even without any features. Some tattered, shimmering tulle trailed from the two spines on the figurine's back, and a little ring between them attached to a delicate chain. Patrick could see how it had been hammered and shaped; he could see the marks of Yu's hands on it. He looked up at Yu with stinging eyes.

"It's your hope." Yu curled his hand around Patrick's with the tiny, fairylike sculpture inside. "But it's also steel, so you can hold onto it without worrying. You can clutch it as hard as you can without fear of breaking it."

Overwhelmed, Patrick put his other arm around Yu's neck and shoulders and pulled Yu close, pressing his face against Yu's smooth skin and inhaling the scent of his hair. "Thank you," he breathed. He could think of nothing else to say, and knew he'd never be able to express what this meant to him.

"You're very welcome," Yu said in a jagged whisper, his breath warming Patrick's ear. "I always want you to hold onto hope. I've never met anyone who deserves it more."

They pulled apart slightly, only a few inches separating the tips of their noses. They just stared at each other, Patrick drowning in Yu's warm brown eyes and both of them smiling. Slowly, Yu moved his hand up Patrick's arm, up his neck, and across his cheek. He ran the pad of this thumb across Patrick's bottom lip, and then he took a handful of Patrick's hair and brought their faces back together. Fireworks erupted behind Patrick's eyes as their lips met, just brushing lightly together at first, then pressing a little closer. Their mouths slid together and parted. The hope sculpture remained encased in their joined hands as they shared each other's breath, tongues venturing out slowly, meeting and exploring before daring deeper.

Patrick clutched the back of Yu's shirt, pulling him closer, wanting to feel him near, feel the heat and hardness of his chest. He discovered the textures of Yu's mouth and teeth as he let Yu take control of the kiss, but with a gentle guidance, like one person leading another in a dance. Patrick heard his pulse inside his head and swore he heard Yu's heartbeat, felt it shaking his body. Yu was so sure, so competent, did everything with such perfect attention to detail, that in no time Patrick disregarded everything around him. Those few minutes, with their lips joined and Yu's silky hair sliding between Patrick's fingers, seemed to exist beyond the bounds of the mundane world. He felt like he'd slipped into a dream.

They broke apart, nipped and suckled at each other's mouths, and touched each other's hair, cheeks, chins, and eyelashes. They kissed a little longer, and Yu's hand wandered down Patrick's back and rested just above his hips, where his boxers extended an inch beyond the waist of his trousers. His touch sent a pleasant shiver up Patrick's spine.

"I've been dreaming about doing that," Yu said when they finally separated. He wrapped his fingers around Patrick's wrist and guided him to the edge of the blanket, where they lay down side by side, the crowns of their heads touching. Yu lifted Patrick's hand, still holding his hope, and kissed the backs of his knuckles. He turned it over and kissed the inside of Patrick's wrist, his lips hot and slick. "You said you've never dated. That means I'm your first boyfriend?"

Patrick wriggled a little closer to Yu and toyed with Yu's foot with his own, bumping their toes together. "Yeah. I… I'm a virgin, if that's what you're asking."

"You've never done anything? Not with a man or a woman?" Yu sounded a little surprised, but not judgmental.

"Only once," Patrick answered. "Back in high school. I used to help the drama club by painting the sets and making props. I liked being anywhere better than at home. I was at the school late one night, working on the castle interior for *Camelot*. A boy named Jake Monroe was working with me, and no one else was around. We went backstage for some supplies, and Jake pushed me up against the wall and kissed me. We kissed for a long time, and then we just went back to work. When we saw each other after that, he never said anything. It was like it had never happened. That kind of hurt me."

Yu trailed a single fingertip over Patrick's Adam's apple and across the prominent collarbones his gauzy shirt exposed, raising gooseflesh on Patrick's skin everywhere he touched. "That boy was probably just experimenting. He probably just wanted to kiss another man to see whether or not he'd like it."

"He liked it," Patrick said softly, remembering Jake's aroused body flush against his own while "I Loved You Once In Silence" played out on the stage. He remembered the smells of paint and plaster, Jake's own unique fragrance. "He liked it. I could tell."

"And you?" Yu asked. "Did you like it?"

"Yeah. I thought Jake was cute. He was one of those tall, lanky guys who always wore tight black clothes and big chunky boots. Even eyeliner sometimes, but he managed to pull it off. I liked it, but it wasn't like kissing you. Not even close. That… that was just amazing."

Without a word of warning, Yu rolled on top of Patrick and captured his mouth again, kissing him even harder than before, kissing him possessively, as if competing with the memory of Jake Monroe. Patrick matched his ardor and twisted his tongue against Yu's. He opened his legs so Yu's thigh could fall between them. It put a delicious, tortuous pressure on Patrick's groin, and he resisted his body's demands to thrust against Yu's leg. Against his belly, Patrick felt Yu's body reacting to him in turn, and he wondered if it was too soon to touch Yu there. God, he wanted to, but instead he dipped his hands inside Yu's shirt and dragged his palms over the silky, damp skin of Yu's back. His touch made Yu press into him, his erection hard and demanding against Patrick's belly. Patrick continued to explore his taut torso, relishing the bumps and cords of muscle that stretched, contracted, and played against each other as Yu moved on top of him. He even dared to let his hand close around the firm crescent of Yu's ass.

"I want to be with you," Patrick panted into Yu's hair. "I want you to be my first. Can we go to your apartment?"

Yu propped himself up on his elbows, his hair tickling the sides of Patrick's face as he stroked down Patrick's cheek with the back of his hand. "You don't have to be in a rush. I don't mind waiting."

Patrick nibbled Yu's chin, making Yu chuckle and his belly vibrate against Patrick's. "I'm not rushing. I want to. Don't you?"

"Of course I do." Yu kissed Patrick's flushed forehead. "I just want you to be absolutely sure of me. I don't want you to regret it later."

"You're kidding, right?"

"No, Patrick. I don't want to mess this up."

"I'm sure," Patrick said, touching Yu's warm, smooth skin and watching his eyes reflect the candlelight. "Or at least I'm sure I like this. I'd like to continue it in private, even if it doesn't lead to… um, completion yet. I just want to keep touching you without worrying someone will see. I like the way you feel, and I like the way you touch me. Can we go to your place?"

"We can't go there," Yu said gently and a little regretfully.

"I don't understand," Patrick said. He pushed Yu off him, sat up, and hugged his knees to his chest. "Why don't you want me to come to your house? If you don't want me physically, just say so. Why lead me on?"

"It's nothing like that," Yu said, also sitting and rubbing the small of Patrick's back. "I'm sure you noticed how I—and my body—reacted to you."

"What, then?"

"It's complicated. I don't exactly live alone. I have a roommate, and me bringing you to the apartment will be awkward. He won't appreciate it, to say the least."

Patrick grinned with relief. He'd really started to think Yu didn't want him. He supposed such doubts came naturally to a person who'd been cast aside by as many people as he had in his life, but Yu didn't deserve to bear the weight of what others had done. Those tender, passionate kisses, Yu's slow, reverent caresses, the way his skin had warmed and his breath had hitched—no one could fake that, especially not Yu, who could barely manage enough civilized deceit to engage in polite conversation. Feeling a little guilty for judging Yu based on the past actions of others, Patrick reached over and clasped his hand.

"Yu, I'm not suggesting we keep your roommate up all night screaming and banging against the wall"—Patrick blushed at the statement—"only that we maybe curl up under a blanket and watch a movie. Eat some popcorn—with truffle oil and Gruyere, of course!"

Yu laughed. "I'd like that, but I can't."

"Why? Does this roommate of yours not know you're gay?"

"No, he knows," Yu said. "He doesn't like people coming to the house, and the truth is, he pays more of the bills than I do, and his name is on the lease, so I have to abide by his rules. Please don't be upset."

"I'm not," Patrick said. "Just a little disappointed. If we can't go to your house and we can't go to mine, where does that leave us? How are we ever going to spend any time alone together?"

Patrick remembered he had some money. Even after he'd paid Tish and Tracy with his prize, he still had a few hundred dollars in tips. He'd almost had a heart attack when he'd counted the rumpled bills. If he wanted to, he could pay for a hotel room, but something about making that suggestion felt way too sleazy. Besides, if he didn't save every penny he could, he'd never accomplish a more permanent solution: a place of his own.

Yu brushed Patrick's hair aside and kissed up his neck until he could whisper in Patrick's ear. "Will you trust me to figure something out?"

With his head spinning and his heart ready to tear itself in half, Patrick just nodded, closed his eyes, and turned his head to find Yu's lips again.

Chapter 12

STENCH and buzzing greeted Patrick when he returned home somewhere on the wrong side of 2:00 a.m. Flies circled the garbage bin and the dirty dishes in the sink. The vomit smell coming from the living room directed Patrick straight down the hall to his own small space. He opened the door and switched on the light. It only took him a few seconds to notice something drastic had changed.

His TV and Xbox, which he'd worked his entire first summer at the Faire to buy, were gone. Only the rectangles in the dust on his secondhand table remained. Most of his games and videos lay scattered over the floor, though a quick inventory told him many of them were missing as well. Irrationally, Patrick checked in the closet and underneath the bed, though he knew he hadn't moved his appliances. He hadn't even been home for two days. Slowly, and though he resisted accepting it, he realized what must have happened.

Violated and outraged, Patrick stormed into the living room and turned on all the lights, exposing all the filth that had built up over the years. He went to the sofa and shook his father's pale, sagging shoulder. The old man only grunted in response, which made Patrick even angrier.

"Where's my TV, you old drunk? Answer me, goddammit! Answer me!"

His father farted and covered his face with his fleshy arm to escape the light and noise.

"No!" Patrick yelled, kicking the wooden leg of the couch until it dented the yellowed plaster wall. "Tell me what you did!"

"Sold 'em," the old man said. "Time you pay your way 'round here. You're a grown fucking man, Patty."

"Why?" Patrick screamed, kicking the couch again. Next door, the small mongrel dog on the chain began to bark, but he didn't care. "How could you do this to me? You had no right! I paid for those myself!"

When his kicks failed to get a response, Patrick used his fists, pummeling the old man's back and shoulders. His father just lay there in a drunken stupor, curling in on himself and ignoring his son. Patrick wanted his father to get on his feet and face him, hit him, even. Anything would have been better than feeling dismissed, invisible, and of no consequence. It soon became clear the bastard wouldn't stir from his coma, and Patrick kicked the end table, sending beer cans flying and the bulb of the lamp shattering against the floor before stomping back down the hallway to his room. He slammed the door and collapsed on the edge of the bed he'd slept in since he'd been six, holding his head and crying.

It wasn't the money; Patrick placed very little value in wealth. It was the betrayal of trust, the desecration of the ten-by-twelve space he'd thought was his. The disregard for his feelings. Damn, he hated to admit it, but he loved that Xbox, loved it even more because he'd toiled to earn it. It had been the first real purchase he'd made with his wages, and it had granted him a sense of independence, like he had a chance of taking care of himself. Sure, he could buy another eventually, but all the characters he'd created and the hundreds of hours of games he'd saved could never be recovered. It wasn't a loss most people would understand, he knew, but before he'd started to perform in drag and at the Faire, those characters had been the outlet for his creativity, his doorway to escape into fantasy and a vicariously satisfying existence. As sad as it sounded, they'd been friends to him, in a way, when he most needed friends. He still had his stereo, so he put on some appropriately depressing music and shut off the lights. My Bloody

Valentine played in rhythm with the blue strobes of his system, and Patrick felt like a stupid cliché as he hugged his pillow and whimpered.

Brand New's "Play Crack the Sky" followed, and Patrick cried a little harder. Something about the shipwreck metaphors in that song and the wish for a little more time, the inevitability of an end to everything, made him emotional on his happiest days. He'd always interpreted it literally, instead of as an analogy for a failed relationship. Like a person couldn't experience more tragedy than a failed relationship. As long as you lived, you had a chance to try again. He tried to believe in hope. Although how could he talk? Here he was, crying over characters in video games and feeling like losing his Xbox had decimated his universe. He thought of his brother and told himself to grow up. Dylan had never had a chance to play a video game or get a summer job. Patrick tried to put his petty tragedy into perspective.

As if the night couldn't get any worse, Patrick's mother called. He ignored her the first three times, until she sent a text message:

I will keep calling until you pick up.

Finally, he surrendered. "Hey, Mom."

"Honey. How *are* you? I'm doing so well. In fact, me and Stan are at a cocktail party tonight in the home of a major producer. Guess who?"

"I don't know," Patrick muttered. Bauhaus came on, followed by the Cure and My Chemical Romance. His personalized soundtrack to despair was never more appropriate.

"Honey, guess! I'll give you a hint. What's the most groundbreaking children's movie of the summer? Well, honey?"

"I'm nineteen, Mom, and I'm working two jobs. How would I know?"

"Well. You don't live in a cave, Patrick. Everyone knows."

"I don't."

"Honestly. Think jungle animals."

"I'm not in the mood to play this game," Patrick said.

His mother exhaled audibly. "Jesus. Have you ever heard of *Madagascar 3D*? Well, I'm at the producer's house tonight, and the voice talent is here too! Honey, who do you think that is? I'll give you a hint. It's a very well-known actor. Who do you think we're having drinks with right now, honey?"

"I don't give a shit," Patrick said. "And I don't understand what kind of satisfaction a grown woman gets out of showing off to the nineteen-year-old son she abandoned. Do you want me to feel sorry for what I missed, not being one of your special, blond, California kids? Do you honestly think you're going to impress me by dropping names? If that's all you want, just leave me alone."

"Patrick Ignatius, you should be ashamed."

"Why? Because I remind you of your white-trash life in Pittsburgh before you got that paralegal certificate and hooked up with your Hollywood lawyer? Sorry to exist."

"You ungrateful little brat—"

"And there's the North Side accent," Patrick said. "Make sure the producer of *Madagascar 3D* doesn't hear you, Mom. Did you want anything else other than to brag about how great your life is?"

"I have a lot of connections, Patrick. I'm respected, and I called because I think I can help you. Have you ever thought about coming out here? Can you imagine working in a *Hollywood studio?*"

"No."

"Oh, and do you have something better lined up in *Pennsylvania?*" She said the state's name like a dirty word.

"I'm doing fine," Patrick said. "Why the sudden concern, anyway, Mom?"

"Oh, like I haven't loved you? Looked out for you?"

Patrick blew air through his nose. "Sure. Thanks for Stan's cast-off polo shirts. Thanks for using me as a way to fish for sympathy from the other Beverly Hills housewives. I need to go. I'm tired, and I have to work in the morning."

"Where are you working?" she asked, all false sweetness and interest.

"Still the Faire," Patrick said. "I have to go. I'm hanging up now. I'll turn my phone off if you try to call back."

"Oh, honey, there's no future in—"

Patrick hung up and waited to see if his mother would call back to brag about her fairy-tale life. It was old at this point, every conversation the same. The next thing she'd ask was if he knew of a charity where she could donate her old clothes, because they were just hanging off her…. Of course, she'd offer them to a shelter in California, but how many homeless women needed a size double zero? They were designer clothes, and they shouldn't go to waste….

"Fuck you," Patrick said aloud. She'd killed his brother and condemned Patrick to the life of squalor he endured. And then she dared to brag about her Hollywood dream of sequins and silicone boobs. He had no mother, just a selfish woman out for herself, and a drunk of a father determined to kill himself. Sick of looking at his shitty room, especially empty of the few things he'd valued and worked so hard to obtain, he flipped off the light. He was alone.

Except maybe he wasn't. Not anymore. Patrick picked his phone up and dialed Yu. After four rings, Yu picked up, though he sounded sleepy.

"Hey, Patrick. Everything all right?"

"No."

That woke Yu up, and he sounded more alert as he asked, "What's the matter? Did something happen?"

"Kind of," Patrick admitted. "But I don't want to talk about it. I just want to talk to you."

"Okay," Yu said. "Okay, talk."

"It's so fucked up, how people decide other people are worthwhile or not," Patrick said, barely whispering. "What do they base it on?"

"I don't know," Yu said. "I'm really not the right person to ask. Their own standards of talent, I suppose. Their own expectations from those people."

"Their own," Patrick repeated.

"Yes," Yu answered. "They tend to base it on the potential to satisfy their desires, become what their lives are lacking, make money and little else. At least that's been my experience."

"I make money, though," Patrick said. "I made so much money on Saturday when I performed. But I'm still of no value to them."

"You are of value to me," Yu said in his scratchy, drowsy voice.

"Really?"

"Yes."

"Yu—God, I know I shouldn't say this, and I don't want to scare you away, but—but I think I love you. You don't have to say it back."

"I want to. Patrick, I've never met anyone like you, and I really want to get to know you better."

"Do you love me?"

"I might," Yu said. "Soon. I almost do, but this is all happening very fast."

"I'm sorry."

"Don't apologize, Patrick. Don't ever apologize for being honest."

"God, Yu. I wish you were here with me. I'm so fucking sick of being alone, facing everything by myself...."

"I'll be at the Faire in the morning. Come to the shop. I'll get croissants and really good coffee."

"You don't have to buy me," Patrick whispered. "I'd be with you for dirty water and wormy hardtack. I'd drink bilgewater."

"Nerd," Yu teased.

"You understood it," Patrick countered.

"I did. Hold on to your hope. Sometimes things can only get better. I'll see you tomorrow, okay?"

"Okay. Yu, I love you."

Yu said nothing for many moments. "Good night, Patrick."

For a long time, Patrick lay curled on his side, staring at the screen of his phone glowing in the darkness. He wished he'd taken a picture of Yu so he could look at his face. God, he had to get out of this house. Tomorrow, he'd lock his games and movies in the trunk of his car. He had little else of monetary value. If his father wanted to kill himself, he'd have to do it without selling Patrick's things. He reached into his pocket and took out the little sculpture Yu had made him, feeling a twinge as he ran his fingers over the smooth metal. How could someone he'd only known for a few weeks care enough to do something this profound, while his own parents wanted him only to bolster their self-esteem, in the case of his mother, or as an emergency source of booze money? Yu filled the empty space in his life, but did that mean Patrick was only using him to replace what he'd always been lacking? No, he knew that wasn't true. He loved Yu and would do anything for him.

Lately he'd felt like he rode a roller coaster, his life reaching impossible pinnacles where only the heavens and clouds surrounded him, like when he'd won the drag pageant or tonight when he'd kissed Yu, but the plummet always awaited just on the other side. That twinkly, fairylike creature called hope was a fickle bitch, one who seemed to appear to taunt him and then retreat just as he reached out his hand. But this hope, the one Yu had given him, was solid, and Patrick held it tight to his chest as he slowly drifted off.

FOR the next few weeks, Patrick worked as much as he could and saved every penny he could spare for a place of his own. Of course, he spent more than a little on costumes, wigs, and cosmetics, especially since Rog worked tirelessly to find him gigs around the area. Lots of clubs wanted to book Titania, who was making a name for herself as something more than a drag performer, something artistic, ethereal, and unforgettable. The increasing popularity meant higher booking fees for Patrick, as bars competed to acquire him, but it also meant traveling as many as three hours away to perform and often working at the Faire the next day on only a few hours of sleep.

That Saturday was July 27, and it took all Patrick's skill to put on a fake smile and perform as Elizabeth's minstrel. If he appeared somber, his friends would only question him, and Patrick would rather not talk today. A few times, as he stood before a crowd, he swore he saw Taylor in the audience. He also thought he saw the pudgy bureaucrat, Mark Emmeck, from the pageant, but running on two hours rest and emotionally stirred up, he couldn't trust his perceptions.

Finally the day ended and Patrick went to the men's dressing room to change, carefully placing the half a dozen white roses he'd purchased beside the sink as he splashed some cold water on his face. Yu was waiting for him when he emerged in a pair of baggy shorts and a faded yellow T-shirt. Yu caught his hand and led him around the back of the building. When they were safely hidden, Yu grasped Patrick's waist, pressed him gently against the block wall, and kissed him. Patrick wrapped his arms around Yu's neck and kissed back, grateful for the comfort. The roses he still held trailed down Yu's back. They pulled a few inches apart and grinned at each other, Patrick looking deep into Yu's soft brown eyes.

"What do you want to do tonight?" Yu asked. "I feel like being outdoors. We could go into the city and walk by the river, or to that roadside rest area you like."

With some effort, Patrick tore his gaze away from Yu's face and stared down at the white toes of his sneakers. "You're good to me," he whispered, resting his head against Yu's shoulder. "Why are you so good? What can you possibly see in me that no one else ever has?"

"What's gotten into you?" Yu asked. "I want you to be happy."

"Why?"

"Because I really like you," Yu said, kissing Patrick softly on the forehead. It wasn't lost on Patrick that "really like" was still the most Yu was willing to say, even though Patrick told Yu he loved him at least every day.

"Come on, let's go get something to eat," Yu said, stroking the back of Patrick's hair.

"I can't tonight," Patrick said. "There's something I have to do."

"Is it something that can include me?"

Patrick considered for a long moment then nodded. "It might be nice to have you with me, but you probably aren't going to have much fun."

Yu nodded back, and they walked to Patrick's car and got inside amidst all the other patrons, actors, and merchants preparing to leave for the day. Patrick rolled all the windows down to let the hot, heavy air escape. He handed his bouquet to Yu to hold while he drove. The setting sun gave everything a fuzzy, gilded quality, even the clouds of dust kicked up by the vehicles' tires on the dirt road leading to the highway. Patrick looked back at the faux Tudor buildings. Leaving the Faire today felt like closing a beautiful storybook to face the ugliness of reality.

"We need rain," Yu said, looking out the window and at the parched grass.

"I know." Watering the rose bushes and gardens around the grounds occupied hours of Patrick's weekdays.

Yu took the hint that Patrick didn't feel like talking; he rubbed Patrick's shoulder before turning on the radio. They drove for an hour without conversation. By the time Patrick reached the neglected cemetery sandwiched between a row of dilapidated houses and a convenience store, the sky had deepened to the rich, velvety cobalt it only ever became for a few minutes before full darkness fell. Patrick parked the car and locked it—this neighborhood wasn't the safest—and opened the rusted gate with a creak. Though someone kept the cemetery satisfactorily mowed, thick weeds covered many of the graves, including the small one Patrick approached, almost hidden beneath a hemlock tree. He set his flowers in the dewy grass and began to pull up the weeds. By the time he'd scraped the moss from the little granite angel beside the modest stone he'd always found woefully inadequate, sweat stained his shirt around the neck and at the armpits. Breathing heavily, he knelt down and placed the roses in front of the marker.

The entire time, Yu stood a few respectful feet away. Finally he asked if Patrick was okay.

Nodding, Patrick stood and brushed shredded bits of vegetation and soil from his knees. "I just can't stand to think of Dylan completely abandoned here." He swiped at his eyes even though dirt caked his fingers. "He'd be sixteen years old today. I wish I could have done something, protected him. Been a real big brother."

"Patrick, you were three years old," Yu said gently. "You can't possibly feel guilty."

Though Patrick took a step closer, several feet still separated him from Yu. "That's the thing. I don't feel guilty. I feel cheated. If he hadn't been killed, I wouldn't have been so lonely. I feel like I would have always had someone in my corner, someone I would have been important to. Someone I could have loved and taught things. But then sometimes I think Dylan got lucky. He got to escape all the pain. When I was little, I used to picture him in a white gown with feathery wings when I felt most alone, like a guardian angel. How stupid is that?"

"It isn't even remotely stupid." Yu closed the distance between them, curled his fingers around Patrick's wrist, and pulled Patrick into an embrace. Patrick, his arms folded between Yu's chest and his own, dropped his forehead against Yu's shoulder and let a couple tears slip down his cheeks. He'd spent years screaming and sobbing over the loss of a brother he barely remembered as more than a peachy pink lump in an old flannel blanket, and the immediacy of his grief had diminished over time. Now it was more like an arthritic ache, still painful but so ingrained in him it just felt like part of life.

When Patrick pulled away, feeling a little self-conscious, Yu touched the apple of his cheek. "Your face is all dirty."

"I have cosmetic wipes in my bag," Patrick said, and both of them laughed to break the tension. Patrick suddenly felt dizzy and a little nauseous. "Can we sit down?"

They moved to a bench near the gate. "Patrick, you look exhausted," Yu said, sounding worried. "Why don't we go sit in a bookstore and get some coffee?"

Patrick shook his head. "I have to perform at Joe's tonight. Yu, why won't you ever come see me? Are you ashamed of me doing drag? Do you think it's sleazy?"

"I admit I don't like the idea of other men thinking of you like that, but I know it's a way for you to earn money and also something you enjoy. I... the truth is, I really don't like crowds. I'm embarrassed to talk about this, but you should know. I get very nervous around large groups of people, especially when they're all talking at once. It's like my mind can't choose what to focus on, and I start to feel like I'm going crazy. It's a big part of the reason I stay in Wade's shop most of the day. I even had to go to a small private school as a child because of it. Does that bother you?"

"Why should it?" Patrick asked. "I'm sure you can't help it."

"Still, it's been too much for more than one man to handle," Yu said. "A few guys I've been interested in said they couldn't be with me if I could never go out and party with them. They saw me as somehow defective."

Patrick took his hand and explored the rough texture of his palm and fingers. "It's going to take a lot more than that to get rid of me."

Yu smiled at him, and seconds later they were kissing. Patrick put his hand beneath Yu's shirt, circling one hard little nipple with his fingertip. "Patrick, what do *you* see in *me* that no one else has?"

"I...."

"Get a room, faggots!" a man yelled from a passing car, and they jumped apart, startled.

"We should probably get out of here," Yu said. "In case he decides to come back. This isn't the most tolerant part of town."

Patrick nodded. "Yu, am I your boyfriend?"

"Where did that come from?"

"I just want to know what's going on with us. Sorry if I'm being melodramatic. I get emotional when I'm tired."

"Do you want to be my boyfriend, Patrick?"

Patrick nodded, feeling like he'd lose it and make an absolute ass out of himself.

"Then of course you are. I thought you knew."

"I wish you would have a talk with your roommate," Patrick said, clutching Yu's arm and cuddling up against him. "It's completely unreasonable of him to expect you never to bring a friend to your own home. I even think it's unreasonable that I can't stay if we're respectful. I really want to spend the night with you."

Yu sighed, probably tired of this argument. "Listen, Patrick. Do you know what next weekend is at the Faire?"

"The Lovers' Hideaway," Patrick said, starting to doze off against Yu's shoulder.

"Well, do you have plans for Saturday night?"

"Uh-uh," Patrick muttered. "I'm performing Thursday and Friday, but not Saturday."

"Good." Yu kissed the part at the center of Patrick's hair. "I have something special planned for you, something I hope will make up for my roommate. Patrick? Are you asleep?"

"No," Patrick said in a whisper. "I love you."

"Come on," Yu said. "I'm going to worry about you driving to work if you don't get some caffeine into you. There must be a Starbucks around here somewhere. You won't be alone there, will you?"

"I don't know," Patrick said. "Roger is performing at a different venue, so Eric won't be there, but I invited Tish and Tracy, and they said they'd try to make it."

"I guess we'd better go so you aren't late."

They stood and left through the squeaky gate. "Bye," Patrick whispered, blowing a kiss as he took a last look at the cemetery.

"I think your brother would be glad you found some happiness in life," Yu told Patrick. "He would be glad you found someone who loves you as much as I do."

"Yu?"

Yu turned to face Patrick, smiling. God, he was so beautiful, the most beautiful man Patrick had ever seen, especially when he smiled. How in the world could anyone not want him? How could anyone throw him away? Overwhelmed, Patrick threw himself into Yu's arms, almost knocking Yu over. Yu laughed, lifted Patrick off his feet, and kissed him. Patrick wrapped his arms around Yu's strong, slender shoulders and held on tight. He never wanted to let go, and he knew Yu would never throw him away, either. They'd hold on to each other.

Chapter 13

SCARLET and ivory roses wound around the lintels of the shops, garlanded the porches, and adorned the arbors of the Faire for the weekend of the Lovers' Hideaway. Their perfume hung in the hot summer air. As cliché as he knew it sounded, Patrick could also feel the love drifting on the light wind as happy couples strolled arm in arm or sat next to the fountains or in the gardens looking into each other's eyes. Vendors sold champagne, and a chocolate fountain had been set up in the center of the food court, surrounded with strawberries and biscuits.

For the weekend, Patrick abandoned his role as a minstrel to play Cupid. He wore a gauzy white shirt with a red velvet doublet, breeches, and muffin-style cap, along with a set of feathery white wings on his back. No one said anything about the circles of rouge on his cheeks or the subtle lip tint on his mouth, and he had great fun skipping around with his bow and quiver, hiding behind columns to aim his fateful arrows at the lovers he saw.

Traditionally, the Duke of Anjou would court Queen Elizabeth this weekend, but they no longer had a Duke of Anjou, and Jen looked more than happy to make her rounds escorted by Sir Henry, offering her blessing to the couples she encountered. Sometimes a wedding even took place at the Faire during the Hideaway, but none had been scheduled this year.

Finale lasted longer than usual, and the songs were bawdier than ever. While children weren't banned from the Hideaway weekend, most patrons exercised common sense and left their little ones behind. Finally Henry and Jen took center stage to perform a very suggestive duet, and Patrick crouched behind them, looked at the audience, and pressed a finger to his lips before targeting the blissful couple. Everyone cheered as he pretended to let his arrow fly.

Patrick snuck away after that, just as it started to get dark. He would no longer be needed, and he couldn't wait to see what Yu had planned this time. Without even changing—he thought he looked rather fetching in the red velvet with his milky skin and auburn hair—he hurried to the blacksmith's shop where they'd agreed to meet.

Yu, his hair wet, dressed in a fresh shirt and deep blue doublet over his customary tight leggings and knee-high boots, offered Patrick a long-stemmed rose. Then he lifted Patrick's hand and kissed the back, never breaking eye contact and showing a mischief in his gaze Patrick had never noticed before. That simple brush of lips sent a tremor to the root of Patrick's body and made his belly clench up.

"You can put those arrows away, My Lord Cupid," he said. "I'm already smitten. You look really good in red. Would you do me the honor of allowing me to escort you?" Yu offered Patrick his elbow, and Patrick took it, his curiosity tearing him apart.

The high grass swished as Patrick walked beside Yu, torn between the urge to run and a desire to slow down, stretch every moment to the breaking point. He wanted to remember the flicker of the fireflies, the moonlight on Yu's smooth skin and shiny hair, the warmth of their intertwined arms, Yu's freshly washed, citrus scent and the smell of the grass and horses, the mélange of anticipation and total contentment he experienced.

Up ahead, a white, octagonal tent with a conical roof and detailed, scalloped edges glowed softly, like a candle inside cupped hands. It sat apart from the rest of the Faire, nowhere near the campgrounds and well past the buildings and shops, almost at the edge of the woods. Yu led Patrick through the open door flap. Patrick blinked rapidly, sure he'd tumbled into a dream. A few glass lanterns provided the fuzzy, golden light he'd seen from outside, along with some candles in iron holders and in jars like they'd been for their nighttime picnic. A mixed bouquet of red and white roses sat on a low table beside a bottle of wine Patrick now recognized as champagne because of the mushroom-shaped cork and the little wire enclosure around it. A tray of fancy, bite-sized foods and a bowl of strawberries sat nearby, all of it next to what looked like an inflatable mattress covered in white linens and dozens of pillows. A radio sitting on a cooler played soft, romantic music—Schubert, Patrick thought. Yu had such excellent taste in everything.

Yu looked more radiant than any of it, though, beaming at Patrick and exuding excited energy, as if he could barely restrain himself from jumping up and down. He looked so proud, as well he should, and the words of profuse thanks Patrick intended to say caught in his throat. No one had ever done anything like this for him before. His parents hadn't even thrown him a birthday party since they'd separated when he was five.

"I hope you don't mind me cooking for you again," Yu said softly, as if afraid speaking too loud might burst the opalescent little bubble they inhabited.

"No," Patrick said. "I mean, no, I don't mind. I can't remember the last time anyone went to the trouble of cooking for me. The most my dad can manage is microwaving hotdogs, and when I stayed with my mom, her housekeeper made all our meals, which were usually strange, gross things like wheatgrass smoothies. I like it when you cook for me. It makes me feel special."

"You are special." Yu held Patrick's cheeks in both his rough palms and just looked at him for a long time before pressing a light, lingering kiss to Patrick's lips. Then he took Patrick's hand and guided him to the mattress, where they sat together on the edge. Yu opened the wine, which he explained was actually Cava, from Spain, chosen to accompany the tapas-style meal he'd prepared. He pinched the end of a toothpick and lifted a small sausage to Patrick's mouth. Patrick accepted it and bit down, a burst of savory juice and heat flooding his palate. He reached for his flute, but Yu gently caught his wrist. "Have some bread instead."

Patrick followed his advice, and the garlicky little slab of bread soothed his mouth. Next Yu fed him an olive stuffed with some kind of pungent cheese, followed by a slice of yellow tomato topped with a creamy chunk of fresh mozzarella and a basil leaf. Patrick realized Yu hadn't eaten anything himself, and he understood what his companion had intended when he'd planned this meal.

Patrick picked up a pale piece of melon wrapped in prosciutto and offered it to Yu. When Yu's full lips parted ever so slightly and Patrick saw a flash of his pink tongue resting against his bottom teeth, extended slightly and wet with anticipation, his hand trembled so badly he almost missed Yu's mouth. Yu made a soft sound of contentment as he chewed, his jaw working and carving small pools of shadow beneath his cheekbones. Watching him savor his food, his pleasure, made Patrick imagine the sounds and faces he might make as he enjoyed other pleasures, and Patrick's body reacted. He scooted a few inches away, feeling like a horny teenager, which he supposed he was. He was also a very nervous and inexperienced young man, terribly afraid of disappointing his partner.

Yu took a sip of his wine and then lifted Patrick's hand and rubbed his cheek against Patrick's knuckles, his eyelids drooping languidly. "Why are you so nervous?" He looked up at Patrick through his dark lashes, a serious expression on his face. "Oh, no. Patrick, I apologize if you're not ready for all of this. I've made you uncomfortable."

Patrick stole a glance at the sumptuous bed and couldn't help noticing the small stack of foil packets and little container of clear jelly tucked discreetly beside it. Looking away quickly, he met Yu's concerned eyes. "It isn't that. This is all so perfect, like a fairy tale. I… I'm just afraid of messing it up."

"Patrick, one of the things I love most about you is the way you let your real feelings show through. You don't do or say things to impress others. I love that I don't have to wonder if you're being sincere. So please don't worry. And I want you to know I don't expect anything. I'd like to spend the night with you, even if that means just lying next to you. I did this so we'd have a chance to be together, and because I want you to be happy. I didn't do it to make you feel like you'd owe me anything. I'm not that kind of man."

"I know you're not," Patrick said, touching the center of Yu's lips with his thumb. "I'm just not used to anyone doing anything just to make me happy."

"Get used to it," Yu said in a commanding tone but with a playful smile. "Let's eat. I'm starving."

Patrick's anxiety drained away, and he fed Yu a prawn that left Yu's lips shining with herbed oil. They looked so delicious Patrick couldn't resist leaning in for a taste, and before long their meal sat forgotten as they licked and nipped at each other's lips. In unison, their mouths parted and their tongues met and bumped impishly together, still discovering and adjusting to each other's rhythm. Patrick ran his hands up Yu's thighs and over his chest, starting on the laces of Yu's doublet when he reached them. In moments he had it hanging open, and he clutched the thin, damp fabric beneath, feeling Yu's hard little nipples just below the gauzy cotton. He moved his fingers up Yu's neck, over his heated cheeks, and into his hair, which he held in his fists as he thrust his tongue deeper into Yu's mouth.

Yu broke away, gasping for breath. "Patrick—" He shucked off his doublet, pulled his shirt over his head, and tossed it onto the bed behind him. Then he curled his fingers around Patrick's waist and guided Patrick into his lap, Patrick's knees beside Yu's hips and their erections barely touching. Yu popped the snaps on Patrick's doublet and lapped at the hollow between Patrick's collarbones. "Patrick, tell me a poem."

"I… I can't think of one."

"Please." Yu cupped Patrick's ass and massaged his cheeks before urging him forward so their cocks pressed against each other. He pecked lightly up Patrick's neck and along his jaw. "Share what you love with me. Tell me the one about the lusty smith."

Patrick chuckled as he wriggled out of his garments, dying to feel Yu's smooth, lean chest against his own, skin against skin, finally. "That's hardly a poem. And I changed it. Made my own version."

"Tell me." Yu skated his fingers down the center of Patrick's chest and belly, grazing his cock through his breeches before journeying back up. His heavy breathing wet Patrick's cheek as he spoke against Patrick's skin.

Even though they were alone, Patrick leaned in and buried his face in the silky, straight hair near Yu's ear. Though he intended to whisper, the verse came out in a husky growl:

"A lusty young smith at his vise, stood a-filing,

His hammer laid by but his forge still a-glow.

When to him a wanton young minstrel came smiling,

And asked if to work in his forge he would go."

"God," Yu panted, wrapping his arms around Patrick and lowering Patrick to the mattress. He kissed Patrick hard as Patrick wrapped his legs around Yu's waist and thrust up against him, feeling dampness in his briefs, afraid he'd come before they got a chance to do anything.

He pushed Yu off. "I… I'm too warm," he said as a feeble excuse.

"Are you saying you want to get naked?" Yu asked.

"Do you?"

Holding Patrick's wrist, Yu pressed his hand against his hard flesh. "What do you think?"

"Okay."

Yu sat up and looked down at Patrick's face, perhaps studying it for any trace of hesitation. He must not have detected any, because he moved Patrick's feet into his lap and slid Patrick's ankle boots off one at a time. Then he leaned forward and placed a trail of featherlight kisses up the side of Patrick's ribs and across his chest until he reached his nipple, which he flicked with the tip of his tongue, making Patrick shudder and fist handfuls of the bedclothes. Yu unsnapped Patrick's breeches and whispered, "Lift up your hips."

Patrick did, and Yu slid the remainder of his clothing—ivory hose and tight white briefs—off and away. He ran his hands up Patrick's thighs, over the outsides of his hips, along his waist and down his arms.

"You are so incredibly beautiful. Everywhere." With his fingertip, he grazed Patrick's tummy from his belly button to where his pubic hair would have begun. "I never would have thought I'd want a man completely shaved, but I like being able to see every inch of you. You have such perfect skin. You're so perfect."

Patrick felt warm and floaty, with the exception of the insistent tightness and throbbing at his root. "You're perfect too. Can I see you?"

Yu smiled and moved to the foot of the bed to stand. He pulled off his boots, snug leggings, and underwear, and stood, completely nude. Patrick basked in the sight, soaking in every detail of musculature more defined than his own, but still lean and graceful, the bumps and divots accentuated by the irregular firelight. Yu's penis was also a little different from Patrick's or any he'd glimpsed in the locker room showers: a hood of skin covered the crown, with the pink tip peeking out at the end. Patrick opened his arms and legs in invitation, and Yu got back on the bed and knelt above Patrick on his hands and knees, kissing Patrick with restrained passion as Patrick explored his taut body.

"God, Yu, I've never even imagined anyone could be so beautiful. I want to be with you. I've wanted you since I saw you…."

"I want you to have something sweet," Yu said.

"What?"

Yu took a strawberry from the bowl on the table and dipped it in fresh whipped cream as he settled against Patrick, sliding their erections against each other. Patrick opened his mouth and bit into the fruit, sweet-tart juice bursting against his tongue. With another berry, Yu smeared cream across Patrick's lips before licking it away, then licked away the flavor on Patrick's teeth and tongue, sharing it, swirling it around where their mouths joined. Patrick fumbled for a berry of his own and tried to feed it to Yu, but in his excitement, he missed and spread cream all over Yu's cheek before finding his lips. Grasping Yu's hair and pulling him closer, Patrick cleaned up the mess with his eager tongue and swollen lips, his balls drawing up tight against him and his inner muscles clenching. "Yu… I'm so excited… I… I might not last…."

"Just do what feels good," Yu said against Patrick's lips. Without separating their mouths, Yu plunged his fingers into the fluffy cream and rubbed it down the center of Patrick's chest and belly, all the way to the base of his cock. He smeared a little on the tip of Patrick's erection. Then he propped himself up on his elbows and ever so slowly licked it all away. Patrick could do nothing but writhe and mutter beneath him, the sensations and emotions his touch evoked so much more powerful than Patrick had ever imagined. His skin tingled and sprung alight everywhere Yu touched it.

Crouching between Patrick's splayed legs, Yu grasped his erection at the base and licked over the tip and across the slit with wide, slow strokes, cleaning away the cream mingled with Patrick's precome. Patrick thought he'd fall apart, and he grasped Yu's shoulders to ground himself. Yu draped his free hand over Patrick's knuckles and met Patrick's gaze as he covered Patrick's corona with his lips. He slid his mouth slowly down Patrick's length and then back up before pausing to circle the ridge between Patrick's head and his shaft with his tongue. After a few moments, he wriggled his hand free of Patrick's grip so he could drag it down Patrick's waist, and then he closed his fist around himself, stroking slowly as he licked and kissed Patrick's flesh. He brought such precision to everything he did, made sure every tiny detail was absolutely perfect, and he certainly didn't rush....

"Yu, I love you," Patrick panted, his whole body prickling as if channeling electricity. "Oh God! Stop! I want you to enjoy it too! Yu, please...."

Yu cupped Patrick's balls and plunged down, once and then twice. The third time, Patrick came, screaming Yu's name and seeing stars. His back arched off the mattress and he let go of Yu and slapped the bed with his palm, overwhelmed at the flood of sensation, his whole body spasming as if he'd been struck by lightning.

"I love you," Patrick mumbled, almost incoherent. "I... Yu, you didn't let me take care of you."

"I enjoyed myself," Yu said, wiping his lips on the back of his hand. He lifted his other hand to Patrick's mouth so Patrick could taste the seed he'd spilled into it.

Patrick moved the bitter, slippery fluid around in his mouth before swallowing. It tasted of Yu, and he loved it, wanted more of it. "You... just from touching me?"

"I've wanted to touch you for a long time." Yu kissed him, the flavors of both of their mouths, skin, and semen intermingling. It was delicious, almost enough to make Patrick hard again. He held Yu and buried his face between Yu's neck and shoulder, savoring the scent of his sweat and satisfaction.

Finally Yu rose to refill their wine glasses, and, both of them thirsty and spent, they drank and collapsed next to each other. Yu rested his palm over Patrick's belly and pecked at his cheek. "I'm sorry. I wanted to make your first time last, but I was so excited."

"So was I." Patrick kissed Yu's forehead and stroked the back of his hair. "When I imagined my first time, it was nothing near that wonderful."

"Really?" Yu whispered, turning on his side and winding Patrick in his limbs as he cuddled close.

"You like it when I'm brutally honest?" Patrick's eyelids felt heavy, and his whole body felt liquid and relaxed, like he could melt and flow into Yu's embrace.

"Yeah."

"Then the only thing I regret is that I didn't last long enough to get my mouth on you. I'd like that, I think. Both of us doing it to each other at the same time...." He yawned and rolled to face Yu, his lover. Wow. His *lover*. Did people say that anymore? He giggled softly against Yu's skin, reminded of the old *Saturday Night Live* skit with Will Ferrell.

"Anything you want." Yu also yawned.

"I want to give you my virginity."

"When you're ready," Yu said.

"Let's rest for a minute.... I love you."

"Love you, Patrick."

Patrick let his eyes close. He'd just rest a little while, and wake up ready to show Yu how much he meant to him....

THE early morning sun turned the canvas walls of the tent to sheets of blinding white. Patrick, lying on his stomach, pulled the blanket over his head and nestled his face against Yu's chest. He couldn't remember the last time he'd slept so deeply or felt so completely safe while he rested. He didn't want to face the world outside their little paradise just yet, but Yu stirred and sat up.

"Good morning, beautiful."

Patrick returned Yu's sleepy smile. "Good morning. Best morning."

"It is." Yu stood up and stretched, looking every bit as beautiful in the harsh light of day as he had in the dreamy candlelight. He went to the cooler, took out two bottles of water, and handed one to Patrick, who drank deeply. The day promised both heat and humidity. "I wish we didn't have to leave."

Those words both woke Patrick up and excited him. He got out of bed and took both of Yu's hands in his, talking fast. "Yu, I almost have enough money saved to move out of my father's house and get a place of my own. Why don't you come with me? We can cook together, sleep together, and wake up together every day. You can get away from your weird roommate, and… and live with me."

Patrick waited for Yu to hug him and enthusiastically agree, but he didn't. Instead, Yu pulled away, scooped his underwear and trousers from the ground, and slowly began dressing, his back to Patrick.

"What?"

Yu stood facing the entrance, his shirt balled in front of his chest. "Moving in together is a very big step after only knowing each other for two months."

"But we love each other!"

"Now. What if that changes?"

Patrick's anger rose, along with his shock. This couldn't be happening. "What do you mean if it changes? Damn it, look at me!"

Yu turned and faced Patrick, though he kept his expression guarded and distant. "Living together is a big commitment. What if we enter into it and then decide it isn't right?"

"I won't," Patrick said, cold uncertainty flowing like poison through his veins. "I love you."

Yu sighed and shook his head. "But what if you decide you want a boyfriend who can come to your shows? Come out dancing with you? What if you eventually decide you don't want a boyfriend who has to work fourteen hours a day, and who will probably never be financially stable?"

"What makes you think I give a shit about any of that?"

"It's been an issue in every relationship I've ever attempted with a man," Yu said, looking down at his bare toes in the grass. "They've always decided I'm not worth it. Every time I think it will be different, they decide I'm too high-maintenance. I… I don't want to be hurt like that again. I just think we should take our time."

Patrick dug his nails into the heels of his hands. "I'm not any man!"

Yu looked up, met his gaze, and smiled sadly. "I know. You are… extraordinary."

"Then… what? Take a chance on me. I love you. I love you just the way you are, and I'm not going to change my mind."

"Oh, Patrick, I know you think so now. But if you do, where will that leave me? Have you ever lived with anyone before? It can change everything."

"It won't. I can't believe what I'm hearing."

Yu took a step toward him, but Patrick retreated. "I am in love with you," Yu said. "I think this is the first time I've really been in love. But we're moving too fast. We have to be sure. I have a decent place to live right now, and I just can't give it up and chance being thrown out again. Try to understand. I don't want to stop seeing you, Patrick. I'm just not ready for this. Not yet."

"Fine." Patrick hurried to retrieve his clothing and pull it on. He couldn't bear to look at Yu's face. It felt like it had with his parents, who had also claimed to love him but only tolerated his presence out of some skewed sense of guilt. "I don't need any favors. I can make it on my own. That's what I need to do, and thank you for helping me finally see that. I guess it's time I grew up. There are no angels or stupid hope-fairies. There's just working for what you want."

"No," Yu choked. "God, no. Growing up doesn't have to mean dismissing beautiful ideas and letting go of beautiful dreams. I don't want to be the one who makes you lose your hope."

"I haven't lost it," Patrick snapped. "I just finally realized I can only depend on myself to fulfill it. I thought… oh, fuck it. I have to get ready for work. I guess I'll see you around."

Patrick smacked the tent flap open and stepped into the relentless morning light. Like the abandoned child he was, he'd clung to any scrap of love thrown to him, but no more. If life had taught him anything, it was not to depend on anyone. They'd all failed him, hadn't they? He'd succeed on his own, he decided. No more panhandling for affection or acceptance. He would have attention and love, love he earned, love from afar. Safe love. One-sided love. Love he received but never reciprocated. Yes. He'd get all the love he needed while basking in the lights of the stage, and he'd never have to surrender his thoughts or feelings to another to acquire it. For once, he'd be the one breaking hearts, denying others his attention when they pined for it. He could only depend on himself, and accepting it made him feel strong.

To hell with fairies and angels. It was time to be a man and venture out into the cruel, spare, dull and dirty territory of real life. It looked like he'd be going alone.

Chapter 14

I'M SORRY, Yu texted after the Faire ended the next day. *I didn't mean to upset you. Can we talk?*

I should go home, Patrick responded.

Patrick, don't do this. Talk to me.

Do what? I don't blame you. I thought there was something there that wasn't and that's my fault, not yours. I was being unreasonable. I realized I was just clinging on to you because I have no one else. I guess I was weak. I won't be again. I'm done living in fantasy land.

This shouldn't be texted. Patrick, can we PLEASE go somewhere and talk?

Have you changed your mind?

No, but I want to explain it to you, Yu wrote.

I'm tired. I have to go home.

Yu sent several more messages, but Patrick didn't look at them as he walked to his car, feeling both broken and strong in his convictions. To hell with Yu. He'd get a place of his own, on his own, and Yu could stay with his psycho roommate. It felt liberating not to depend on anybody else for happiness or success, or at least Patrick tried to tell himself so as he stomped across the crunchy grass.

Someone waited next to his car. Something about the stranger's bulk and posture seemed familiar, and Patrick hesitated, wishing he'd learned to use a weapon. Wishing he had a weapon to brandish even as an empty threat. With most of the Faire staff and vendors gone for the night, the field stood almost empty. Patrick decided to go back through the gates and wait for someone to escort him. He retreated a few steps before deciding it was just another form of dependence. He needed to be able to get through life on his own, without waiting for someone to love or save him. He'd succeed or fail by his own devices, and let no one else take credit or responsibility. He'd do it without an angel on one shoulder and a fairy on the other. Still, he made sure he had his phone ready in his hand as he approached his car.

His worst suspicions were confirmed as he recognized the older man from the night of the pageant: this Mark Emmeck who worked for the state government and thought that gave him the right to claim Patrick as his property and decide what was best for him. With the hair on the back of his neck standing up, Patrick stopped several feet from where the man blocked his driver's door.

"Get away from my car, please," Patrick said, trying to sound authoritative even though the stain of fear soaked through like the sweat through his heavy costume.

The man held up his empty hands and took a step closer to Patrick, who tensed. "Whoa. Hey, there. There's no need to be nervous. I just want to talk to you, Patrick."

"I'm on my way home," Patrick attempted.

"It won't take long."

Patrick held up his phone. "If you don't leave me alone and get away from my car, I'm calling the police."

"Oh, are you?" the man asked, closing in. "And who do you think they'll believe, a well-respected government employee or a swishy little boy who prances around in his underwear and takes money to let men grab his ass?" He smacked Patrick's hand with the back of his own, sending Patrick's phone flying into the high grass several feet away.

Patrick darted in the direction it had gone, but the larger man grabbed both his wrists and pressed them together painfully.

"That hurts! Let go of me!"

"I don't want to hurt you," the man said, leaning in so Patrick choked on his abundant cologne. "I'm trying to be nice to you. I wanted from the beginning to be nice to you, Patrick, but you wouldn't listen to me." He swung Patrick around and pressed Patrick's back against the car. "Now be good and listen, okay? I'm not a bad guy, so don't make me hurt you. Meet me halfway here. That's the least you can do, isn't it?"

"Okay," Patrick said through gritted teeth, buying time until he could find some way out of this. "What do you want to say?"

"I could do a lot for you if you'd let me, Patrick. I'm an important man, and a fairly wealthy one."

"I'm not a whore," Patrick practically spat.

"Oh, I know you're not," the man crooned, his face so close Patrick saw the beads of sweat across his upper lip, saw perspiration staining the armpits of his lavender shirt, smelled what his expensive cologne attempted to cover. "But what if we could be friends? I bet you'd like to move out of your father's house, and I can make that happen. I can set you up with a nice apartment and pay the rent, and all I ask is for you to return the favor, let me come and see you, say, once a week. And be discreet about it, of course. I'm not into anything weird, and I'll be gentle with you."

Patrick couldn't listen to any more. He felt like he'd be sick. "No. Not interested. Let me go."

"Oh, Patrick. We could have done this the easy way. I'm not a man you want to upset." He pressed his soft, sweaty body against Patrick, pinning Patrick to the hot metal of the vehicle. His erection pushed against Patrick's belly, and Patrick saw no alternative but to lift his knee and drive it into the man's groin as hard as he could. Dancing had strengthened his legs, and the other man staggered back a few feet, gagging as he doubled over to cradle his testicles. Patrick scrambled to get his car keys from his pocket.

"You little bastard," the man choked. "You're going to pay for that." With his shoulder lowered, he ran at Patrick and caught him in the ribs, slamming Patrick against the car and knocking the wind from his lungs. He grabbed the front of Patrick's shirt and pulled their faces together. "I like that you're feisty. But it's time to stop pretending you don't want it. You need what I can offer you."

"Fuck you." Patrick attempted the same move—the limits of his fighting repertoire—but this time the man expected it and stomped down on the top of Patrick's foot with a sinister grin. He liked causing pain and controlling people; that much was obvious. "I'd never let you touch me. I hate guys like you, who think they rule the world because of some meaningless desk job. You're nobody, and I don't care if you have money. Money isn't important to me. Character is, and if you had any, you wouldn't have to resort to bragging and threats!"

"You'll find out how much you appreciate money when you're not so young and pretty anymore." The man slammed Patrick against the car, smacking his head against the window. Patrick twisted and writhed, beating his fists against the man's chest, but he couldn't get away.

"I'll make it on my own!" Patrick yelled, and thank God, he attracted some attention.

"Patrick?" someone called. "You okay, buddy?"

Henry. Oh thank God, Henry! The man tried to clap a hand over Patrick's mouth, but not before Patrick managed to call out his friend's name. A moment later, Mark Emmeck was pulled off him and tossed to the ground. A cloud of dust rose around him where he landed. He tried to get to his feet, but Henry, still looking like a shining, storybook hero in his armor and tabard, drew his sword and pointed it at the stranger's throat. He turned to Patrick. "Is this prick giving you a hard time?"

"Yeah," Patrick panted, rubbing the back of his head. "Tell him to get the hell out of here."

Emmeck moved to stand, but Henry closed in, almost poking him with the point of his blade. "I think maybe we should call someone."

"No!" Patrick said, remembering what the man had said and envisioning answering questions about his performances, being painted as some kind of slut. If the authorities wanted to talk to his father, he'd find himself thrown out before he had quite enough money for an apartment. No, he had to keep it hidden just a little longer. "No, Henry. It's no big deal. I just want him to leave and never come back. Please?"

The young knight backed away, allowing the older man to stand and retreat. "I ever see your face again, and you're gonna be shitting your teeth, asshole!" Henry said, waving his weapon and making the man flinch. After a final warning glare at Patrick, the man turned and ran clumsily across the field.

Safe now, Patrick felt drained and dizzy. He grasped Henry's arm, and the two of them sat down in the grass.

"What the hell was that all about?" Henry asked. "You know that guy?"

Patrick found it hard to catch his breath as he pulled up clumps of grass and let them fall from his trembling hands. "Kind of. He gave me some trouble after one of my performances."

Henry nodded. "Jen said she wanted to see one of your shows. What exactly do you do?"

Patrick swallowed. "I… I'm a drag queen."

"Oh, all right."

"It doesn't bother you?" Patrick asked.

"Why would it?"

"I don't know," Patrick answered. "That guy bothered me after a show until the bouncers scared him away. I didn't think I'd see him again. God. How did he know my real name? Or that I live at home with my dad?"

"Dude, he sounds like he's stalking you," Henry said. "I really think you should call the cops, get a restraining order or something. A friend of my sister's had a problem like this in college, and the guy didn't stop. He assaulted you, and I witnessed it. If something happens, you want the cops to have a record of this kind of thing."

"I can't," Patrick said softly. "If my dad finds out what I've been doing, he'll kick me out. I just need another month or two to save up for a place of my own, but I have to keep it a secret until then. Um, Henry?"

"Yeah?"

"I think I want to learn how to fight, if you're still willing to teach me."

"Absolutely, man," Henry said. "I'd pay money to see you kick that pompous jerk-off's ass. If you'll be here later in the week, come by any day around four. We're always practicing in the arena around then. I'm trained in theatrical combat, but I also grew up in the Hill District, so I can show you how to fight dirty if you have to. I can teach you a couple of easy moves to protect yourself."

"Thanks," Patrick said.

"Faire's family," Henry said, patting him on the shoulder.

"What's all this?" Jen asked, coming up behind them and leaning down to kiss Henry on the cheek. "Is everything okay with my two favorite men in the world?"

Patrick and Henry looked at each other and an unspoken concern passed between them. They didn't want to worry Jen, who would probably set out looking for the man who'd threatened Patrick if she heard the story. They nodded, and Henry said, "We were just thinking about getting some dinner."

"Oh, cool!" she responded. "I'm starving. Should we go to the Stew?"

"You two can go ahead," Patrick said. "I actually have to get home. Need some sleep."

"Well, we're coming to your next show," Jen said. "I can't wait. You'll have to let me know when it is. You'll come too, Henry?"

Henry stood and brushed dried grass off his backside. "I wouldn't miss it. In fact, I hope to see Patrick here use some of the moves I'm going to teach him." He elbowed Patrick in the arm, the simple bastard.

"In the show," Patrick hurried to say, glaring at Henry.

"Yeah, sure," Henry said. "Anyway, I'll see you sometime later this week, around four." He winked, and Patrick rolled his eyes and extended his hand to Henry.

"Thanks again, for everything," Patrick said. He stood and walked to his car as his friends headed up the hill toward the tavern. Before he got in, he remembered his phone and went to search the grass where it had fallen. He found it after several minutes of pawing dried vegetation, with a cracked screen and another message from Yu. He swore, but if he wanted to get his own place, he wouldn't be able to replace the phone anytime soon. Ignoring the jagged lines bisecting the letters, he read Yu's message:

Stop ignoring me. If you don't want to see me anymore, just say so.

Patrick considered. He really didn't want to stop seeing Yu, and in retrospect, he knew he'd overreacted and probably behaved like a child. Yu had treated him like a prince, and he had no reason to apologize for not wanting to live together after such a short time. Patrick was probably lucky Yu hadn't written him off as a lunatic and dismissed him altogether. He thought about how to respond.

I want to see you. I'm sorry about the way I acted. You were right about moving too fast. I didn't mean to be such a baby. Forgive me?

Of course I do. What are you doing tonight?

I have to go home.

Are you sure? Yu wrote. *I think we should talk. I don't want you to think I'm being selfish.*

I don't, Patrick responded. *I have to go home. Haven't been there in days. Dad will be worried.*

I understand.

Yu, I still love you.

Text me tomorrow, Yu responded, and Patrick's heart plummeted. He got into his car and started the engine. The highway whizzed by through his windshield, just yellow and white lines he barely noticed, and before he knew it, he pulled up in front of the run-down little house and got out.

"Where have you been?" Patrick's father asked when he walked in the door.

"Working," Patrick said.

"Bullshit." His father approached him, stinking, as always, of old sweat and alcohol. "You ain't been home in two nights. I'm not a fool, boy. Where have you been?"

Patrick was too tired for this. He'd learned long ago the futility of arguing with his father when he was drunk. "I've been working."

"All night?"

"Dad, why do you care?" Patrick asked.

"You're my son."

"Since when?" Patrick shouted, his anger bubbling up past his good sense. "Why would I want to come here and watch you drink yourself to death while your friends make jokes about raping me?"

"I—" his father stuttered. "You're still my boy."

The old man's skin hung from his bones like soggy paper, a yellowish cast to his eyes and complexion. Swaying, he put a hand on the cluttered kitchen table to steady himself. It stank in the little house, of rotting garbage, of decay and death.

Patrick took his father's clammy hand. "Dad, you should get some help," he dared. "You're killing yourself. God, you're only in your forties. You could get cleaned up, get back to work, and have a life. It isn't too late. I love you. I don't want anything to happen to you."

His father pulled away. "What the hell do you know about anything, boy? Have you ever had a wife and two kids to support? You seen all your dreams dry up yet? You think I wanted this? No? Then don't tell me what to do!"

"I'm just worried about you," Patrick said, tears gathering. "If you keep going like this, you'll die."

"So what," his father said, slumping into the recliner. "Who cares?"

"I do, Dad."

"Oh, fuck off, Patty," his father said, waving his hand. "You're a little faggot, ain't ya?"

"No, Dad."

"Everybody says ya are."

"They're wrong," Patrick said.

"Just fuck off. Go t'bed."

"All right," Patrick said, dimming the living room lights. "I do love you, Dad. I know you did the best you could."

Only snores responded to him, and Patrick went into his room and stripped off his clothes before getting into bed, so tired it hurt. He knew he couldn't keep being responsible for his dad; he had to let him sink or swim on his own. He couldn't feel guilty about moving out, but he did. If his father died in this house, he'd feel responsible. But what could he do if his father refused to get help?

Just before falling asleep, Patrick checked his phone. Yu had sent him a text message:

I still love you too.

Patrick just stared at the words. He wasn't sure what love meant, and he didn't think Yu knew either. Maybe they could find out together, but maybe they'd just end up causing each other pain. As much as Patrick wanted to take a risk on Yu, find out what might be, he didn't know if he could handle any more pain in his life. Hope seemed more fragile and elusive than ever, a glowing, gossamer thread that had grazed his hand only to slip through his fingers. Fate, it sometimes seemed, would always be victorious.

AS HE drove to the Faire the next morning to help clean up after the Lovers' Hideaway, Patrick received some good news when Roger called. He'd booked several more shows for Patrick, including something special coming up in a few weeks.

"There's a huge pageant coming up toward the end of August." Rog always talked fast when he got excited. "A documentary filmmaker will be there, along with talent scouts from modeling agencies. Oh, and I almost forgot the best part! There's a $5,000 prize! Do you want to sign up? There's a fifty-dollar entry fee, but it all goes to charity. I'm going to do it, and so are Aouli and Shawn."

"Me, compete against the three of you?" Patrick asked.

"Well, why not?" Rog asked. "You don't have to worry about our friendship. No matter which of us wins, we're sisters. But it isn't an amateur pageant, honey. You'll be competing against other professionals."

"Wow, I could really use that prize money," Patrick said. "I'd have more than enough to get an apartment and even some left over for furniture and things. I guess it can't hurt to try."

"Fantastic! And listen, even though we'll be competing against each other, I'll still help if you need me. You're still my little girl, okay?"

"Thanks, Rog," Patrick said as he pulled into the nearly empty Faire parking lot. "It's nice to have people like you and Eric. I wish you'd been my parents. I love you, Mama."

"Aw, I love you too, honey. I'll text you the link to enter the pageant. Start thinking about what you want to do. You'll have to bring something really special to win this one."

Ideas flitted through Patrick's imagination all day as he worked around the grounds, but he couldn't decide on a song or pin down a solid concept. He wanted to top even his first performance and do something really surreal, something his audience would never forget. He wanted to bring art in its highest form, something to transfix those watching, make them forget about the troubles of their lives, forget everything but him, while at the same time wondering just what they witnessed.

He wanted to go shopping. Maybe he'd find a pair of shoes or a piece of jewelry to serve as a springboard and bring everything together. He considered calling Jen or Aouli to see if they'd like to join him, but he smiled and dialed Yu's number instead.

Yu answered, and Patrick beamed at the sound of his voice. "Hey, what are you doing?"

"Working," Yu answered.

"Well, yeah," Patrick said, shaking his head as he imagined the confused look on Yu's face. "Tom's letting us finish up early because of the heat. You must be ready to collapse at the forge. Do you want to wrap it up and come do something with me?"

"Like what?"

"I have a big competition coming up," Patrick said, feeling a little silly all of a sudden, "and, well, I thought I'd start doing some shopping for my costume. I know you're probably not into that kind of thing, but we could maybe go for ice cream afterward. If you want. I understand if you don't."

"I do," Yu said quickly. "That sounds like fun. I have to stop by the showers first, though. I'm filthy."

Maybe because he felt like hope had returned to hover just over his shoulder, sprinkling its intoxicating dust into his face, Patrick said, "I could meet you there." He glanced over his shoulder even though he hadn't seen anyone else all day.

Yu hesitated for what felt to Patrick like hours. Finally he whispered, "Okay," and Patrick sighed with relief and excitement.

"See you soon," Patrick said, as giddy as a child about to open the door to a surprise birthday party. He wondered how he'd ever gotten so lucky to have such wonderful people in his life and so much opportunity before him as he jogged to his car to retrieve a change of clothes. He felt like he had wings of his own, and his feet barely seemed to touch the ground as he ran through the idealized Elizabethan village for the shower house.

Steam and the soft hiss and patter of water met Patrick inside. The air felt heavy and clouded the row of mirrors above the sinks along the wall. Yu's gray pants and white shirt sat neatly folded on a shelf with his boots beneath. Patrick toed his sneakers off, stripped his sweaty clothing away, and placed his things next to Yu's. Then he slowly opened the plastic curtain.

Yu stood beneath a silvery spray of water, his golden skin wet and glistening, accentuating all his graceful muscles. He turned, raked his wet hair out of his face, smiled, and held his hand out to Patrick. Patrick took it and joined him in the shower, the lukewarm water refreshing as it flowed over his sweaty skin. He let it soak his hair and trickle down his back as he stood belly to belly with Yu, resting his hand over Yu's hipbone. Yu pushed Patrick's bangs back, held his cheek, and kissed him softly. Patrick moved closer and drew Yu's lip between his teeth, suckling at it and running his tongue over the slick, swollen flesh. Both of their bodies reacted, hardness sliding against hardness as they began to rock against each other.

Yu moved his hand down Patrick's neck and rolled Patrick's nipple between his thumb and finger. "I've missed touching you," he said, bending in to nibble beneath Patrick's jaw.

A jolt of sensation tumbled down Patrick's spine and his balls huddled against his body despite the heat. He let his head fall back so Yu could kiss his neck and moved his fingers down the sparse trail of hair beneath Yu's belly button. God, his skin was so soft in contrast to the wiry muscle under it. "You're so beautiful, Yu. I'm sorry for the way I acted...."

"Let's forget about that." Yu nipped Patrick's earlobe, and while it didn't hurt, Patrick yelped with surprise. Then both of them laughed and found each other's lips again. As they kissed deeply, Yu held Patrick's waist and spun him, holding him tight so Patrick wouldn't slip on the wet tiles, and guided him to the wall. It felt cold against Patrick's back at first, but he soon dismissed it as Yu arched into him and rubbed their bodies together from their throats to the bases of their erections.

Patrick felt his release building, and he decided he wasn't going to let go until he got his hands on Yu. He wriggled his hand between their bellies and curled his fingers around Yu's shaft, making Yu hiss with surprise and pleasure. Patrick squeezed, and Yu's cock bucked against his palm. "You feel so good," Patrick said, moving up Yu's length, eager to explore his hood and the dusky pink crown he'd glimpsed peeking from beneath it. The skin easily drew back beneath

Patrick's thumb. It fascinated him. He pushed it back up over Yu's cockhead and back down. "That doesn't hurt, does it?"

Yu chuckled. "No, it feels good. Here, I like it like this." Placing his hand on top of Patrick's, he guided Patrick's fist back down to the base of his erection and slowly back up, giving a slight twist at the tip. After a few shorter strokes, he led Patrick's hand leisurely back down his length until Patrick learned just what he enjoyed and took over, Yu moaning against his lips as Patrick rubbed him and cupped his balls.

Just as his tummy started to flutter with irregular breaths, Yu peeled Patrick's hand from his cock and switched places with him, his hand beneath Patrick's on Patrick's erection. "Now show me," Yu whispered.

Patrick moved Yu's hand over his flesh just the way he moved his own in the shower at home, or beneath his bedsheets when he was alone. It felt a hundred times better than he'd ever been able to manage on his own, though, especially with Yu's tongue bumping against his, Yu's body taut and slick against him, and the scent of Yu's wet skin enveloping him. Yu's palm was a little rough, but within minutes Patrick's precome eased the way. He let Yu take over and grasped Yu's rigid flesh again, stroking him just as he'd instructed. Soon, they both became too distracted to even kiss and just stood with their flushed lips pushed together, panting into each other's open mouths. At the last minute, Patrick looked down to see his white seed splash against Yu's golden-brown belly before the water washed it away. Trembling all over, barely managing to stay on his feet, Patrick grasped a lock of Yu's hair to steady himself as he stroked Yu, watching with delight as his foreskin moved back and forth. With a muffled cry, Yu came in Patrick's hand and over Patrick's knuckles.

Afterward, they just clung to each other and kissed lazily as the water trickled over their tightly pressed bodies and interlaced limbs. Patrick closed his eyes and rested his forehead against Yu's. "I could stay here with you all day. I love you so much."

A man cleared his throat loudly and dramatically. Patrick and Yu jumped away from each other. "Boys, this may be hard to believe," Tom said, his voice coming from near the entrance, "but I was once young myself, so I understand what's going on here. Still, I think you'd best finish up. I'll just pretend I wasn't here."

"Oh my God." Patrick clapped his hand over his mouth and giggled, more out of nervousness than because he found it funny.

Yu just smiled languidly and touched Patrick's cheek. "Look at you blushing. Your cheeks are so red. So is your mouth. I—I'd better not look at you like this, or we'll never get out of this stall."

Yu turned away, picked up a bottle of shampoo, and began lathering his hair vigorously. Patrick had to tear his attention away from Yu's beautiful form to wash himself, and he wanted to suggest how nice it might be to live together and shower together every day, taking all the time they wanted, lingering over each and every inch of each other's skin, but he didn't want to upset Yu again, so he hurried to wash, dry, and dress. On their way out of the bathhouse, Tom gave them a knowing smile and an obligatory wag of the finger, muttering, "Young knaves."

They took Patrick's car downtown, to the thrift stores and consignment shops he'd visited with Roger. Yu patiently perused the knickknacks on the shelves while Patrick sorted through gowns and inspected the jewelry in the cases by the registers. Patrick loved to shop, and carefully inspected all the garments so he didn't miss anything. He worried it might bore or annoy Yu, but every time he looked over at his friend, Yu just looked up from whatever pile of books or old records had caught his interest and returned Patrick's smile. He was really just too perfect to be real, Patrick thought.

By the time they reached the third store almost two hours later, Patrick had yet to find anything that inspired him. He and Yu walked past the secondhand furniture in the front of the charity thrift shop to the cast-off wedding gowns and dresses near the back. Patrick stretched out an ivory sleeve adorned with faux pearls. "It's kind of sad how all these ended up here, isn't it?"

"Why do you say that?" Yu asked, coming to stand beside him and placing his hand over the center of Patrick's back.

"They just, I don't know, symbolize lost love. These were somebody's dreams at one time, and now they've been abandoned."

"Things just don't always work out," Yu said. "They don't work out more often than they do."

Patrick wanted to ask Yu if that was why he didn't want to move in together, because he didn't see much chance of their relationship lasting, but they'd had a nice time so far and he didn't want to sour it, so he moved to the next rack, which held more colorful gowns. Instead of wandering off to pour over the bins of paperbacks and rows of salt and pepper shakers, Yu helped him sift through the rainbow of musty-smelling taffeta and chiffon.

"Do you really think it's so impossible for two people to meet, fall in love, and make it last a lifetime?" Patrick asked. He didn't want to upset Yu, but he decided tiptoeing around on eggshells whenever they spoke would get them nowhere. If he couldn't share his hopes and fears with Yu, they might as well just give up.

"I don't think it's impossible," Yu said, "just highly unlikely."

"Why?"

Yu considered. "I can't say what happens with everyone else, but for me it's always been a matter of someone having a picture of their ideal mate in their minds, and trying to shape me to match that vision. There's always the honeymoon phase before the reality sets in and they decide I'm too much work for too little reward. I suppose I'm also to blame, since I'm not willing to change to suit their needs. I just know neither of us will be happy if I do."

"It sounds like you've had a lot of relationships," Patrick said, holding up a leopard-printed sequin dress and draping it over his arm as a possibility.

"A lot of very brief ones," Yu said. "I figured out very early on that I can't please everyone, and I'll lose myself if I try. I couldn't be the son my parents wanted—I almost killed myself trying to live up to their expectations and always fell short—and I couldn't be the ideal boyfriend most men want. I decided after the first few to wait until I found someone who could really accept me. I—don't mind being alone as much as most people do. It gives me time to design and work. I like the quiet, and I think best when I'm alone."

"I hate being alone," Patrick said softly.

"I can tell."

"Is this our honeymoon phase?"

"I don't know," Yu answered. "I hope not. I just worry that you need—and deserve—more than I have to give."

Patrick didn't know what to say to that, so he returned to the dresses. Yu's blunt honesty could be a double-edged sword sometimes. "Some of these are just hideous, aren't they?"

"Look at this one." Yu held up an emerald-green gown. "Why on earth would someone want a dress like this?"

The top of the dress was fitted, with puffy cap sleeves and a wide strip of flesh-colored nylon from the neckline to the navel that gave the illusion of it being open and exposing skin. Layers and layers of green tulle made up the lower half, with a shorter layer of green satin overtop. It looked like the bastard child of a disco outfit from the seventies and a ballerina's tutu. Still, a larval idea began to grow in Patrick's mind. "How much is it?"

"Are you serious?" Yu looked at the tag. "Seven dollars, but it's so ugly."

"Think of it as raw material," Patrick said, taking the dress from Yu. "Most people can't look at a piece of steel rebar and see an ornate rapier, but you can. I can see beyond what's here, and I have an idea. If it doesn't work out, it's only seven dollars, right?"

"I suppose," Yu conceded. "I think you should wear red. You look really good in red."

"Um, thanks," Patrick said, his cheeks heating as he approached the clerk at the register. He purchased the green dress along with the sequined one for less than fifteen dollars. Then he and Yu walked to a small café down the block. They ordered frozen lattes and found a table outside.

"It's nice having another artist as a friend," Yu said, sipping his drink. "I think artists see the world differently from other people. They see the potential in things, just like your ugly dress. I hate to sound self-aggrandizing, but I think artists function above the mundane, to an extent. For me, my work is more important than ever making a lot of money. Would you agree?"

"To an extent," Patrick said. "I don't want to be rich, and I certainly wouldn't trade performing for sitting in a boardroom somewhere for money, but right now, I need some. My costumes can be expensive, and I'm spending a lot of money on gas getting back and forth to shows. I have to move out of my dad's place, but no matter how much I save, I just can't seem to get quite enough. So I guess I at least want to do well enough to be able to live."

"True," Yu said, "but I think I'd rather be destitute than give up all my time doing something meaningless. Most people—"

Patrick held up his hand to stop Yu as a dark-blue Dodge Caravan with state-issued plates parked across the street. Patrick recognized the driver even behind his dark sunglasses. He grabbed Yu's wrist and practically toppled Yu's chair pulling him to his feet. "We should go. Now."

"What's wrong?"

"I want to leave."

When Yu looked across the street, the older man who'd been bothering Patrick sunk a little lower into his seat. Patrick pulled against Yu's arm, but Yu stood firmly, looking back and forth between Patrick and Mark Emmeck.

"Patrick, do you know him?"

"No. Kind of." Patrick proceeded to give Yu an abridged version of his dealings with the other man. When he finished, Yu balled his fists and scowled, all of his elegant composure seared away with his anger.

"I'll kill him." It took all Patrick's strength to keep Yu from bolting across the street.

"Please don't, Yu. I don't want you getting in trouble."

"It will be worth it. Let go of me."

"Please don't."

The government employee, Mr. Mark Emmeck, according to his business card, pulled away with a screech of tires as Yu glared at him and trembled with rage. Only when the van had sped through the nearest traffic light did Yu relax a little and turn to face Patrick. "I can't believe you didn't tell me about this."

"I had no idea how strong you really are," Patrick said, trying and failing to defuse Yu's unexpected rage.

Yu tossed his half-finished drink into the bin and took hold of Patrick's arms. "This isn't a joke. You have to report this. Do you know this man's name?"

Patrick chewed his lower lip. He couldn't lie to Yu, especially not after seeing this passionate, protective side of him, but he couldn't let Yu do something they might both regret. "Um, I think I still have the card he gave me after the pageant somewhere."

"We have to go to the police right away," Yu persisted. "Right now. Get a restraining order. Henry saw him threaten you? And Eric and Roger? That should be enough evidence."

"Wait…."

"We're going," Yu said. "Now. Before something happens to you and we wish we'd gone when we had a chance."

"Wait," Patrick said a little louder, resisting when Yu tugged against his arm. "Listen to me. I can't go to the police. Imagine how it will sound. He's a respected state employee and I'm a guy who struts around in women's underwear."

Yu's features softened and he rubbed Patrick's shoulder. "That doesn't take away your right to be safe and not be harassed. He's no better than you are, Patrick. He's trash, and I won't let him hurt you."

"I'll be careful," Patrick promised. "I just can't let this get out. Not yet. If my dad finds out what I've been doing, he'll kick me out for sure. I have to stay there until I have enough saved for an apartment, or I'll have nowhere to go. I almost have enough, I think."

"Your father has nothing to do with this," Yu said. "You're an adult."

"Come on, Yu. I know you understand. I just have to stick it out a few more weeks until I have enough saved for a security deposit and the few things I'll need. I'll sleep on the floor, I don't care, but I don't want to be homeless in the meantime. After that, if that guy gives me any more trouble, I promise I'll call the police. Okay?"

"I don't like it," Yu said. "How did he know you'd be here today? How did he find out your real name, or that you work at the Faire? He's stalking you and it's dangerous."

"Please, Yu."

"Fine, but I want to know his name."

"Why?" Patrick asked, suspicious and flattered at the same time. "I already said I don't want you getting into trouble because of me. What are you planning to do?"

"Nothing. But if something happens or I can't get a hold of you, I want to know where to look."

"Thank you for defending me," Patrick said.

"I love you." Yu fished some change from his pocket and bought a newspaper.

"What are you doing?" Patrick asked.

"Checking the classifieds. You should start looking for an apartment now. It can take quite a while to find what you want for the right price." Yu perused the ads as they strolled leisurely down the street, though Patrick couldn't quite relax and watched every car that passed them carefully.

Some large, colorful drawings in the window of a tattoo parlor caught Patrick's eye, and he stopped and put his hands on the glass. "Yu, do you plan to get any tattoos?"

"Oh, I don't know. My mother would have a heart attack. There's still a stigma associated with them for some Japanese Americans."

"I think I'd like to get one," Patrick said, tracing the petals of a bright flower through the window. "A rose. Or a few roses, here on my ribs." He traced his hand down his side. "Red and white. Do you think that would be sexy?"

"Yeah, I do," Yu said in a husky tone.

Patrick pointed to some kanji on another board. "And look! This one means hope!"

Yu chuckled and rolled his eyes. "No, it doesn't. The brushstrokes are wrong. Make sure you bring me with you when you decide to get it done. I'll make sure they don't mess it up. In fact, I'll write it for you."

"Of course I'll bring you," Patrick said. "That would be so cool if you wrote it on me and then it became permanent. I wish I could afford to get it done now, so I could always look at it and remember today. Do you think you'll ever want to get one with me?"

"I don't know," Yu said. "We should be getting back to the Faire. I still have a lot to do."

"You have to go back to work?"

"I don't mind," Yu said. "I'm working on a really fun commission: a Roman-style shield, cuirass, and helmet, steel with bronze detail and some engraving. I'll make a good amount of money when I finish it, too."

"Okay," Patrick said. "I should stop by Tish and Tracy's and ask them if I can borrow a sewing machine."

"Are you performing tonight?" Yu asked as they headed back toward Patrick's car. "Do you want to come by my shop for a bit when you're finished?"

"I can't," Patrick said. "I have to meet up with Shawn. He's teaching me dancing and gymnastics, and I have to be back at the Faire first thing in the morning to help mow the parking area. Then Henry's going to start showing me how to fight."

"You look really exhausted," Yu said. "Maybe you should take a day off and rest. You know Tom will understand."

"I just really need the money," Patrick said. "I have to do this for myself, and nobody's going to do it for me. If I want my own place, I have to make it happen or it never will."

Yu looked a little shocked and hurt, but said nothing as he got into the car. Patrick wished he could be more like Yu, strong like tempered steel instead of ephemeral like a gossamer wisp, someone who wouldn't bend to the desires of others, who'd stay true to himself no matter what. Patrick knew he wasn't that man. It irritated him to realize he'd change anything about himself Yu asked him to change just to keep Yu with him. He'd already changed, gone from saying anything he wanted to restricting himself to what Yu wanted to hear, gone from lapping up affection and begging for more like sweet berries and cream to worrying about crowding Yu and making sure he gave Yu the space he seemed to need. Worst of all, he knew Yu loved him *because* he said what he meant, *because* he displayed his emotions so openly. Damn it, this was all so confusing, and being dead-on-his-feet exhausted didn't help. Still, Patrick swore he'd tell Yu the truth about his feelings from now on, at least the important parts. He owed both of them that.

Chapter 15

THAT Friday night, Patrick performed with Aouli at Joe's. He'd spent
the morning looking at apartments, and most of the ones in his price
range had been dumps in dangerous neighborhoods. Then the Realtor
had shown him a beautiful studio loft in Shadyside, in a fully restored
Victorian building with private parking, a secure lobby, and even a
private courtyard. It had beautiful hardwood floors, oak crown
molding, a gas fireplace in the living room, and while small, Patrick fell
in love. Two of the ten apartments in the building were vacant, the
Realtor had said, but they wouldn't last at that price. She'd told Patrick
he had excellent references, and if he could pay the deposit by the
beginning of the next week, he could move in at the beginning of the
next month.

The rent was a little more than he'd budgeted for, and paying the
deposit would almost wipe out his savings. He'd hoped to start his new
life with at least a few hundred dollars for necessities like dishes and
furniture, but Patrick loved that apartment. He loved the old trees lining
the sidewalks and the little balcony overlooking the veranda. He loved
the mix of Victorian aesthetic and modern convenience. He really,
really wanted to live there, and so tonight, as he danced, he allowed
men a little more liberty than he usually tolerated, at least if they were
willing to pay. All his tips for the evening could go to things like
curtains, bath towels, silverware, and maybe even some food.

For their first number, Patrick and Aouli, or more appropriately, Queen Titania and Miss Anita Lei, dressed as naughty schoolgirls in miniscule plaid skirts, knee socks, high-heeled Mary Janes, white shirts that exposed their navels, and ties. Both wore wigs with blunt-cut bangs and huge, teased-up ponytails, Patrick's hot pink and Aouli's electric blue. They strutted onto the stage licking oversized, rainbow lollipops as the music began to play. Patrick handed his lollipop to the first man who waved a twenty-dollar bill and began lip-synching along with the cheery, squeaky vocals of Runo and Hatsune Miku's "We Are Pop Candy!"

Patrick flashed his audience a smile as he remembered Yu trying to help them learn the Japanese lyrics; they'd managed only just enough to be convincing, but they knew the English refrain and the tossing of their hair and kicking of their slender legs distracted from the rest. If anything, he'd been much more nervous dancing in front of Yu for the first time than he was now. He'd wanted so badly to be perfect, to impress Yu, to turn him on. At the same time, he'd worried as he'd rubbed himself against Aouli in Eric and Rog's backyard while Yu sat at the picnic table. Performing just for Yu, Patrick imagined they made love without touching, every movement of his hips and bend of his waist the foreplay. Though he'd danced with Aouli, his gaze never left Yu's eyes, and he imagined it was Yu's body moving against him, which resulted in a much more provocative display than he'd intended. When the song ended, sweat sparkled above Yu's lip and his mouth was slightly open. He hadn't looked jealous or offended, just aroused. When Aouli had gone inside to get water for them, Yu had grabbed Patrick's hips and pulled him into his lap. "Will you dance with me like that? For me? Somewhere no one else can see?"

They'd gone back to the Faire and stood beyond the light coming from the Stew, dancing to the music spilling from the tavern. Soon, they'd found themselves in the wet grass, kissing hard, hands down each other's pants, groping and stroking each other as if oblivious to the dozens of people who could come out of the bar and discover them.

Tonight, Patrick sauntered to the edge of the stage, turned, and smacked the back of his skirt, making it fly up to expose the lacy panties he wore underneath. Hands moved up the backs of his legs and over his ass, slipping money into his satin undergarments. He turned and put his foot on the center of the nearest table and bent down to sing to the men sitting there, holding his collar away from his neck so they could slide more bills into his shirt.

Aouli, pretending to be jealous, grabbed Patrick's tie and dragged him back to the center of the stage. Dancing more suggestively together than the innocent little song probably warranted, they both licked the lollipop Aouli still held. Patrick imagined Yu watching him as he swirled his tongue over the edge of the sticky candy and looked up from beneath his thick fake eyelashes. The crowd threw money at them, especially when Aouli buried his face in Patrick's small, false breasts before dragging it down Patrick's body while Patrick arched backward. As the song ended, Aouli rubbed his chin against Patrick's crotch while Patrick sucked the lollipop provocatively. Then the lights went down, and they hurried to collect their earnings before exiting the stage.

Aouli hugged Patrick and jumped up and down, his heels clicking on the concrete floor outside the dressing room. "Girl, we made so much money. We'll have to do this again."

"Absolutely," Patrick agreed. They hurried to change for their next performance.

The next time Patrick appeared, the stage was completely dark except for a baby spotlight following his every move as he crawled on his hands and knees, his smoky-painted eyes on the washed-out faces in front of him as he lip-synched to Angelspit's "As It Is In Heaven." He wore the black corset Tish and Tracy made, black panties, garters and hose, knee-high boots, and a bobbed platinum wig.

As they'd practiced, Aouli came up behind him in a red vinyl dress and set a folding metal chair on the stage. He took hold of the faux leather band Patrick wore around his neck and pulled him to his feet. Then he turned Patrick around, pushed against his back so he bent over, and pretended to spank him. The audience roared their approval. Aouli led Patrick to the chair, pushed him into it, and handcuffed Patrick's hands behind him. With a red silk scarf, he blindfolded Patrick and pushed Patrick's legs open to dance between them. Though he couldn't see, Patrick felt little flutters against his bare arms as the audience tossed bills. He felt Aouli's backside brushing against his groin, and he couldn't help finding it exciting. The beat of the music coursed in his veins as he wriggled and writhed in his bonds, receiving little taps from Aouli's crop for misbehaving. The loss of his sight enhanced all the odors of the bar: smoke, alcohol, and the men's sweat and cologne. When the song ended and Aouli removed his blindfold, Patrick couldn't believe how much money littered the stage.

"Do you want to stay in drag and dance for a while?" Aouli asked. "We can probably make even more tips."

"Okay," Patrick agreed, feeling confident and sexy as he always did after performing. Besides, he could hide behind Titania. He could let the men adore him and shower him with affection without risking showing anything of himself. "Actually, that sounds like fun."

Aouli took his hand and led him to the floor as the house music began to play and the lights flashed in lime and electric blue around them. At first they just danced with each other, touching and grinding a little, but nothing like they'd done in their act. Soon they attracted the attention of the other men in the club, who encircled them and queued up for a turn to be one of their partners. A few women even joined in the fun. Patrick enjoyed himself, and sure enough, he found more money slipped into his hose. He couldn't help wishing Yu could be here dancing with him, but he wouldn't want to pressure Yu into doing something he wouldn't enjoy. Yu was more than understanding about the nature of Patrick's performances—he'd seen him practice with Aouli—and Patrick vowed to finally be the man who accepted Yu exactly as he was. Still, he missed him.

Thirsty, he wandered over to the bar where Matt, the bartender, had his Coke with cherry syrup waiting. Patrick leaned his back against the bar and watched the dancers as he sipped at it. He flinched when he thought he saw the man who'd been following him sitting alone at a table at the edge of the pulsing light. People moved in front of him, blocking Patrick's view. When he caught a second glimpse of the table, it was empty. He blinked hard and shook his head. Exhaustion and paranoia had started to mess with his mind, and he found he craved some quiet conversation and, if he got really lucky, the chance to get Yu naked and run his hands all over Yu's beautiful body. He set his empty glass on the bar and waded back through the sea of undulating bodies to Aouli.

Leaning in, Patrick shouted in his friend's ear to be heard over the loud music. "I think I'm going to get cleaned up and go home."

"I'm going to stay for a while," Aouli yelled back, holding Patrick's shoulders as they swayed to a slower song. "I've got my eye on somebody. Can we divide up the tips later?"

Patrick kissed his cheek. "You're my sister. I trust you."

"Okay, hon. Tell Yu I said hello."

Patrick went back to the dressing room to change, wash up, and pack away his costumes. Even in his street clothes, it took him a while to say good-bye to everyone who stopped him and get out of the club. The night was hot and hazy, with a wormy-smelling mist rising from the wet asphalt. Patrick fished his keys out of his shorts pocket and turned to say good night to the bouncer with the spiderweb tattoo, Murph, when his blood went watery and cold. The dark-blue van sat across the street.

"Something wrong, sweetheart?" Murph asked.

"Yeah," Patrick said in a disjointed whisper. "A man's been following and threatening me, and I think he's waiting in that van. I'm really scared."

The warm weight of Murph's big hand on his shoulder calmed Patrick a little. "I'll see you get to your car," the big bouncer offered.

"Thanks," Patrick said, forcing a smile. "But I'm afraid he'll just follow me home, or wherever I go."

"Do you want me to call someone for you?"

Patrick considered. Like him, Yu had to be up early and working at the Faire tomorrow, and he'd barely convinced Yu not to go after the man earlier in the week. Eric and Roger were out of town. Who did that leave? Henry? Or Jen? Patrick knew they'd come if he needed them, but he couldn't bear to impose upon them like that. "No. I don't really have anyone."

"What do you want to do?" Murph asked. "Call the cops? They might not be sympathetic."

"I know. I just don't want him following me home, knowing where I live," Patrick said.

"Here's what we'll do." Murph put his heavy arm around Patrick and guided him back toward the door. "Go back inside and wait until he leaves. Me and some of my brothers can patrol the area and make sure he's really gone. Encourage him to be on his way, if you know what I mean. We can encourage this douchebag pretty hard if we have to."

"Thanks," Patrick said.

"You're family, baby," Murph said. "Get inside, and we'll drive this son of a bitch off and let you know when it's safe to go home."

AROUND 3:00 a.m., long after all the patrons had left Joe's, Murph shook Patrick's shoulder to let him know it was safe for him to drive home.

Patrick woke with a start, forgetting where he was for a few seconds. He looked around the small office as the events of the night returned to him. He stood from the chair where he'd fallen asleep with his head on the desk. He thanked the bouncer again, drowsily dug his keys out of his pocket, and picked up his duffle bag. Except for three other men in leather vests standing by the motorcycles, Patrick found the parking lot completely deserted. Barely able to keep his eyes open, Patrick drove home, stumbled to his room, fell into bed, and slept in his clothes for two and a half hours until he had to wake up to perform at the Faire.

When the alarm on his phone went off, Patrick truly wished the devil would appear and offer him a Faustian bargain: his soul for another two hours of sleep. He'd have accepted without hesitation, but since scarlet smoke and the smell of sulfur never materialized, he dragged himself into the shower, washed, and put on his costume.

The morning was cooler than it had been in weeks, and dark thunderclouds gathered over the western horizon. As he drove to work, Patrick watched the lines on the highway blur. He cranked the radio up and rolled the windows down even though the first sporadic raindrops splashed against his face. He just couldn't seem to wake up, and even felt a little dizzy. He gripped the steering wheel harder because his hands felt weak. He needed to stop for coffee, and soon. He shook his head and tried to clear the lingering fog. His chin bumped against his chest, and he realized with horror he'd closed his eyes for a second without even intending to. The shock didn't wake him up as much as it should have, and his head lolled back against the seat's headrest....

EVERYTHING hurt when Patrick woke up: his head throbbed, his ribs ached, and his body felt like one giant bruise, tender everywhere it touched the firm surface he lay on. Even the weight of the stiff sheets over him exacerbated the dull pain. He smelled antiseptic and heard hushed whispers. Slowly, he opened his eyes and looked with confusion at the stark white ceiling above him and the mint-green blanket covering his legs. Except for a few strips of reddish-orange light spilling in from the vinyl blinds over the window, the room was dark.

When Patrick tried to sit up, he felt a sting at the inside of his elbow and reached down to find a plastic tube taped in place. Another tube was taped to his nose, feeding oxygen into his nostrils.

"Don't try to get up," said a familiar voice: Eric. He came to the bedside and pushed a button to incline the bed, then turned on the lamp on the stand.

Along with Eric, Rog, Shawn, Aouli, and Tom stood in the small room, all of them looking worried. "What happened?" Patrick croaked.

"It looks like you fell asleep driving," Tom said. "The hospital staff found our numbers in the contacts on your phone and called us. You're going to be all right, but you have to start taking better care of yourself. The doctors say you're exhausted, dehydrated, and likely suffering from anxiety. Luckily, they think your foot slipped off the gas pedal when you passed out, so you just veered off the road and were going pretty slow when you hit the guard rail. They did chest X-rays and a CT scan, and everything looks all right. You're very fortunate, Patrick."

"They want to keep you overnight," Rog said. "Other than being banged up, they say you're fine, but you really need to get some rest. They want to do some more tests in the morning, maybe an MRI, I think. They gave you the IV to try to replenish some of your fluids."

"We tried to get a hold of your parents," Shawn said, "but neither of them picked up."

"Yu?" Patrick asked.

"We got his voice mail and left him a message," Rog told him.

His neck ached and felt too weak to hold his head up any longer, so Patrick let it droop back against the pillows. He felt so stupid, but at least he wasn't alone. The people who really cared about him were here, waiting to make sure he'd be all right. Rog reached over and squeezed his hand, and Patrick managed a wan smile. "I'm sorry all of you had to come here and spend the day in a hospital room. I feel like an idiot. I guess I didn't realize I was that tired."

"We're just glad you're okay," Aouli said, brushing the hair off Patrick's face. "It could have been a lot worse. Promise me you'll start looking out for yourself. I don't ever want to get another phone call like that. I was worried sick you really got hurt. And you can't imagine how awful it felt to see you on that board, being carried out of the ambulance with that collar around your neck and the mask over your face. I don't ever want to be that scared again. Baby, I don't want to lose you."

"Sorry," Patrick said again. His brain still didn't want to work properly. The oxygen tube hurt his nose. "Is Yu coming?"

"I'm sure he will," Eric said, but Patrick didn't miss the worried glance he exchanged with Rog. "Probably as soon as he checks his messages. Jen and Henry will be here as soon as the Last Huzzah is over, and I think Tish and Tracy are coming too. You scared quite a few people today. We all care about you."

"Sorry."

"You don't have to apologize," Eric said. "You just have to promise you're going to start sleeping enough and stop spreading yourself too thin. Okay?"

"Okay."

"You're taking the week off from the Faire," Tom said.

"No," Patrick said, remembering his beautiful little apartment. "No, I'll be fine to work in a day or so."

"I won't hear of it," Tom said. "I said you're taking the week off, and you're taking the week off. I never said you wouldn't be getting paid."

"Thanks," Patrick whispered, a little ashamed of his desperation but grateful to Tom for understanding and looking out for him, the way he'd always imagined a father might. Then another thought occurred to him. "Is my car okay?"

Eric and Rog looked at each other, and Patrick knew from their faces the news wouldn't be good. Eric took a deep breath as if to brace himself before speaking. "It wasn't totaled. Your front end is pretty smashed up and there was some damage to the engine. My cousin's husband owns a garage. I had him tow it there, and I can promise he'll treat you fairly. He can't be sure yet, but he thinks he can get everything fixed for just under a thousand, parts included. He can make it a priority and probably have it done by the end of the week."

"A thousand." Patrick's hope of moving into the pretty little apartment tore into a million pieces and drifted away, like little scraps of tissue paper on the wind. Tinsel. While he could still pay the deposit on it and maybe make the first month's rent, he'd never make the second and get his car repaired. He needed his car to get to the Faire and to his drag shows. This would set him back at least another two or three months. The idea of staying in his father's house that long made him want to curl into a ball and sob. Instead, he blinked back his tears and thanked Eric for having his back yet again.

Someone knocked softly on the door, and a moment later a young doctor with her dirty-blonde hair in a ponytail came into the room. She smiled at everyone and then said, "If you could all give me some time to examine my patient, you're welcome to come back in about an hour; however, what Mr. Harford needs most is plenty of sleep."

"No problem," Eric said. "Get some rest, Patrick. Just call if you want us to come back; otherwise, call when they discharge you and I'll come pick you up. Try to get some rest."

"Thanks," Patrick said weakly.

The doctor shone a light in Patrick's eyes and had him follow it with his gaze. She drew the covers back and checked his bruised ribs and belly. "You're very lucky you didn't sustain any broken bones or internal injuries. I'd like to talk to you about what happened." Thankfully, she removed the oxygen tube from his sore, dry nostrils.

"Okay."

The doctor sat in the chair beside the bed. "Are you having problems with drugs or alcohol?"

"No," Patrick said.

"It's just very unusual for a person to fall asleep while driving like you seemed to. We didn't find anything on our initial tox screen, but that doesn't always give us the full picture. If you're struggling with substance abuse, help is available. Your medical assistance will probably even pay for some of it, and I can refer you to some free support groups in the community."

"It's nothing like that," Patrick told her. "I've just been working a lot, trying to save money to get my own place. I work during the day at the Renaissance Faire, and I have a second job in the evenings. I guess it just caught up with me."

She nodded, but Patrick wasn't sure she believed him. "Okay. Just try to make sure you don't get so run down again, or next time you might not be so lucky. If you need counseling, the GLBT center...."

"No," Patrick said emphatically. "No, I'm fine. I just dozed off because I've been working too much."

The doctor left Patrick's room, and not long after, an orderly delivered his dinner: chicken, a biscuit, some steamed vegetables, fruit salad, and chocolate milk. Though the food was bland, Patrick had eaten worse and decided he needed to keep his strength up. Jen, Henry,

Ian and Carlton arrived just as he finished his meal, and he ate a few of the cookies Jen had brought from the bakery at the Faire. Tish and Tracy came to visit with gifts of English toffee and a little pink teddy bear wearing a lacy ruff they'd probably made themselves. Patrick appreciated seeing his friends, but he wondered why he hadn't heard from Yu. Word of what had happened had likely spread to everyone at the Faire by now, and he couldn't imagine why Yu wasn't with him yet. Not for the first time, Patrick wondered if he placed more value on the relationship than Yu. Maybe he saw something between them that wasn't really there.

After everyone left, Patrick used the remote to turn on the little TV mounted on the wall above his bed and found a documentary about coral reefs. He didn't pay much attention to it, thinking instead about the apartment he'd never get to live in now. Alone, he let his tears come, even though crying made him feel weak and silly. He'd find another place to live in a few months; it wasn't the only apartment in Pittsburgh. Thinking about it led his mind down all kinds of thorny paths, though, to his guilt over leaving his father alone and to Yu's refusal to move in with him or even let Patrick come to his apartment. He understood about taking their time, but right now, with the prospect of returning to that filthy dump looming over him, it felt like a betrayal. Worse yet, Yu still hadn't come to see him or even called. Patrick started to wonder if Yu cared about him at all.

Patrick punched his flat pillows and buried his face in them, crying until he tired himself out. Afterward, he felt a little better. It might take a little longer than he liked, but it would be okay. He loved his work and had plenty of people to lend him a hand and help him up if he faltered: his friends from the Faire and his drag mama and sisters. He had himself, and he'd begun to unearth a strength in himself he'd never known was buried there. He thought back to everything he'd survived and decided he'd make it through this too. It might be a fragile little thing, frivolous and mercurial, more delicate than a rose petal, but hope always seemed to find him when he needed it most. He'd even started to understand the fluttering little creature a bit, how it was all bound up with and dependent on his confidence and willingness to keep going even when it hurt to take another step.

Maybe this accident wouldn't ruin his plans after all. If he won the upcoming pageant, he'd be able to make his rent and get his car fixed. Ideas about his costume and act flooded his brain. He decided to risk everything and perform and dress just as he envisioned it. If everything worked out as he imagined, it would be a bizarre and beautiful dream. He would either win hands down or he'd fail spectacularly. Having the week off would give him plenty of opportunity to finish his dress, and he'd have an excuse to go to Madame's. He could hardly imagine a week away from the Faire.

Patrick pushed the button to flatten out his bed and lay watching colorful fish drift by on the TV screen. It soothed him to watch them, and before long he grew very tired again. He waited a few more minutes, still not giving up on Yu, and then he turned out the light and rolled onto his side to sleep.

Sometime later, well after dark, Patrick woke to a nurse checking his IV. As she left, the shaft of light from the hall fell on someone asleep in the chair by the bed. Patrick blinked a few times to make sure he wasn't dreaming.

"Yu?"

Yu lifted his head and rubbed his eyes. He reached over and stroked Patrick's cheek. "How are you feeling?"

"Okay, I guess," Patrick said. "Tired and sore. Embarrassed I let this happen. Happy to see you. I was starting to think you weren't coming. You don't have to spend the night here. You can't be comfortable in that chair."

"I don't want you to be alone."

Patrick took Yu's hand and held it against his cheek. "Thanks. I really screwed up, didn't I?"

Yu leaned in and kissed Patrick's forehead. "You're trying to do too much, and you're exhausted. I really wish you'd take as good of care of yourself as you do of everyone else."

"I don't have any choice. The only way I can get the money to live on my own is by working, and I can't stay in that house with my father anymore. Did you know he sold my TV and Xbox for drinking money?"

"No. I'm sorry, Patrick."

"Are you?"

"What do you mean?"

Patrick rubbed his face. At least it hadn't got smashed up, or he'd have no chance in the upcoming pageant. "I was planning to move out within the next week or so, but with what it will cost me to get my car fixed, I might not be able to make my rent for long. Why won't you let me come to your apartment?"

"We've talked about this," Yu said, straightening his spine and moving away from Patrick. "My roommate doesn't want people at the house."

"And his feelings are more important than mine?" Patrick asked. He'd had enough of this; he'd say what he felt and either gain some ground with Yu or go down in flames. At least he'd know if they had a future together. "We can't even watch TV together? Yu, that's really weird. I'm sorry if I seem desperate or naïve, but I feel like if you cared about me you'd let me stay until I could get a place of my own. I'd sleep on the couch, or even the floor. I just can't take living with my dad anymore. I just want a little help."

"Patrick, I wish I could."

"Why can't you? It doesn't make any sense."

"The situation with my roommate is very complex," Yu said.

"Tell me."

Yu opened his mouth as if to speak but then shook his head.

"Tell me," Patrick repeated.

"Fine. My roommate is a successful older man. We… used to see each other. I moved in with him when my parents cut me off. We aren't involved anymore, but you can see how he might react if I brought another man to the house he's letting me live in."

"He's your ex." Patrick pulled his hand free of Yu's grasp and moved to the opposite edge of the bed.

"Technically."

"You're living with your ex-boyfriend, and you have to keep me a secret so you can keep stringing him along," Patrick said. "Are you still sleeping with him?"

Silence.

"Oh shit. You are. You are, aren't you? Yu?"

"No, not really."

"What the fuck is 'not really'?" Patrick's voice rose as he forgot he was in a hospital in the middle of the night.

"After I broke up with him, it happened now and then," Yu said, his voice soft with shame. "Not... not full sex or anything. I... I sucked him off every once in a while, or I used my hand. But I haven't been with him for months now, certainly not since I started seeing you. He even asked me, and I said no. I never betrayed you, Patrick."

"Why the hell do you stay there?" Patrick asked. In his mind, it was almost prostitution. "You'd rather stay there than with me?"

"I need a place to live," Yu said, sounding a little defensive. "When my parents stopped paying for my dorm, I had nowhere to go. I have a nice, safe place, and if that means I can't parade my boyfriends in front of James, well, I have to respect his wishes. He's been good to me. He was the first man not to just toss me away. I'd be out on the street if it wasn't for him. He understands that I want to be an artist, and he's trying to help me. He's a very kind man."

"In exchange for an occasional blow job," Patrick said, rolling on his side with his back to Yu. "You're such a fucking hypocrite, you know that? Always going on about how money isn't important to you, and yet you're too fucking scared to give up your cushy apartment and take a chance making it on your own. With me. I guess everything you said about being willing to starve was bullshit. It's fine in theory, but not when you have to actually leave the penthouse."

"I should go," Yu said, standing.

"I agree."

Yu got up, walked to the door, and stopped. "I didn't let him lay a hand on me, Patrick. Not from the day I met you at the barbeque. From the minute I saw you.... Never mind. It doesn't matter anymore."

"I guess not."

Yu left, disappearing into the washed out light of the hall, and Patrick tried to convince himself he didn't care. As soon as Yu was gone, he got out of bed and stood on wobbly legs, then dragged his IV pole behind him as he went to the night table and picked up the bouquet of red and white roses, took them to the small bathroom, and dumped them into the bin.

Chapter 16

PATRICK had always seen the Faire as some sort of magic kingdom, with its idealized Tudor-style buildings and rose-lined, cobblestone lanes, but it wasn't. It was just a business, hoping to make a profit the same as any fast-food restaurant or mall clothing store. He was just an employee, and he did his job to the best of his ability, but he concentrated on the pageant, only a week away now. The prize money was his only chance of keeping the lovely little apartment he'd already paid the deposit for. If he failed, he'd be stuck living with his dad for another two or three months, and he didn't think he could stand that.

After finale, Patrick went to Madame's to use the sewing machine. Yu had texted him a few times after their argument in the hospital, but he seemed to get the hint after Patrick failed to respond. Life was no fairy tale, Patrick now realized, and true love was probably bullshit. He had more important matters to worry about, and little time to waste on thinking about Yu and what they could have shared.

Patrick finished his sewing well after dark, then helped Tish clean up the shop. With Halloween coming, the sisters had plenty of commissions. Finally they turned out the lights and walked to their cars. Patrick found a note wedged under his windshield wiper. It read: "You'll be sorry."

"Oh my God," Tish said. "Do you think it was Taylor?"

"Taylor." Patrick wished. Taylor was simply pissed because he'd lost his job. Patrick could deal with him. The motives of his stalker, Mr. Mark Emmeck, district manager of the Pennsylvania State Liquor Control Board, remained more elusive, and Patrick felt sure he, not Taylor, had left the note. He crumpled it up and threw it into the high, brittle grass. "It's not him," he said to Tish. "Another sicko has taken an interest in me. He can't accept that I'd rather die than have anything to do with his fat, bald ass. I don't have time to worry about him right now."

"I've been there," Tish said. "Plenty of perverts think because me and my sister make corsets we're down with wife swapping or worse. We've been propositioned loads of times. So many of these dicks ask us for a three-way. It gets annoying, but I guess it's part of the job." She loaded some boxes into the trunk of her silver Volkswagen.

"They should respect you," Patrick said. "You just make clothes."

Tish draped her tiny arms over Patrick's shoulders. "Sweetie. If you were straight, I'd be all over you, Patrick. I love you, hon."

"Love you too," Patrick said, returning her embrace. "Faire's family, right?"

"Right. But I think you should report this to the police." She found the crumpled note where Patrick had thrown it in the grass. "You should probably hang onto this too. It's evidence he's been threatening you."

"Okay. You're probably right," Patrick said, since he didn't want to explain his reluctance to go to the authorities and get into another argument. He hugged Tish again. "Thanks. For looking out for me. For everything. You and Tracy will be at the show next week?"

"I wouldn't miss it for the world," she said with a smile and got into her car.

Patrick got into his car and started the engine. As he hooked his phone to the charger, he noticed another text message from Yu:

Are you still at the Faire?

I'm just about to head home, Patrick wrote. He couldn't see any reason not to at least be civil.

Can I talk to you for a few minutes? Please?

After staring at his phone's cracked screen for several minutes, Patrick wrote, *Okay. I'll wait by my car.*

Patrick got out and sat on the hood. The night was clear and the stars shone brightly above him. A half-moon had just risen above the hills. It was cooler, already starting to feel like fall. The idea of the Faire soon closing up for the year filled Patrick with a strange melancholy. It wasn't like he wouldn't be back next summer, and he'd keep in touch with his friends, but it somehow felt different this year. Maybe, Patrick thought, his sadness came from the realization of his childhood ending. He'd soon be twenty years old, and he'd missed out on enjoying what everyone said were the magical teenage years. He'd never gone to a dance or to a movie with a date. He'd never spent the weekend at the beach with friends. Now he had to work and make his own way, be practical before he'd ever had a chance to be whimsical, impetuous, or cavalier. Thinking back on the time he'd spent with Yu, he didn't even know if he could say he'd had his first boyfriend. Nothing between them had gone the way it did when people dated on television or in books.

"Hey." Yu stopped and stood about a dozen feet from Patrick, still in his Faire garb, white shirt, leggings, and boots with his straight dark hair hanging loose around his shoulders.

"Hey." Patrick could smell the smoke from the forge, and he fought against the urge to touch Yu's smooth face and run his fingers through his hair. His gaze lingered on Yu's full lips as he remembered how they'd felt pressed against his, how they'd tasted….

"I've really missed you, Patrick. Has everything been going well for you?"

Patrick shrugged. "I got my car back. Eric's friend did a nice job for me."

"That's good." They stood in silence for a few more minutes. "Look, I've never been good at idle chatter, saying meaningless things. I came to ask if it's over between us."

"Is that what you want?"

"No. I've never met anyone like you, and I know I should have told you the truth about my roommate. I don't want to lose you. I didn't tell you because I didn't want to lose you. I knew you wouldn't take it well."

"I just don't know if I can be okay with you living with your ex," Patrick said. "He obviously still wants you."

"He still wants to sleep with me," Yu said. "James doesn't want a relationship, especially not with me. Our interests are just too different, and he's looking for a partner who will have money someday, who will want to invest in things with him. He's also very social, so we just agreed it would never work between us. Still, he's been a good friend to me. You were right when you called me a hypocrite. I suppose I'm also a bit of a coward. I'm afraid of having nowhere to go."

"You could make it on your own," Patrick said, hope tickling him with the edge of its gossamer wing even though he wanted to swat it away. "That's what I'm trying to do."

"You almost killed yourself," Yu said. "James doesn't make me pay much to live there, so I can make it on smithing until I get established. Is... is this a deal breaker for you?"

Patrick felt like he stood on the edge of a precipice, and he chose just to leap. "We could share my apartment. Between the two of us, we should be able to afford it. We'll make it work somehow."

"It's funny," Yu said, looking sullen and shaking his head. "There's you who dresses up in satin and lace and me who shapes steel, and you're so much stronger than I am. I'm afraid."

"Of what?"

"Of you changing your mind," Yu said, meeting Patrick's gaze. "I'm your first boyfriend. Do you know how astronomical the odds are that you'll end up with the first person you ever dated? You're around gorgeous men all the time. What if you meet someone else, or decide you're not ready to settle down? You're nineteen. What if you want to experiment? Then what will I do?"

"I'm not that fickle," Patrick said. "I know what I want, and it's you. That's not going to change. I love everything about you. I love that you'll always tell me exactly what you're thinking, and that you don't have to talk all the time. I love that we can just sit together, just be together, and it's enough. I love that you value art and following your dreams above money. I love your talent, and your elegant way of moving. You're so beautiful. So passionate. Take a chance on me." He closed the distance between them and took Yu's hand.

"I just can't," Yu said. "It's too soon for me. I have to be sure it's going to last."

Patrick pulled his hand away, feeling like he'd been kicked in the gut by a horse. "Whatever happened to defying fate?"

"I can't," Yu repeated, his voice cracking.

"I guess that's it, then," Patrick said.

"Tell me we can still be friends," Yu said, his eyes sparkling. "I need you in my life."

"Yeah," Patrick said, a lump the size of a walnut filling his throat. "I can't hate you for making the decisions you think are best for your life. They're your choices to make."

"You make it sound like I'm choosing staying at the apartment over you."

Patrick said nothing, and he couldn't bear to look at Yu's face, so he gazed out over the parking lot at the trees in the distance.

"I don't want to stop seeing you," Yu continued. "I'm completely in love with you, and I never cheated on you with James. I never will. It's just a living arrangement. I wish you could trust me, but I understand if you can't. I hope we'll still spend time together now and then."

"I have a show next weekend," Patrick said. "It's a pretty big deal. I'm sure you won't want to come, though."

"Well, I wish you the best of luck. I guess I should go. I'm… I'm really sorry if I hurt you." Yu reached up and stroked Patrick's cheek, and Patrick closed his eyes and leaned into the touch before he gave it a second's thought.

Choking, he took Yu's shoulders and pulled him close, burying his face against Yu's neck and breathing his scent, pressing his cheek flush against Yu's warm skin. He wound his arms around Yu's waist and held him tight. He didn't want to let him go, not now or ever. "I still love you. Yu, I can't just turn it off. I just wish you could believe in me. Believe I won't throw you away."

"I'm sorry," Yu said. He pulled away and brushed Patrick's bangs aside to kiss him on the forehead. "I've been thrown away too many times. Good-bye, Patrick."

Yu wandered back through the gates and disappeared. Patrick stayed on the hood of his car, scrubbing at his eyes with the side of his fist. It hurt that he hadn't been worth Yu giving up his cushy apartment, but he supposed it made sense. This was real life, not a fantasy. Yu was probably right; people didn't end up spending their lives with the first person they dated. Most people Patrick's age had already dated several people, and few of them had found a soul mate or partner. Patrick had just been so sure of Yu; he'd known it when he'd first seen Yu at the joust. He'd wanted to spend the next hundred years with him, even if they had to live in a tent in the Faire's parking lot. Yu just didn't agree.

Eric had been right on that night back at the beginning of the summer when he'd told Patrick he'd never be in love like the first time. Patrick knew he'd never feel this way again, never experience the soaring thrill he got just from Yu looking at him or brushing his hand. Eric had just neglected to tell him how much the first heartbreak would hurt. At least he didn't think he'd ever feel this pain again. In comparison to losing Yu, money, performing, and even the pageant seemed trivial. What did it matter if he couldn't share his success with the only person he wanted beside him through life?

AT HOME, Patrick knew something was wrong as soon as he walked in the door. His father sat at the kitchen table with a stack of papers spread out in front of him and a half-empty bottle of cheap vodka next to his elbow. Dust motes eddied in the yellowish light and the kitchen smelled of bad food.

"Well, I guess I know why you've been out all night," his father slurred out. "You sick little son of a bitch."

"Dad?" Patrick felt cold all over, and his hands shook as he took a few steps closer to the table. Over his father's shoulder, he saw dozens of photographs: him tied to a chair with Aouli running a crop down the center of his body, him grinding on a pole wearing his vinyl miniskirt and Union Jack T-shirt, him strutting in his bloomers and corset. The photographs he'd taken with Tish and Tracy in their powdered wigs and lacy unmentionables, all of them draped decadently over a powder-blue upholstered chaise and some of which Rog had photoshopped into flyers and promotional posters for Patrick, lay off to the side. "Where did you get these?"

"I found 'em on the porch." His father stumbled to his feet, one of the pictures still clutched in his fist. "How could you do this to me? To our family? This is a fucking disgrace!" He swung, but he was drunk and Patrick's reflexes had improved since training with Henry, and he dodged the blow.

"You little queer. How could you bring shame like this on me? Out prancing around in ladies' underwear. Sucking dicks, just like everyone tried to warn me. I didn't believe them, because I thought you were my son. Well, you're no son of mine. I wish you'd been in that car with your brother. I'd rather see you dead than out there whoring yourself out to a bunch of faggots. Making me look like an ass."

Something inside Patrick snapped. Anger over his brother's needless death and the life he'd had to endure welled up in him like lava and erupted. "Like you need my help to look like an ass, you sorry old drunk!"

"You're gonna talk to me like that, you little cocksucker?" He swung again, and this time Patrick wasn't fast enough. His father's fist caught him in the mouth, splitting his lip and spilling blood down the front of his shirt.

Patrick staggered backward, seeing stars and momentarily disoriented. His back smacked the edge of the counter. His father grabbed him by the collar and pinned Patrick with his superior size and weight. He hit him in the face twice with the back of his hand, and pain exploded behind Patrick's eyes and across his cheeks. The next punch connected with his left eye, and Patrick did the only thing he could think of to save himself: he drove his knee into his father's groin. The old man stumbled backward and bent in half, but in less than a minute, he was back on his feet and holding the vodka bottle.

Patrick hurried to take his phone from his pocket, thankful he'd remembered to charge it. "Stop!" he yelled, his whole face throbbing and his eye swelling shut. "I'm leaving, and you'll never see me again. You'll be free to drink yourself to death and wallow in your own filth. You can let me walk out of here and forget I was ever born, just like you always wanted to, or I can call 911 and you can spend the night in jail."

"Go on, you miserable little faggot," his father yelled before taking a deep gulp from the bottle. "I should have thrown your fairy ass out of here the day you turned eighteen. You got no family now, boy. I hope you're happy."

Though he didn't know why he bothered, Patrick said, "You don't know the meaning of the word family. You've never supported me or stood up for me. You were never a father to me. I have people who care about me now, people who want to see me succeed and be happy, who'll have my back if I need them. I have a family. What the hell do you have, besides that bottle?"

"Get out!"

"Fine, I'm going. Jesus, Dad, I tried to love you in spite of everything." Patrick stormed out into the night and took a long, last look at the run-down little house before getting back into his car. All of his drag, his Faire costumes, the picture of his brother, his games, movies, and CDs were in the backseat and the trunk, and he even had several changes of street clothes. It wasn't worth trying to retrieve the rest of his things from his room. Why did it hurt to know he'd never come back here? He supposed it was the only home he'd ever known, but living there had been hell.

He looked at himself in the rearview mirror. God, his face was a mess, lips split and eye black and swollen. A bruise across his cheekbone. Blood drying on his mouth and chin. His injuries could very well cost him the pageant, he knew. Who wanted to look at a beat-up drag queen? If that happened, he'd lose his apartment. Then where would he go? He'd dreaded the thought of staying here for a few more months while he saved money, but now, with no roof at all over his head, he wished he still had the option.

Who could have sent those pictures? Taylor? Or maybe Mark Emmeck? Did it matter?

God, where would he go? His adrenaline wound down, and despair quickly took its place. Patrick didn't think he had enough strength to shift his car into reverse and pull out of the driveway. He wanted Yu, wanted to be held and told things would somehow be okay. But Yu had made his choice, and Patrick couldn't go to the apartment he shared with his sugar daddy. He could think of only one place to go, and with a great effort, he pulled onto the road and drove to the Faire.

When he reached the grounds, Patrick pulled around to the camping area and parked not far from the shower house, positioning his car beneath the boughs of a large oak tree. As far as he could tell, he'd be living here for at least a few weeks. At least the Pennsylvania cold hadn't set in yet. If he won the pageant, he could move into his apartment on September 1.

If not—

Patrick went into the shower house and washed his puffy, bruised, and aching face at the sink. He looked like hell, and he didn't know if makeup would cover it. After he washed up, Patrick went back to his car and reclined the front passenger seat. He took one of his sweatshirts from the backseat and balled it up for a pillow. He had to work in the morning and needed at least a few hours of sleep. How would he explain his injuries?

Patrick picked up his phone. After several rings, Yu answered in a scratchy voice. He'd obviously been sleeping. "Patrick?"

"Hi."

"Is everything all right? What do you need?"

"Nothing. I just wanted to hear your voice. I'm sorry I bothered you."

"No, it's okay," Yu said. "Are you sure you're all right?"

"Yeah. Yeah, I just wanted to tell you good night. And that I still love you."

"I still love you too."

"Yu… never mind. Good night."

"Good night, my beautiful Patrick. I'm here if you need me, for anything. Anything. Okay?"

Patrick seriously considered asking Yu to come to the Faire and just sit with him for a while. He felt sure Yu would agree. He shook his head. "Okay. I'll see you."

"Bye." Yu ended the call, and for a long time, Patrick just stared at his name on the broken screen. He had to move past what they'd shared, he knew that. But right now, he wanted to hold Yu so badly his whole body ached and his insides felt shredded. He opened his glove compartment and took out the hope charm Yu had made him. Turning on his side and holding the little steel creature next to his heart, Patrick finally managed to fall asleep.

Chapter 17

NOT only did Patrick's face hurt twice as much the next morning, it also looked far worse. The bruises had darkened and his eye had swollen almost completely shut. His lower lip looked grotesque and disproportionate, half of it puffed out and bisected by a thick scab. Sleeping in the car had left his neck and back stiff. He opened the door to step into the harsh morning light and found Eric glowering at him with his arms crossed.

"What the hell do you think you're doing?"

Still drowsy, Patrick just shrugged. "Um…."

"What the hell happened to your face?" Eric demanded. "Who did this?"

"My dad," Patrick said, feeling like he'd confessed to some wrongdoing of his own. He was ashamed of what he'd let happen, of not being able to defend himself. "Somebody sent him pictures of me performing. He wasn't too happy, but it was bound to happen eventually. It's over now. I just want to try to forget about it."

Eric nodded. "Why the hell didn't you call us if you needed a place to stay?"

"I don't know. You and Rog have done so much for me already. I… I should try to clean up and get to work."

"You can't work like that," Eric said. "Have you seen yourself? I'm going to talk to Tom—don't worry, I won't tell him anything you don't want me to—and you're going to go to the house, put your things in the spare room, get cleaned up, and get some rest."

"But—"

Eric held up a hand. "That wasn't a request, princess. Jesus, if Jen sees you, she'll be at your father's house with a baseball bat, and the National Guard won't be able to stop her. And what do you think Yu will do?"

Patrick knew Eric was right. "It won't do any good for Yu to get himself in trouble. It's over, and him getting angry and doing something he'll regret won't change what happened."

"I know that," Eric said. "You know that. He won't. If I saw Rog looking like that, I'd be out for blood. Something just happens to guys when somebody hurts the man they love. The logical part of the brain shuts down. Think about it. What would you do if somebody beat the crap out of your boyfriend?"

Patrick balled his fists. "I'd kill someone if they hurt Yu."

"See?"

Patrick nodded. "I don't want to lie to him either."

"I understand," Eric said. "Give it a few days. Hopefully he won't fly off the handle as much when your face has started to heal. Leave Tom to me."

"I don't want to lose my job here," Patrick told him. "I love this place. As stupid as it sounds, this is the closest thing I've ever had to a home or a family. I messed up again. First that car accident, now this. Tom is going to start seeing me as a liability. What if he decides I'm more trouble than I'm worth?"

Eric rolled his eyes and patted Patrick gently on the shoulder. "You are a part of this Faire, and taking a week off to heal won't change that. Nobody here wants to lose you, least of all Tom. I promise it will be okay. Have I ever led you astray before?"

"No."

"Good. Now if Rog is your mama, then that makes me your father. So just do what I tell you and don't argue, okay? Go home and rest. You're not working until the pageant."

Overcome with gratitude, emotion overtaking him, Patrick sniveled and hugged Eric, choking back a few sobs against Eric's broad chest. Eric embraced him protectively, shielding Patrick in his strong arms.

"Eric, I'm sorry if this sounds stupid, but I have to say it. I never had a father, not really. I don't know what would have happened to me if it hadn't been for you and Rog. You were the first people who ever cared what happened to me. Everything I know about the kind of man I want to become, I've learned from you. Thank you."

"Patrick—" Eric hugged him tighter, and Patrick swore his breath hitched a little. "Home. Now. Do you want me to bring you some ice cream?"

With something between a laugh and a sob, Patrick shook his head. "Aouli says I have to watch my weight until the pageant. He'd never let me live it down."

"So, chocolate or strawberry, then?" Eric asked, petting the back of Patrick's hair.

"Peanut butter cup?"

"Peanut butter cup it is. Go home, honey. I'll call Rog and try to calm him down before you get there. He'll be on the warpath, but I'm good at making him see reason. Then I'll talk to Tom. What do you want me to say?"

"Tell him the truth," Patrick said. "I trust Tom, and… and he knows about me, at least partially. He caught me and Yu in a shower stall together. He was cool about it."

"Okay. I just want you to take care of yourself, Patrick. You're good to everybody but yourself. I'll see you at home. Don't let Rog fawn over you too much, but let him a little. It'll be good for both of you. We love you. You know that, right?"

"I know," Patrick said, his eyes stinging. "It feels good to be loved."

PATRICK spent the rest of the week in blissful lethargy. He'd never known such a peaceful time as he did waking up to Rog making waffles, lounging around in his pajama pants until almost noon, watching the news, and putting finishing touches, like beading and glitter, on his costume and accessories. It certainly beat the week he'd spent at his father's house after his accident, trying to stay out of the old man's way. After lunch, he helped Rog around the house or went out back to prune the bushes or pull up the weeds at the base of the hedges. In the afternoons, he practiced dance moves and gymnastics with Shawn and, against Eric's advice, made his way to the Faire a few times to continue his lessons with Henry. He wanted to be able to take care of himself the next time he was threatened.

When Henry had first seen Patrick's face, he'd simply said, "Dude. I hope the other guy looks worse," and he'd picked up his sword.

The night before the pageant, Patrick helped Shawn make a special dinner for all the competitors. They didn't prepare anything that would have impressed Yu, but Aouli, Rog, and Shawn obviously enjoyed the grilled steaks, shrimp, corn on the cob, baked potatoes, and salad. They sat in the backyard, around the chiminea, just as they had at summer's beginning.

"No matter what happens tomorrow, we're family," Rog said, lifting his glass of wine.

"Amen," Shawn said.

"We are going to be the four hottest bitches in that show, and no matter which one of us wins, we're sisters," Aouli said. "That's forever."

"Sisters," they all said, clinking their glasses together.

Aouli brought out the baked Alaska he'd made, and they had their dessert and another glass of wine. Rog suggested they get an early night, and all of them hugged before Aouli and Shawn left for the night and Patrick, Rog, and Eric went inside.

Rog and Eric went straight to their bedroom, and Patrick knew they needed some time alone. He hoped he'd one day have something as wonderful as what they shared, and he could only imagine sharing it with one man. He went to the guest room, sprawled out on one of the lace-canopied beds, and dialed Yu.

"Patrick?" Yu answered. "Is everything okay? I haven't seen you at the Faire all week."

"I got hurt and had to take some time off."

"My God. Are you all right?"

"Yeah, Yu, I'm fine. I'm just getting ready for the contest tomorrow. I really need that money to keep my apartment. I'm nervous."

"I'm sure you'll be wonderful," Yu said.

"I don't know. My performance will be edgy. I wish you could be there."

"Where is it?" Yu asked.

"At a club called Wonderland, just across the Ohio border." Patrick wanted to ask Yu to come, but he couldn't bear to hear him say no, so he stayed quiet.

"I'll be there if you want me there," Yu said.

"Really?"

"Really. I promise."

"Yu, can't we—"

"What?"

"I want to spend my life with you," Patrick said. Screw it; things between them couldn't get worse. "I want you, forever. I think I'll spend my life alone if I can't be with you. Shit, I know you're not ready to hear something like this, but I am. I'm ready. I'm ready to share my life with you, if you want me."

Yu said nothing; Patrick could hear him breathing slowly on the other end of the line.

"I'm sorry, Yu. I had to tell you. I need you to know. I... maybe I'll see you tomorrow night. If I don't, I understand. If I don't, I hope you'll be happy. I want that for you. I want you to realize your dreams."

"I don't know what to say, Patrick. I've never met anyone like you. You kind of scare me."

"I don't want to scare you," Patrick said. "I've thought a lot about how you must feel, always being told you're not good enough. I understand why you'd think I found you lacking, but I swear to God, I don't. I don't, Yu. I can promise I'll never toss you aside. I'll be with you through anything. I know it's only words, but I mean them. If you can put up with my bullshit, I can easily deal with your issues. I... I love you so much."

"I love you too, Patrick. I have never been so enthralled with another person. You're so different from anyone I've ever known. So authentic. So damn brave."

"I'm here if you want me," Patrick said. "All you have to do is say yes."

Yu said nothing.

"Well, I guess I'd better get to bed," Patrick said to break the silence. "I have a hell of a long day tomorrow. Um, take care of yourself, Yu. God. I absolutely fucking adore you. I love you."

"I love you too, Patrick. Good luck tomorrow."

"Thanks."

"Good night. *Oyasumi.*"

"That sounds familiar." Patrick thought maybe he'd heard it in a video game, but he wasn't sure. "What does that mean?"

"It means 'good night' in Japanese. My mother used to say it to me. I... miss hearing it sometimes."

"Good night, Yu. I wish you were here beside me. I miss you. Good night. *Oy—oyasumi* to you, too." He hung up his phone.

THE next morning, Patrick woke, showered, shaved everything, and packed his costume into his garment bag. He rode with Rog, Eric,

Shawn, and Aouli to Wonderland. In the dressing room, he went behind a screen to tuck everything away and slip on his tight, flesh-colored panties. Unlike other queens, he didn't pad his hips or buttocks—his friends said it made him look willowy, young and vulnerable, which audiences seemed to like. He did wear a light waist cincher, bustle, and small faux breasts, which he kept in place with surgical tape.

With his preparations done, Patrick put on his gown. He'd transformed the ugly green dress into something he felt was exquisite and completely different from the costumes the other queens wore. He'd cut away the satin in the front and left the layers of tulle beneath tattered and uneven, revealing his long, slender legs from the tops of his thighs to the tips of the emerald velvet ankle boots. He'd attached some fake ivy to his silk stockings and the tops of his shoes. More ivy covered the bodice of the dress, the leaves overlapping in a way that almost looked like scale armor. Tendrils curlicued over the full skirts and twisted down Patrick's left arm. When he looked at himself in the mirror, he'd achieved just the effect he'd wanted: mystical and ethereal, a fairy queen covered in a frock of nature.

Patrick tucked his hair beneath a stocking and sat down on a stool in front of a mirror. First, he attached long, pointed, latex ear tips made by a Faire artisan to his ears with spirit gum. Then he mixed a few drops of icy green body paint with his porcelain foundation and sponged it on his face and neck. He brushed on his highlights and lowlights to accentuate the contours of his face before setting it all with a thin layer of pearlescent powder. When he was satisfied, he set to work on his eyes, using all the tricks he'd learned to make them look slanted and catlike. He lined his lips with dark green and brushed a paler green on their centers. To finish, he coated his mouth in green glitter. Patrick hardly recognized himself by the time he finished. He looked like a creature glimpsed in a dream, and that was exactly what he wanted.

"I have had a most rare vision. I have had a dream, past the wit of man to say what dream it was," Patrick whispered softly.

Only his wig remained. He'd ordered it from the cosplay site Tish had recommended, but he'd done a fair bit of custom work to the long, mint-green tresses, twisting some of them into knotted locks, winding vines around others, and attaching some sticks and branches he'd spray-painted silver. He wanted it to look wild, befitting a fey queen wandering the wilds beneath the summer moonlight. When he put it on everything came together, and Patrick didn't think he could have done anything more to make himself perfect. Delight in disorder.

Patrick wondered what Yu would think of him, if Yu would be watching. For the final touch, he put the hope sculpture Yu had made around his neck.

Finally, one of the men working at the bar came into the dressing room to announce it was Patrick's turn to go onstage. Patrick took a deep breath and fluffed his hair a bit more in the mirror. This was it— time to get out there and show the world what he could do, to draw the audience and judges into his vision and leave them wondering if they'd stumbled into a dream.

The lights were low and fuzzy when Patrick stood at the edge of the stage. He stretched his neck and looked into the audience, though most of the men watching just looked like hazy black silhouettes. Shadows. His eventide fairy court. At a table not far from the edge of the stage, Patrick saw Eric, Henry, Ian, Carlton, Tish, Tracy, Jen, and even Tom. His family—all the people who cared about him had come to support him. It hurt a little not to see Yu among them, but Patrick ignored the wound, because he knew he was very, very lucky to have such wonderful people in his life. He focused on what he'd been blessed with instead of what he lacked as the song he'd chosen began to play.

He'd decided to gamble everything on what he loved and had chosen an electro-medieval song by the German band Qntal, who performed pieces from history with industrial touches. "Name Der Rose" blasted from the sound system, starting with some low, somber chanting, and then Syrah's lilting, angelic voice held the audience in a siren-like fugue. No one made a sound as Patrick lip-synched along with the Latin lyrics. No one would understand them, but hopefully they'd grasp the beauty and romance behind them.

The song had a steady enough beat for Patrick to dance to, but the almost operatic vocals allowed him plenty of pause to demonstrate some of the acrobatic moves he'd learned from Shawn. Within seconds, the thrill of performing had lifted Patrick on the crest of a wave and he thought about nothing but moving his body to the music, looking into the faces of the men in the audience, seducing them into his dream. They stared up at him, spellbound. Some of their mouths even hung open as Patrick dropped into a split and made serpentine movements with his arms, as if he could pull all of them up on stage with him by some invisible thread.

Patrick slid onto his belly and crawled to the edge of the stage, reaching out his arm as the song neared its conclusion. The men who could reach stroked his exposed skin and touched his hair, as if they needed to convince themselves he really existed. The lights faded to black just as Patrick dropped his head. The dream had ended, and he hurried to leave the stage before the lights came up, so he appeared to be the fairy queen who faded into memory with the coming of dawn.

Silence stretched for a few minutes before the first smatterings of applause began. Just as Patrick wanted, they hadn't known what to think of him. They'd been utterly disoriented by his performance.

Patrick stood in the hall catching his breath along with the other drag queens. All of them looked nervous, and few of them spoke to each other. Some checked their cell phones while others fidgeted with their hair and costumes. Seeing Rog, Shawn, and Aouli, Patrick walked over to them. They had all performed before him, while he'd been getting ready, so he'd missed their acts. Rog looked like a Golden-Age Hollywood starlet in a gorgeous, gold-sequined gown and blonde wig. Shawn wore purple silk, and Aouli wore a sundress with a cherry print and big red sunglasses. All of them held hands as they waited for someone to call them back to the stage.

A few minutes later, all of the drag queens stood in a line on the stage. Twenty of them had performed, all beautifully polished professionals. Patrick still felt he had a chance; none of them had taken a risk on an act quite as unique as his. A camera crew waited near the front of the stage, along with men and women in business suits. Patrick hadn't noticed them when he'd performed.

It seemed to take an excruciatingly long time for the older queen in the turquoise gown to address the audience and thank them for coming. Finally, she began to read the names of the runners-up. When

Patrick didn't hear his name among them, he felt certain he'd won. He'd really done it. Not only could he pay for his apartment and live comfortably for the next few months, the world had finally acknowledged his worth. He began to think of what he would say—he had so many people to thank—as the emcee spoke into the mic.

"And now the moment we've all been waiting for. Gentleman, this hasn't been an easy decision. We've seen some absolutely beautiful queens here tonight, and as far as I'm concerned, all of these lovely ladies are winners. Let's give it up for them!"

The audience cheered. Patrick kept his coy smile in place as he waited for them to get on with it.

"Okay boys. Without further ado, it's time to announce the winner of the $5,000 grand prize and a photo spread in *Out* magazine. I give you the gorgeous, the talented, the incomparable Lady Regina!"

Patrick barely noticed the applause or the words Roger said as he accepted his prize, one he deserved. It all felt surreal. All Patrick's hard work, everything he'd gone through, had been for nothing. He looked down at his sparkling green fingernails. He'd failed, and now he would have to ask the Realtor to return the deposit he'd put on that wonderful little apartment, a place he'd already starting thinking of as his own. As home. Slowly, he left the stage along with the other disappointed performers, trying to convince himself he was happy for Rog.

In the dressing room, Patrick packed up his costume and cleaned up. The mood was somber, and none of the drag queens spoke much. Both Aouli and Shawn came up and hugged Patrick, and he saw his disenchantment mirrored in their faces.

"There'll be other shows, honey," Shawn said, and Patrick nodded.

"Regina is a beauty," Aouli said, shaking his head.

"Yeah," Patrick agreed. "She really looked great." He turned away and went to the mirror, removing the last of the illusion of Queen Titania. Then he slipped his faded gray hoodie on over his T-shirt and went down the hall and out the back entrance, wanting some air and to be alone for a few minutes before he had to pretend to be happy for Rog.

A few of the other queens, men again now, stood smoking cigarettes. One of them extended an open pack to Patrick, but Patrick shook his head and leaned against the building.

"Patrick."

Turning toward the sound of his name, Patrick saw Yu. Without thinking, he hurried into Yu's arms and buried his face against Yu's neck. "What are you doing here? I thought you hated crowds."

Yu hugged Patrick back and stroked his hair. "I do. They make me crazy. That's why I'm out here. I needed to see you, talk to you. Tell you I was wrong."

Patrick pulled away just enough to look into Yu's eyes. He saw determination and resignation behind them. "What do you mean?"

"I should have taken a chance on you. From the beginning. You're all I want, and the last week has made me realize that. I've been miserable without you. You might eventually decide I'm not right for you, but I want to take the risk. If you'll still have me. God, I know I don't deserve you."

Patrick pressed his lips against Yu's, tears coming in spite of how hard he tried to dam them. "I'll live in a ditch with you. God, it might actually come to that. I didn't win the pageant. I didn't even place. I... I can't afford the apartment now. But I don't care. We'll figure something out. Won't we, Yu?"

Yu stroked Patrick's cheeks, wiping his tears away with his rough fingertips. Then he leaned in and pecked and nibbled at Patrick's lips. "I have some money saved. Between the two of us, we should be able to make it. At least I hope so. I got into an argument with James about moving out. He thought I was being very foolish. Everything I own is in the back of my car. I... I didn't even know if you'd still want me, but I had to try. I had to take that chance. I love you. I couldn't keep being a coward and hiding behind his money. I think about you all the time. You're the first man who's ever been more important to me than my work, or even my safety. I just came to understand none of it mattered if I couldn't be with you. I was afraid of getting hurt, but I'll risk pain later to get rid of the pain I feel now."

"Of course I still want you," Patrick said. "I always will. I tried to tell you. And I'll never, ever hurt you on purpose. You... you're my dream come true. My hope."

They kissed, oblivious to the others, clutching at shirts and chests and bellies, pressing close. Patrick squeezed Yu until he worried he'd break Yu's ribs, and Yu returned the force of his embrace. When both of them needed some air, they stood forehead to forehead, hands still wandering, both of them grinning wide and panting hard.

"I've been told I'm a nightmare to live with," Yu said softly as he moved his fingers up Patrick's spine beneath his shirt. "I have to have everything in a certain order, with nothing out of place. I'm picky about cleanliness. I'm probably going to drive you crazy. Are you still in?"

"I'm in," Patrick said, letting a strand of Yu's silky hair glide between his fingers. "I'm in forever." They kissed again as Yu backed Patrick against the aluminum side of the building and rubbed his erection against Patrick's. Patrick cupped his ass with one hand and cradled the back of his neck with the other as his skin heated beneath Yu's ministrations. "I love you so much."

Their kisses, blistering with passion at first, soon turned slow and tender as they took their time to taste and explore each other. For Patrick, his failed pageant, the club, the other men, everything, faded into the distant past. He only perceived Yu, his wet, swollen lips gliding along Patrick's mouth, his strong, rough hands gripping Patrick just above his hipbones, his full, dark lashes fluttering with pleasure, the scent of his skin and hair. Yu had risked everything to be with Patrick, and Patrick loved him even more, loved him so much he thought his chest might cave in and he'd forget how to breathe. Of all the wonderful things others had done for him, this was the most profound. Patrick knew Yu was afraid, that he was vulnerable despite his strength and reserve, but he'd faced all of it for Patrick.

"Do you want to go back in the club?" Patrick panted near Yu's ear.

"Not at all," Yu answered. "I was actually hoping we might break in that new apartment. *Our* new apartment."

Patrick laughed because he was just so happy he couldn't hold it all in anymore. "It's not technically mine, ours, until September 1."

Yu poked out his lower lip, pouting and looking so adorable Patrick couldn't resist bending in to nibble the slick pink flesh. "I should go inside and let the others know I'm leaving, or they'll worry. Then we'll go somewhere. I don't care where. I… I don't even know where we'll sleep tonight, but I don't care. This has already been the best night of my life. That hope I always imagine is sitting right on my shoulder, flapping its wings."

"I love the fanciful way you think about things. I hope I won't let you down."

"Stop it," Patrick said. "Seriously. I want you to stop doing that. I know people have told you that you aren't good enough, but I haven't, and I won't. No matter what you say, I won't. Because I think you're perfect."

Yu smiled and shook his head. "I think you read too much love poetry."

"Really?"

"No. You know I like it when you say things like that, and I love it when you recite poems for me. We're such a couple of nerds. We'd probably be hopeless if not for each other. Go say good-bye to your friends. I want you all to myself. And soon."

"Not coming in?" Patrick asked.

"I'd rather wait here. I've had as much of the noise and chaos as I can handle for one night."

"You were inside?"

Yu smiled and traced the line of Patrick's brow with the tip of his pinky. "Did you think I'd miss your performance? You are truly an artist. You looked so beautiful, I could barely believe you were human. Standing there, watching every man in that club wishing they could be with you, even touch your dress, and knowing you were mine—it really made me proud."

"I'm glad you got to see me," Patrick whispered, overwhelmed and ready to break down with emotion.

"I had some ideas," Yu said. "Things I could make for you, like armor. I sketched them out while I waited for you"—he pointed to his car in the lot around the side—"if you'd be interested."

"Absolutely." Patrick held onto Yu and just looked at his skin beneath the artificial amber light.

"What's wrong?" Yu asked.

"I'm afraid. Afraid as soon as I take my eyes off you I'll realize this has all been a dream."

Yu kissed him softly, wound their tongues together, then said, "We're a real pair. We have to stop being afraid. Both of us. I'm not any of the people who hurt you, and you aren't the people who hurt me. I—I want to get past feeling like I'm just waiting for the bad things to happen, and I want you to get past it too."

"I'll try," Patrick said, pulling away from Yu. "Be right back."

"No. No, I'll come with you." Yu took his hand and gripped it tightly. "I can do this. For you."

Patrick didn't doubt him a bit as they hurried back inside to congratulate Rog, share his good news with his family, and tell them good night. He didn't plan on staying at Eric and Rog's; the things he wanted to do with Yu shouldn't be done in a little girl's canopied bed.

Inside, Patrick found his friends at a table sharing a magnum of champagne. When he told them what had happened, they all hugged, kissed, and hurried him off, promising to help them settle into their new apartment. Rog agreed to see to Patrick's costume and have it waiting at the house. No one seemed to mind Patrick cutting out early, and he couldn't wait to spend the evening with Yu.

Yu's hand trembled against Patrick's palm. His gaze darted back and forth, and a sheen of sweat coated his face. His breath grew quick and shallow. "Patrick, would you mind if I waited outside? I... I really need some fresh air. This is a little too much for me. It's hard for me...."

Patrick smiled and kissed Yu's cheek. "I don't mind at all. Thank you for doing this for me. I know what it means. I'll be right there."

"I love you," Yu whispered before he kissed Patrick back and literally sprinted for the door.

"He's very uncomfortable around crowds," Patrick explained. "It took a lot for him to come in here."

"I think he's a keeper," Aouli said, kissing Patrick on the cheek.

"This is the best time of your life," Eric whispered in Patrick's ear as he hugged him. "You'll never feel like this again, so enjoy every second of it, princess. I'm so happy for you."

"Thanks, Eric, but I think I'm going to feel like this forever."

"Get going," Eric said. "He's waiting for you. It obviously wasn't easy for him to do what he did. Go show him you appreciate it."

Grinning like a fool, Patrick nodded and hurried out of the club through the front door. He rounded the corner, and what he saw quashed his joy, cold fear taking its place.

Yu stood against the building, his hands held out in front of him, and Mark Emmeck stood facing him in a sweat-stained, striped pink shirt. Patrick had enough experience with drunks to know by the way Emmeck stumbled and swayed that he'd been drinking heavily… and he had a gun.

Chapter 18

RETREATING back around the corner before he could be seen, Patrick pulled out his phone and dialed 911.

A dispatcher answered and asked Patrick if he had an emergency.

"I do," he said, just loud enough for the man on the other end of the line to hear. "A guy's been following me and threatening me, and now he's threatening my friend. He has a gun, and I don't know what he's going to do. God, please help. I—I should have called sooner. Everyone said I should. I should have called—if something happens to Yu—"

"Please calm down, sir. I'm sending an officer. What is your location?"

Patrick told him the club's address. "Please hurry. This guy is dangerous."

"The police are on their way. Are you in immediate danger?"

"Not me," Patrick said, starting to panic. "My friend—"

"I need you to stay calm and give me some details," the dispatcher said, but Patrick ended the call. He wasn't about to stand by while anyone threatened Yu, and the fear he'd felt turned to anger.

Life had taken everything from him, swatted his hope down into the gutter again and again. Just when things had started to go his way, this pompous ass dared to threaten what he loved. No. Not this time.

Patrick might have been too young to save his brother, but he'd save Yu, one way or another. It surprised him how sharply and clearly he thought as he peeked around the corner of the building and listened to the conversation.

"What do you think you can offer him that I can't?" Emmeck yelled at Yu. "I'm a successful man, and I want the best for Patrick. Why are you trying to ruin it for him? I can take care of him. Why are you trying to come between us?"

"You misunderstand," Yu said slowly and calmly. "I would never stand in the way of Patrick's happiness. He's a good friend to me, nothing more."

Emmeck waved the gun in Yu's face. "You think I'm stupid, you little bastard? I saw you kissing Patrick. My Patrick! I know I can make him happy if he'll give me a chance. But people like you and those queen friends of his are always getting in our way."

"I never intended that," Yu said.

"Stop fucking with me!" Emmeck yelled. "I'm not stupid! You should show me some respect! I'm more successful than you'll ever dream of being! Me and Patrick belong together! I can take care of him!"

Patrick had to do something, but he didn't know what. He'd never been in a situation like this, and he didn't know whether to go back inside and get help or just wait for the police to come. Either of those things could spook Emmeck, though, and Yu could be gone in seconds if he pulled the trigger. Maybe he was being stupid, but Patrick knew he had to stop this himself. He crept around the back of Yu's SUV, where he had a good view of Emmeck's back. The back hatch was ajar and held closed with bungee cords, all Yu's worldly possessions packed into the vehicle. He'd literally packed up his whole life to be with Patrick, and Patrick decided he'd rather die than let this arrogant, entitled pig put an end to that.

Among the suitcases, garment bags, and taped-up cardboard boxes, Patrick noticed some of the weapons and armor Yu had been working on, some rough and others finished and polished. A mace, little more than a heavy steel ball covered in blunt studs on the end of a thick handle, lay atop a stack of clothing and bath towels. It lacked the fine detail of Yu's finished pieces, but Patrick supposed it would do. He carefully and quietly unhooked the rubber cords and eased the hatch open a few inches, just enough to grasp the handle of the mace.

It was heavier than he'd expected, but anger and adrenaline let him hold it aloft as he crept up behind the drunken, ranting man. Henry had taught him what to do. Yu's eyes went wide when he noticed Patrick, and he shook his head. Emmeck must have noticed, because he turned to face Patrick, fumbling to aim the pistol he held in Patrick's direction but clearly inebriated and off balance. He opened his mouth to speak, and Patrick struck, swinging the mace with all his strength, aiming for Emmeck's flushed, pudgy face. He missed and connected with Emmeck's shoulder, but the blow sent the man to his knees, the gun dropping a few inches from his hand. He reached for it, but Yu kicked, his heel striking Emmeck under the chin and snapping his head back. When he collapsed on his side, Patrick hurried to kick the gun out of his reach. Sirens sounded in the distance, and minutes later, flashing blue lights flooded the parking lot.

Patrick held the mace over Emmeck as four cruisers squealed to a stop and officers hurried out, weapons drawn on all three of them. Patrick dropped the mace and it landed with a heavy clang. He and Yu lifted their hands and spread their fingers as the troopers patted them down and led them away from Emmeck, who bled from his nose, mouth, and shoulder as they hauled him to his feet, cuffed his hands, and guided him to the ambulance that arrived a few minutes later. By then, nearly everyone in the bar had come outside, drawn by the commotion.

Patrick ignored most of the chaos as he ran his hands over Yu's face and chest, checking to make sure he hadn't been injured. When he knew Yu was all right, he crumpled against Yu and wrapped his arms around Yu's neck, weak in the knees and barely staying on his feet. It took every scrap of will he owned not to be sick all over the asphalt.

Several different officers questioned Yu and Patrick about the events, and Patrick had to sit down on the curb before long. The whole incident felt distant, like it had happened years ago. He relayed what had happened again and again, and hours passed as the police questioned everyone who'd been in the bar or witnessed Emmeck's previous threats. The film crew even tried to sneak a few shots for their documentary before the authorities chased them off. They asked to interview Patrick, but he declined. He wanted to make a name for himself as a brilliant performer; he didn't want to be known for or associated with this incident.

Patrick was drowsing against Yu's shoulder, Yu's arm around him, when a man in a suit and tie cleared his throat. He introduced himself as Detective Somebody, but Patrick was too tired to process or remember the name.

"You young men are free to leave," the detective said. "We have your statements. We have a pretty clear picture of what happened here. We'll need you to produce the evidence in your possession, and you may be asked to testify if this goes to trial. This seems like a classic case of self-defense to me. I suggest you go to the authorities in your area and file for a restraining order against this man. He might make bail, and, well, you can't be too careful. These stalkers are living in a fantasy world, and they can be dangerous. Unfortunately, I've seen things like this end very badly."

Yu tightened his grip on Patrick's shoulders protectively. "Thank you, sir. Will Mr. Emmeck be prosecuted here in Ohio?"

The detective nodded. "Yes, this happened in our jurisdiction. The police in your area may want to file separate charges for the previous threats and assault, and I encourage you to cooperate with them. The longer this guy goes away, the safer your friend will be."

Yu stood, helped Patrick up, and shook the detective's hand. "Please just let us know what we need to do. Thank you for getting here so quickly."

The detective nodded once before approaching a group of uniformed officers. Eric and Rog hurried over, followed by Shawn and Aouli.

"Jesus, what a night," Eric said. He looked meaningfully at Yu. "We should have done something about that asshole a long time ago."

"Agreed," Yu said through gritted teeth. "I assure you, he won't get within a mile of Patrick again."

"Good," Eric said.

"The building we're moving into has excellent security," Patrick offered weakly. "Nobody can get in the front door unless we buzz them up."

"That's good, baby," Rog said, taking Patrick's hand. "But you have to take precautions when you're performing too. I don't want you going anywhere alone. Not after this."

"He won't be," Yu said.

"Yu?" Patrick asked. "You hate bars and crowds."

He looked at Patrick, his eyes as hard and blazing as heated steel. "I love you. I'll deal with it. I won't let you be threatened again."

"You kicked some ass, girl," Shawn said. "Nice."

Patrick blushed. He couldn't deny it had felt good to defend himself and the man he loved, but he wished it had never progressed as far as it had. "I should have listened to everybody and called the police when the jerk started giving me trouble. If I ever thought he'd put Yu in danger—"

"Hey," Yu said, "no harm done." He nuzzled against the side of Patrick's face. "I had you to look out for me."

"Always," Patrick said. "You really make some top-notch weapons. I'm sorry the police had to take it as evidence."

"I'll make another," Yu said. "I sort of enjoyed seeing it in action. Weapons are made to fight, to defend, not just to look pretty."

"Beautiful things can also be strong," Patrick said.

"Can we go home now?" Aouli asked. "You two look like you're ready to fall over, and I feel like I'm going to die."

Rog held up his hand. "Everybody is coming to our house tonight. No. Don't start, bitches. Nobody needs to drive home at this hour. You can stay with us, and we'll sleep till noon, get up, and cook a huge, fattening brunch."

"I can cook," Yu offered. "Do you have miso?"

"Oh no," Rog said, his taunting a sure sign he'd accepted Yu into the family. "I heard all about you, foodie psycho. We're having bacon, eggs, and pancakes with syrup. Not quail's eggs, either, so don't ask. Maybe a mimosa. Now let's go."

Patrick and Yu followed the others. After they'd showered, they fell into bed in the guest room and were asleep in seconds, twined tightly together in the narrow bed.

AT THE Faire, Patrick became a bit of legend, though he didn't feel he deserved it. Gradually, as summer became fall, the exaggerated tales of his exploits grew stale in anticipation of the upcoming Wine Festival and Halloween. He continued his role as the queen's troubadour, and Yu worked for Wade at the blacksmith's shop. The reputation of his quality weapons and armor spread, with many patrons traveling from other states just to visit his workshop.

One day, while Patrick sat eating a sandwich near the woods, Tom approached him and crouched down next to him in the grass. "I've had some ideas for next season, based on your performance in that pageant."

"Okay, I'm listening."

"Well, I thought we could perform a Shakespearean play, in the Elizabethan fashion, with all the women's roles played by men. Of course, I want you to play Titania."

"Wow," Patrick said. "That sounds amazing. Do you think the audience will respond well, though?"

Tom shrugged. "That's how they did it back in the day. I say we give it a try. I'd also like to incorporate it into the Faire. Imagine, the queen of England hosting the fairy queen. A fairy-themed weekend could be a lot of fun for our patrons. They revel in the fantasy. Imagine a fairy ball. A fairy tournament. I'd like you to help me organize it."

"I'd love to," Patrick said. "I just don't want who I am to be a detriment to the Faire. I love it here, and I don't want to harm this place."

Tom chuckled, adjusting his kilt as he stood. "You think you're going to shock this crew of misfits and ne'er-do-wells, lad? Bah. We'll get together at the end of the season and throw some ideas around. Patrick, you looked amazing in that show. If nothing else, I need you to help with the costumes."

"I've always loved working with the costumes," Patrick said with a smile, already forming some ideas.

"Good. I think this will be good for the Faire. You're good for the Faire, lad. I'll be in touch." Tom shook Patrick's hand and left.

Patrick got another surprise at the end of the day when Taylor met him at the gate. Luckily Yu was with him, and Patrick grasped his hand when he saw Taylor, his first instinct to reach for the dagger Yu insisted he carry at all times.

"What the hell are you doing here?" Yu asked, stepping in front of Patrick.

Taylor held up his hands. "Chill, man. I'm here to apologize. I need to talk to Patrick. Please?"

Yu reluctantly stepped aside, and Taylor shoved his hands into his jeans pockets, looking at the yellowed grass. "Look, I was pissed at you because of what happened with Jen. I was a dick; I know that now. I—I was the one who told that Emmeck guy your real name. I swear, I had no idea he'd try to hurt either of you. He met me after the Faire one day and offered me money to answer a few questions about you. I admit I wanted him to make you uncomfortable, see you humiliated, but I didn't know—I swear, I didn't know, Patrick. I felt like complete shit when I heard about what happened. I want to say I'm sorry, and that if you need me to talk to the cops or anything, I will."

"Thanks, Taylor," Patrick said. "I know this can't be easy for you, and I appreciate it."

"I never wanted anybody to get hurt," Taylor said again. "I feel like a tool."

"You should," Yu said.

"I know. And I'm sorry. Look, I learned my lesson," Taylor said.

"You need to start respecting people," Patrick couldn't help saying. "What you said about Jen was mean and petty."

"I know," Taylor said. "I know. I apologized to her too, and to Tom."

"Well, at least that's something," Patrick said. He couldn't forgive Taylor yet, but he respected the effort. "Thanks, Taylor. For being honest."

"Okay," Taylor said. "I just wanted you to know I'm sorry. I-I'm not okay with what you guys do together—I don't think it's right—but I never wanted anybody to get hurt, and I'll help in any way I can. I-I'm really sorry I had my head so far up my ass." He hurried away as Patrick and Yu looked at each other, struck dumb by the change in the other young man.

"That was unexpected," Yu said.

Patrick nodded. He didn't know what to say. He hoped Taylor's apology would help Jen get past some of her anger, but at this point, Henry had probably wiped her memory of every other man she'd been involved with from her mind. Yu had done the same for him. Looking at Yu in the crisp autumn light, Patrick still couldn't believe his good fortune. For once, he didn't let himself worry someone might take it away.

Epilogue

OCTOBER 10 was Patrick's birthday. His mother had sent him a baseball-themed card with a long letter detailing her husband and family's recent achievements, along with some blurry pictures of supposed celebrities. Patrick just shook his head. He didn't expect her to change any more than he expected a call from his father. Yu and his friends had helped him start to realize his family's dysfunctions weren't a reflection on his worth. He still loved them, and he worried about his dad, but he accepted that he'd have to live his life without them. He'd decided he'd rather let them go than let them continue to hurt him.

Yu had been in the apartment's small kitchen most of the day. Patrick sat in the living room enjoying the savory smells filling their home. He looked around. Fine examples of Yu's weaponsmithing—swords, daggers, shields and breastplates—hung on the walls. The sculptures he'd made in art school—androgynous figures similar to Patrick's hope charm—sat on the hardwood floor. Yu had framed some photographs of Patrick, including those he'd taken with Tish and Tracy. A faded picture of Dylan sat on the mantle next to a vase of red and white roses Yu had bought at the market down the street that morning. Most of their furnishings were secondhand and rather worn—things gathered from friends and relatives of friends who no longer needed them, or bought from thrift stores—but the forty-six-inch flat-screen TV and the black Xbox beneath it were brand new.

One by one, their friends began to arrive for the combination housewarming and birthday party. Patrick gave Eric, Rog, Tom, Tish, Tracy, Jen, Henry, Shawn, and Aouli a tour of the small apartment while Yu set out the German, Oktoberfest-inspired meal he'd made buffet-style and opened some wine. All of them filled their plates and ate and talked.

"So how does it feel to be a full-fledged adult?" Rog asked. "You're not a teenager anymore."

Patrick looked around at his cozy little home, his beautiful partner, and the smiling faces of his friends. "I'm happier than I ever thought I'd be. I can't believe the luck I've had."

"You worked for it," Shawn reminded him.

"And you deserve it," Eric said.

"I also had a lot of help," Patrick said in a humble whisper. These people were like angels watching over him.

"We have a gift for you," Tish said, handing Patrick one of the pink and black boxes from their shop. "Open it."

Inside, Patrick found a beautiful pale blue corset with an irregular print on the right side: two white foxes beneath a full moon surrounded by stylized plum and cherry blossoms. He couldn't believe the detail in the design, or the exquisite feel of the silk beneath his fingers. He'd never seen Tish and Tracy make anything like it. "This is incredible," he said. "You didn't have to do this."

"It's made from a piece of a vintage kimono," Tracy said. "The original piece dates from before the Second World War, and was badly damaged. But we thought, hey, nothing is ever so badly damaged it can't be made into something beautiful. We thought it sort of symbolized both of you, what you've made together. We like having a little brother, and you've certainly helped our sales. Money aside, we love you both."

"Thank you," Patrick said, reaching over to squeeze Yu's hand.

"We have something for you too," Eric said, handing Patrick a box wrapped in bright blue and gold striped paper. "Nothing as glamorous, I'm afraid."

It contained something they really needed: a high-end coffeemaker, a bag of fragrant beans from Kona, and two ceramic mugs made by the potter at the Faire. Patrick recognized his delicate glazes.

"Thanks, Eric," Patrick said. "Thank you, Mama."

Aouli and Shawn got them a glass casserole dish and some glass napkin rings, also made by an artisan at the Faire and accented by shimmering bands of gold. Tom had brought a set of stainless steel cooking utensils and a bottle of Silver Oak Cabernet Sauvignon to put in the steel wine rack resembling grapevines Yu had made, and Jen and Henry had gotten them a copy of *Call of Duty: Black Ops II*, a game Patrick really wanted to play, and it had a co-op mode, so Yu could play with him, if they ever found the time. Lately their minutes together had been short and stolen, especially since Yu had returned to his classes, but that made them all the more precious. Simple things like ordering takeout and falling asleep on the sofa watching TV had taken on a magical dimension. Even cleaning up the kitchen together felt like a wonderful privilege.

"Forgive me for saying this," Eric said, "but I didn't think you two would make it at first. I'm happy to have been proven wrong."

"After what we have been through, I think Patrick and I can manage to choose our drapery," Yu said sarcastically. He was ever full of surprises.

"Amen," Shawn said, and Tish, Tracy, and Jen clapped. Yu stood to serve the almond and pear torte he'd made, along with a dessert wine from Germany.

"Foodie lunatic," Rog said, pretending to complain. "But this is incredibly delicious."

"I don't cut corners," Yu told him, grinning. He'd smiled more tonight than Patrick had ever witnessed.

"I hate to bring this up," Jen said, "but whatever happened with that Emmeck guy? I just want to know you two will be safe."

"Oh, it's okay," Patrick replied, smiling to assure her. "He'll be going to jail for a while. It came out during the investigation that he's done this kind of thing before. Some of his former employees even came forward. I guess he was a real bully at work and harassed quite a few of them, trying to intimidate them into... um, intimate relationships. He really screwed himself when he threatened Yu with a gun, though. The last I heard from our lawyer, there will be some civil suits, too, and his wife filed for divorce."

"At least he's out of your lives," she said.

"Man, I would have paid to see you whack him with that mace!" Henry said, shaking his head. "The student has become the master." He offered Patrick an exaggerated bow.

"I... I guess I cracked his collarbone," Patrick said, a little guilty at how pleased he sounded. "So I guess you were a good teacher, Henry."

"It certainly didn't hurt that you wielded such an exemplary weapon," Yu said, arching a brow, and all of them laughed, then the conversation returned to lighter matters.

After a few hours, their friends departed and Patrick and Yu tidied up. They'd both taken the day off, but Yu had school in the morning and Patrick planned to go to the Faire and share some of his ideas for next season with Tom before they started preparing the grounds for Halloween. He'd also been volunteering at the community center, working with gay and lesbian kids. It surprised him how many of them had been thrown away by their families; he just couldn't comprehend people tossing out those they loved over something so trivial. Some of their stories were more horrific than his own, and he really wanted to help them in any way he could. He even considered entering a program to become a social worker, but that was in the future. Right now, tonight, he didn't want to think about anything but Yu.

They went into their small bedroom, stripped off, and deposited their clothes in the hamper as they usually did. Tonight, instead of falling exhausted onto the double bed they'd acquired from Henry's aunt's unused guest room, they stood looking at each other in the bisected light of the streetlamps through the blinds. Yu stroked down the side of Patrick's hair, neck, chest and ribs before letting his hand settle above Patrick's hip.

"This is a fairy tale."

"What do you mean?" Patrick asked, moving closer so their bellies brushed together and wriggling his hand inside Yu's briefs to skim the crescent of his asscheek. He dragged his lips slowly along Yu's jawline, feeling the first catch of stubble against his mouth.

"Nothing." Yu glided his hands down Patrick's ribs and hooked his thumbs in the waistband of Patrick's boxer briefs. "I just can't believe I'm this lucky." He tugged Patrick's underwear to his knees and rubbed Patrick's erection. "Does this happen in real life?"

"Apparently," Patrick groaned, snapping his hips toward Yu's warm, rough palm. "Eric calls me 'princess'. Well. I met my prince, and if I have anything to say about it, we'll live happily ever after."

"Nerd."

"Like you're not," Patrick whispered before capturing Yu's lips and slipping his tongue between them, relishing the heat and texture of his palate. Yu urged him back toward the bed—covered in red satin at Yu's insistence, one of their few splurges—and Patrick sprawled across it when his knees met the edge.

Yu kissed, licked, and nibbled up and down Patrick's body, and Patrick shivered as his hot, wet lips moved up the outside of his thigh, over his hipbone, up the muscles of his waist and along the ticklish spots on his ribs. Yu traced over the four large roses, following the curve of Patrick's body from just below his chest to the top of his groin. They covered most of his right side. "They've healed up nicely," Yu said, "and they're sexier than I ever imagined."

He used his other hand to toy with Patrick's nipple, his expert ministrations driving Patrick almost out of his mind. Over the last few weeks, Yu had learned exactly how to turn Patrick into a whimpering, quivering mess, and Patrick had learned just what Yu enjoyed. Yu liked to go slowly, to take his time exploring every inch of Patrick's body, and he did it with the same care and precision as he did everything else. He also liked to watch, so Patrick turned on the lamp on their bedside table. Patrick felt just like a shard of metal in Yu's forge: heated to blistering, malleable and liquid.

He buried his fingers in Yu's hair and enjoyed the play of Yu's shoulder muscles with his other hand as Yu moved up his body, the soft skin of his chest and belly dragging along Patrick's erection. He'd never get tired of the feeling of Yu's skin against his. Finally their lips met, and they kissed languorously as Yu slowly lowered his weight onto Patrick. They circled their hips, rocking against each other and making their cocks slide together. Patrick inclined Yu's head to kiss up the side of his neck, and Yu rewarded him with a low groan and a harder thrust. He liked being kissed there. Patrick opened his legs and Yu settled between them, taking both of their erections in his fist and pressing them together as Patrick kneaded the taut muscle of his ass and arched his back off the bed to get even closer.

Many nights, they satisfied themselves like this, just by kissing, touching, and rubbing against each other. Yu seemed to have other ideas tonight, and he wrapped his arms tightly around Patrick and rolled so Patrick lay on top of him. "Sit up," he said, and Patrick did, looking down at Yu's face, flushed and sparkling with sweat, his lips swollen and his eyes dark and dilated.

Patrick reached down and touched Yu's cheek, making Yu exhale a shuddering breath. "God, you're so beautiful," Patrick said, and Yu turned his head and sucked Patrick's finger into his mouth. With his other hand, he caressed Patrick's chest and belly, lavishing attention on every inch of his skin and making Patrick's eyes roll back in his head and his breath catch in his throat.

"Come here," Yu said, pressing lightly against the small of Patrick's back to urge him forward.

The sparse hair of Yu's body tickled Patrick's clean-shaven backside as he slid toward Yu's face. Yu wet his lips and moaned hungrily, and Patrick almost exploded all over him. Everything he did, his every gesture and sound, was just so sexy it almost destroyed Patrick. Yu stroked down his belly and took hold of Patrick's cock at the base, then sucked just the tip into his mouth and swirled his tongue around the crown, flicking the tip against the sensitive groove on the underside.

"God!" Patrick's inner muscles clenched, and he grabbed a handful of the bedsheets with one hand and Yu's shoulder with the other. He clamped his eyes shut and for a few minutes lost himself to the exquisite sensations. When he opened his eyes and looked down, the sight of Yu's shiny lips stretched over his cock and Yu's eyelids drooping with pleasure almost finished him. Patrick bit down on his lip and tried to concentrate on holding back. He wasn't ready for the night to end yet.

He pulled away, and his cock slid from between Yu's lips with a little pop. He bent down to kiss Yu, tasting his flavor on Yu's tongue, before swinging his leg over Yu and turning around. Yu took hold of Patrick's hips and guided him back down, sucking Patrick's balls into his mouth, first one and then the other.

Patrick loved this position. He raked his nails through the sparse black hair framing Yu's erection, and Yu trembled beneath him. Yu could be overly generous in bed if Patrick let him, putting Patrick's needs far ahead of his own. Not tonight. Patrick cradled Yu's balls as he swiped his tongue across the tip of Yu's crown poking out from his foreskin. The little hood of skin still enthralled Patrick, and he thumbed it back before closing his lips over the tip of Yu's penis. He loved the texture of that smooth flesh, the taste and the heat it radiated. Yu did the same, and they fell into a slow rhythm, neither rushing, both just enjoying the feel of each other. If Patrick got what he wanted, this was still just foreplay.

He relaxed his throat and took Yu all the way in, stilling and swallowing until he adjusted to the sensation. Since they'd started living together, Patrick had gotten more comfortable doing this for Yu and also found he thoroughly enjoyed it. He began to bob his head, and Yu groaned, the sound vibrating through Patrick's cock and into his belly. Yu wet one of his fingers and slid it over Patrick's cleft, the moisture cool and slick. He circled Patrick's opening, and Patrick pressed back against him to encourage him to delve deeper. Though he'd still never been touched there, tonight Patrick finally felt ready. He released muscles he hadn't realized he'd been clenching, and Yu's finger slipped inside.

It didn't hurt, but Patrick grunted at the strange new sensation and fought his body's instinct to close off. It excited him, being touched like this, entered in the most intimate way. Then Yu touched a spot inside, and an intense jolt of pleasure shot through Patrick. His whole body flinched with the overwhelming sensation, and he whimpered around Yu's cock. If Yu kept rubbing that place, Patrick wouldn't be able to hold back. He lifted his head and panted, "Stop. Yu, stop."

Yu moved his finger out of Patrick and they turned to face each other, sitting on the bed with Patrick's legs folded and resting in Yu's lap. Yu stroked his calves and looked at him with a concerned crease between his brows. "Did it hurt?"

Patrick shook his head. "It was amazing. I… I didn't know it would feel like that. It was too good, Yu. I almost couldn't take it. There's… something else I hoped we might do tonight."

Yu cupped Patrick's cheek, and Patrick relaxed into his hand, letting Yu support the weight of his head. "What?" Yu asked.

"I hoped we could finally make love," Patrick said, his cheeks burning. He met Yu's gaze and just watched his dark eyes. "Like… full sex."

"Are you sure?"

Patrick nodded again and kissed Yu softly. "I really want to. And it's my birthday."

Yu pulled Patrick into his lap, their cocks pressed tightly together between their flat bellies. He held Patrick close and whispered, "How do you want to do it? Do you want to be on top?"

"You've done that before?" Patrick asked. "Let someone else be on top? You like it?"

"I have, and yeah, I like it. With you, I'll love it. Don't worry, I'll let you know how I want it."

"It's not that," Patrick said, nervous but getting so damned excited he shook all over. "I've thought about this, and I always imagined it the other way around, imagined looking up at your face while you made love to me, imagined feeling you moving inside me."

"Okay, if you're sure," Yu said, lifting Patrick and then gently lowering him to a stack of crimson pillows against their headboard so Patrick half sat and half lay down. Patrick watched his every move as Yu slid open the night-table drawer and set a condom and small bottle of lubricant on top. He flipped its lid open and drizzled some of the clear liquid into his palm. With his other hand, he pushed Patrick's knees apart so he could crouch between his legs and rub the slippery lotion between his cheeks. "I'm not going to hurt you, Patrick. I love you too much to ever hurt you, but...."

"What?" Patrick gasped out, surprised he managed to speak at all.

"It can be a little uncomfortable the first time."

"I trust you. Yu, I love you. I want to."

"Okay." Yu propped his forearm against the headboard and leaned down to kiss Patrick, his tongue pulsing against Patrick's and swiping along his lips and teeth. He spread the lubricant along Patrick's cleft and eased one and then two fingers into him. Patrick sucked air through his teeth at the sting and burn. "Just relax," Yu said, his breath wetting Patrick's cheek. "Push down against me with your inner muscles. It will help you open up."

Patrick did as he said, and his body soon acclimated to the feeling. Yu slid his fingers slowly in and out, grazing that magical place inside and driving Patrick closer and closer to the edge of release. His back arched off the bed, and he wrapped his arms and legs around Yu, pulling him closer and holding tight. He rubbed his leaking erection against Yu's belly as Yu spread his fingers, getting Patrick ready.

"Do you still want to?" Yu asked.

Patrick nodded, senseless with love and arousal, feeling like he'd die if Yu made him wait much longer. Yu tore the condom wrapper and rolled the thin latex over his cock, and then he smeared more lube over top. He lifted Patrick's legs and rested Patrick's ankles on his shoulders, his gaze never leaving Patrick's face, an alluring mixture of anticipation and concern on his features. He positioned himself and slowly pressed against Patrick's hole. At first, it felt like being torn in half, and Patrick cried out and clutched Yu's shoulders, digging his nails into Yu's golden skin.

Yu paused with just his tip inside Patrick and stroked Patrick's face with the back of his hand. "Should I stop?"

"No. No, I love you."

"I love you too, Patrick. So much." He dared forward a bit more, and Patrick thrust against him. "Is it okay?"

"Yeah, I like it. Love it. Love you. Inside. Filling me. Please keep going, Yu."

Yu fell forward, kissing Patrick and driving Patrick's knees against his chest. Slowly, he sank all the way inside Patrick until their skin met. Then he paused and looked at Patrick's face again. "I love you, beautiful. You feel so good. God, you feel so much better than I ever dreamed."

"You feel good too." Patrick grasped Yu's hips and urged him on. "Come on."

"I'm not in a hurry," Yu said, playing with Patrick's nipple. "I want our first time to last. I want you to remember it was wonderful. I want to remember how amazing it feels to be with you like this, inside you."

"It is wonderful," Patrick said, taking a handful of Yu's hair and pulling their faces together as he circled his pelvis and ground against him. Yu began to make love to him with long, slow strokes, and Patrick lifted his hips to meet him. They established a leisurely rhythm at first, Yu's cock rubbing against Patrick's prostate and pushing the first droplets of precome out to pool on Patrick's belly. Then their mutual desire and need for release compelled them faster, and Yu thrust deeper into Patrick, kissing him hard as their skin slapped together. Patrick moved to wrap his calves around Yu's waist and held Yu tight with his legs and rocked up against him, trembling and panting against Yu's neck as his orgasm built. Then they slowed and stopped to look at each other and kiss again. Patrick just enjoyed the sensation of Yu filling him, connecting with him, and he squeezed Yu's cock with his muscles. Gradually, Yu began thrusting again.

When Yu reached between them to stroke Patrick, Patrick came screaming Yu's name and holding onto him for dear life as bursts of light erupted behind his eyes. Wave after wave of pleasure rolled through his body until he didn't think he could take anymore.

Yu buried his face in Patrick's hair, moaning with every breath. He snapped his hips forward a few times and whimpered. "Patrick. Oh,

Patrick, God! You're just amazing. I... I love you." He collapsed against Patrick, slipped out, and they lay panting, sweating and holding each other.

Patrick was so happy he wanted to cry. Every cell in his body hummed with satisfaction, and he'd never imagined being in love like this. It almost hurt. He giggled and touched Yu's hair, then his face. Yu laughed too, and they rolled to face each other, pecking all over each other's faces until Yu went into the bathroom to get rid of the condom.

"How would you feel about doing away with these things, if I get tested?" Yu asked, stretching back out beside Patrick. "I'd really like to feel you with nothing between us, but I understand if you aren't ready."

"No, I'd like that," Patrick said. "Would you really like it if I topped?"

"I'd love it," Yu said, rubbing his calloused palm against Patrick's. "Would you?"

"There's one way to find out," Patrick said with a grin.

"I look forward to it," Yu said, kissing Patrick's knuckles.

"Tomorrow night," Patrick said, nestling in next to Yu and pulling the rumpled red covers over them.

Yu set the alarm clock on the stand and wound his arms around Patrick, pressing his forehead against Patrick's on the pillow they shared. "Great. Now I'll be walking around campus all day tomorrow with a semi. You... you don't have to use anything when you do."

"Yu...."

"No. You were a virgin. I know you're clean, and I want to feel you come inside me. I've never let a guy do that, you know."

Patrick groaned, his own semi brushing against the treasure trail on Yu's belly. "If you don't stop talking, neither of us is going to get any sleep tonight. We have tomorrow, and the next day. We have forever, don't we?"

Yu kissed Patrick one last time before letting his eyes close. "Yeah. Forever. I believe that."

Smiling until his face hurt, Patrick fell asleep against Yu's warmth. Somewhere, up near the light in the center of the ceiling, he felt sure he saw the glowworm green of the little fairy creature he thought of as hope hovering above them. It might be a feeble, translucent thing, but no matter how many times life and fate swatted it down, it always returned to Patrick, fluttering next to him on its tinsel wings.

Author's Note

Here's a list of poetry alluded to in the story, should you be interested. The poems should be easy to find in their entirety online, one of the best sites for the literature of the period being luminarium.org.

"Delight in Disorder" by Robert Herrick

"My Love is Like a Red, Red Rose" by Robert Burns

"Sonnet 18" by William Shakespeare

"To His Coy Mistress" and "The Definition of Love" by Andrew Marvell

"The Minstrel Boy" by Thomas Moore

AUGUSTA LI is the author of several short stories, novellas, novels, and yaoi manga scripts, created either on her own or with her partner in crime, Eon de Beaumont. Gus and Eon are also artists and are currently hard at work on many manga and prose projects. They would love nothing more than to see the yaoi/BL genre flourish in the West. Video games, manga, and anime have been huge influences on Gus's work. Xbox Live calls Gus away from work far more often than it should.

Visit Gus at http://www.BooksByEonandGus.com or keep an eye out at anime conventions and Goth clubs around the East Coast.

Fantasy Romance from AUGUSTA LI

Ash AND Echoes

Book One of the
BLESSED EPOCH

AUGUSTA LI

http://www.dreamspinnerpress.com

Also from AUGUSTA LI

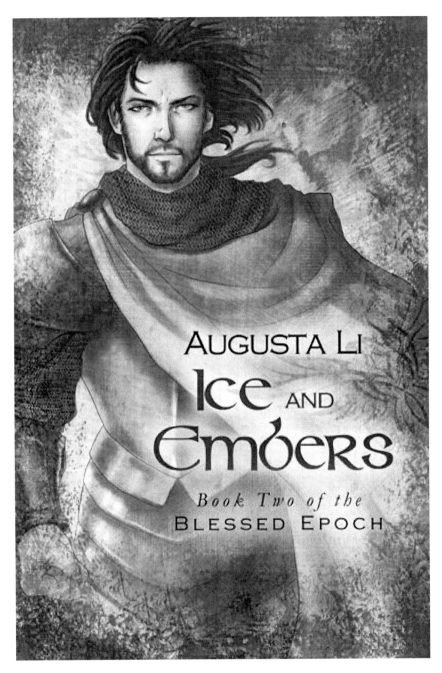

AUGUSTA LI
Ice AND
Embers
Book Two of the
BLESSED EPOCH

http://www.dreamspinnerpress.com

STEAMCRAFT AND SORCERY from AUGUSTA LI
And EON DE BEAUMONT

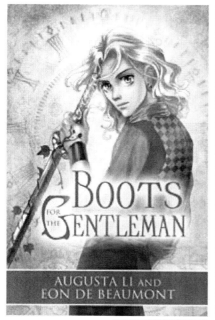

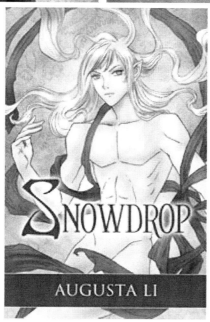

http://www.dreamspinnerpress.com

Contemporary Fantasy from AUGUSTA LI

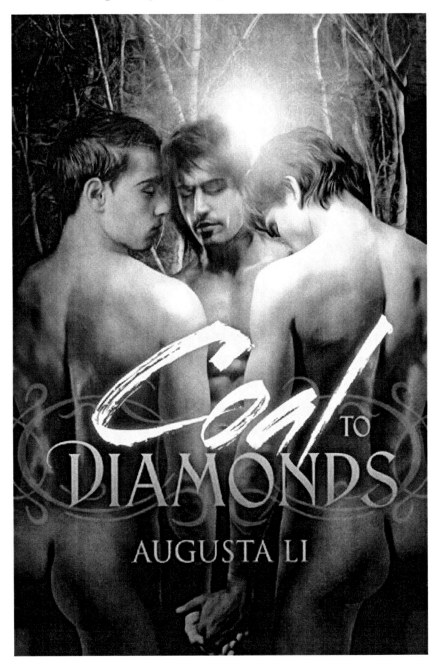

Coal TO DIAMONDS

AUGUSTA LI

http://www.dreamspinnerpress.com

Bittersweet Dreams from AUGUSTA LI

Romance from DREAMSPINNER PRESS

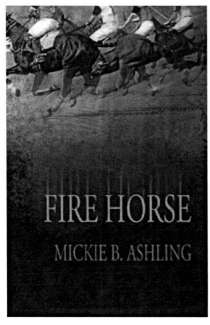

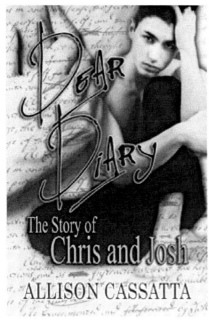

http://www.dreamspinnerpress.com

Also from DREAMSPINNER PRESS

A SENSES AND SENSATIONS MYSTERY: 2

Love in
Plain Sight
Susan Laine

http://www.dreamspinnerpress.com

Lightning Source UK Ltd.
Milton Keynes UK
UKOW031847150713

213846UK00018B/1692/P